TRANSCENDING
FIRE

E. K. BLALOCK

Black Rose Writing | Texas

This is a work of fiction. Names, characters, businesses, places, events, and incidents are either the products of the author's imagination or used in a fictitious manner. Any resemblance to actual persons, living or dead, or actual events is purely coincidental.

ISBN: 978-1-68513-066-4
PUBLISHED BY BLACK ROSE WRITING
www.blackrosewriting.com

Printed in the United States of America
Suggested Retail Price (SRP) $23.95

Transcending Fire is printed in Calluna

*As a planet-friendly publisher, Black Rose Writing does its best to eliminate unnecessary waste to reduce paper usage and energy costs, while never compromising the reading experience. As a result, the final word count vs. page count may not meet common expectations.

Cover design by Aleksandra Bezukladnikova

"For my Dearest Husband, Jonathan. Without you, this story would not be possible and my life would be incomplete. You and our sweet son Jeremy are the fire in my soul, heart and mind. Love, Emily"

TRANSCENDING
FIRE

CHAPTER 1

A flood of tears abruptly blinded Alex as she lay in the tall grass at the break of dawn. They came out of nowhere. No. Not now. She clapped one hand over her mouth to stifle a sob and pushed her face toward the dirt to hide her contorted face. Allowing her men to witness her uncertainty now was not an option. She had to focus, to think of the good that would come of this sacrifice. Finally, the war between two grieving families that had ravaged both an empire and a kingdom for over a hundred years would end. This was a good day. A great day. For the Luxorians at least...

Just over the top of the hill, she and fifty of her men surveyed a vast enemy war camp. The sounds of legionnaires rousing themselves in the early morning sun made them all uneasy. They would spot them if one of their men stepped too close to the base of that hill for a piss, but this was still the best vantage point. After a deep breath meant to abate the swell of bile in her throat, she lifted her head just above the long, green grass, soon to be painted red, to get a better look at their demise.

It was a strange sight to behold. Most Luxorian war camps she had encountered were the epitome of order and efficiency, but what she saw now were irregularly spaced rows of tents, many with gear piled in front of them in unceremonious heaps. No palisade walls fortified this camp, and no moats had been dug. This glaring flaw in their normally impervious armor made her nervous; what artifacts must they have at their disposal to make them feel so safe?

"Do you have your target?" she dared to whisper. Her eyes shifted from the camp to the grizzled archer kneeling a short distance away from her. Her heart would have liked to stop when he propped himself up over the grass line.

"Yes. I have three," he replied in a gruff murmur, his arrow drawn back and at the ready.

Following his gaze, Alex spotted three legionnaires—light cavalry stationed at the edge of the camp to serve as lookouts. All three were dozing on their imperial stallions with war horns hanging from their saddle horns and short-bows held loosely in their hands.

"Good, but we need to get closer. Kaden, grab the horses when those men hit the ground," she quietly commanded the massive, redheaded giant whose hands she knew to be the gentlest of bear paws. He was having the hardest time of them all, keeping himself crouched below the tops of the tall grass. It was a comical sight that normally would have had Alex snickering.

He nodded. "Your last glorious conquest and all you ask of me is to wrangle beasts?" he asked with a hefty sigh and a roll of his big brown eyes.

"It's important," she insisted. "If those horses get spooked, they'll run off with our chance for a surprise attack and give the Luxorians all the time they need to assemble. So, can you do it?"

"Easily enough," he assured her with a stiff nod. He shifted his weight a bit before letting loose a whistle that carried through the valley. There were already a few early birds up and eager to catch their breakfast, so his song blended in with the sounds of nature.

Her throat seized when the scared faces of her most loyal men silently marched by, one by one. These men had been with her from the beginning and they had trusted her to lead them to victory. She closed her eyes to strengthen her resolve. This was for the best.

"Do it now," she whispered, calling forth the beginning of the end.

The archer loosed his arrow. When the arrow found its mark, the legionnaire's wet gurgle of surprise was the only noise that escaped before he fell from his horse, dead. The tip of her archer's arrow shot through the second legionnaire's left eye before he could identify the source of that strange sound that startled him awake. The final legionnaire scrambled to bring his horn to his lips, but by the time his lips puckered, her archer shot him through the throat and all that came out was a sound like the croak of a toad.

Her men slid down the hill to secure the horses while the others spread through the camp like wildfire. Across the camp, the imperial tent was like a beacon, beckoning her onward. She had to get there before all hell broke loose. Looking over her shoulder, she glimpsed three of her men slithering back to the shelter of the tall grass. Her cousin hadn't trusted her to execute this attack, after all. No time to curse their names now; she had two royal deaths to secure.

Alex mounted her stolen steed and heard the dreaded cry of alarm and the blasting of horns.

"Sound assembly! The enemy attacks! Legionnaires and praetorians, to me!"

The voice belonged to Marcus Evandrus. Their armies may have clashed a handful of times over the years , but she had yet to face the man personally.

Damn him! He couldn't have failed to notice her every move, just this once? Time was almost out, for all around them, Luxorians scrambled to abandon their breakfasts, their whores, and their shit piles to grab their weapons and join the fray.

That was when she saw the man believed to be evil made flesh: Antonius Evandrus. Snug, silver armor gleamed in the rising sun, accented by his stylish black chain-mail. The royal crest emblazoned his imperial blue surcoat, making him easy to identify even across a chaotic campground turned battlefield. He was a handsome man with long, black tresses, an angular jaw, and a chiseled physique. She doubted that his soft, uncallused skin had ever experienced the bite of a blade.

Prince Antonius took his time to don a circlet of silvered laurel leaves about his brow. He clearly wanted no one to doubt his status as a prince of the empire, even as his legionnaires were being slaughtered less than a hundred yards away. He must have heard the thunder of her horse's hooves, for he turned to look at her with a devious smile.

Alex came within twenty feet of him before the ground beneath her horse's hooves crumbled, revealing a shallow pit studded with spikes as wide as her biceps and as sharp as any blade. The horse screeched an otherworldly cry and writhed in agony as the hidden spears impaled him. He couldn't escape, but she could.

In a flash, she kicked her feet free of the stirrups, threw herself forward, and used that momentum to catapult her body across the pit. She landed hard, but was quick to her feet.

"Coward," she spat, incensed by his use of magic. A privilege she'd never had, nor never would. Annoyed that he had access to magic, but she did not. His men fell in around her, blocking her direct line of sight. Bitterly, she ripped her eyes from where he knew he stood as the Luxorians raised their swords high. She had to move. Her body flowed through the movements of battle as a courtly woman would move to the sound of a waltz. She was born to dominate the battlefield, and it showed. Her hair swirled around her like a halo of gold as she ducked, spun, and kicked like a dervish.

Her soldiers crossed the moat on either side and raced into the fight, their armor of garnet and gold reminiscent of a dying flame being swallowed by the sea of blue that surrounded them. The distraction of their presence could keep her alive for a moment, but only just. She needed to end this quickly or risk all their deaths being for naught.

"Back down, men. She's mine," she heard Antonius drawl in a loud voice, his command peeling his men off her like the skin of an onion. He weighed her with his eyes and an arched brow meant to mock her. His firm lips showed his contempt for the soldiers that had failed to kill her. Even with a sword in her hand, this man regarded her as an object to be toyed with, rather than as a threat to be feared. Nothing could have breathed life into her more.

"The whore was in such a rush to get into my tent that she nearly died. The least I can do is let her have a taste of my blade," he taunted. Without warning, he stepped in with a brutal overhand swing of his broadsword, as though he sought to crush her resistance with a single stroke. His eyes were alight with a crazed rage unlike anything she'd ever seen, but not unlike anything she'd ever felt. The strike would have cleaved clean through her chest if she had stayed in its destructive path. Instead, her blade flashed up, striking with the shrill screech of steel on steel. She diverted his blow to the left and spun to the right, tucking her body away from him.

With the first swing cleared, she turned back to him with a confident grin. "If your sword arm was as quick as your tongue, I might be worried." She lunged forward and swung her sword down hard, to put him on the defensive and get a feel for his ability.

His face flared red as a rush of fury seemed to overtake him. With gritted teeth, he began striking her low and high, driving her back. His blade cut through the air like an angry wasp, demanding all her attention just to stay ahead of it. Ducking and darting out of the path of death and redirecting crushing blows was all she could manage. In a contest of pure force, she knew she was no match for Antonius. She needed speed and leverage.

Inevitably, her stamina ran out. A blow came thundering down that she could not avoid; the blade crunched into the joint of her left shoulder, denting the armor and striking her hard enough to throw her to the earth. He cut her, but it was not severe and not on her sword arm.

"It's about time someone showed you your place beneath my heel, Princess." He spat the last word as though it were fouling his mouth and brought his sword down on her again in rapid swings.

Alex rolled left, barely staying ahead of the succession of blows, and finally tucked her feet under to regain her stance. She was faster than he was, and she had been certain that she would have more stamina than him on the field, but she was playing a dangerous game. Eventually, this brief rush of adrenaline would fail her. She had already gotten lucky once, but she couldn't count on the god of fortune to smile upon her again. She needed to end this. Suddenly, it felt as though time slowed just for her, and she caught sight of an opportunity: there was a rip in the chain-mail under his left arm.

She became the aggressor, emboldened by the opening she found. She couldn't avoid the bite of his blade, but she could stop his heart with just one touch of hers. His blade came down on her for the last time, slicing through her armor and into her bicep. At that moment, she thrust upward, the tip of her blade piercing his blackened heart and releasing his soul.

With a cry of triumph and pain, she wrenched her sword back out with a violent twist and kicked him away from her. Antonius collapsed in a heap, dead before his head hit the ground. Alex spent her entire life avoiding the eyes of the dead, but she couldn't block out his dying words. "It can't be..."

Without a moment to breathe, her next opponent sprang forward to engage her in another life or death struggle. She threw herself into the fight, her eyes searching desperately for a pocket of her men that she could rejoin. A vengeful cry that stood above all the others interrupted that thought.

Twisting her head, she sliced a soldier across the throat to clear her view of the source of that cry. There stood the only living heir to the throne. Marcus

Evandrus kneeled beside his fallen brother, checking for a heartbeat with tears of rage in his eyes.

In stark contrast to his ostentatious brother, who lay lifeless in his quivering arms, Marcus' light brown hair was in a simple soldier's style, and his face showed the weathering of a man who lived outdoors. He wore standard legionnaire armor, with the markings of his rank upon his chest and the crest of the helm that lay beside him. He stared in disbelief at what the princess had done to his brother, disbelief widening his eyes and leaving his mouth agape.

Seven praetorians surrounded him and more were gathering by the second. As eager as she was to take advantage of his grief and end this nightmare, she knew she needed a clean kill. If she jumped into that swarm of death, she would be lucky if her blade even met his armor, let alone his skin.

"You're his younger brother, aren't you? Why don't you rise to avenge his death and leave your nursemaids behind?" Such insults would have easily provoked his arrogant older brother. She had to make this quick, but come to find she could not goad him so easily.

"For years, I've wished to meet you outside the battlefield to talk of peace. You always seemed like an honorable foe to me," he confessed as he rested his brother's head on the ground and slowly rose to his feet. "I never thought that I would find such a bloodthirsty fool, but you will not manipulate me. Fight me here and now or go die with your men."

Marcus rolled his right shoulder out of the grip of his praetorians so he might raise his blade.

"You expect me to fight you amidst your ring of personal guards? Hah! Unlike your mother, mine didn't suffer a fool. Fight me with honor or cower between their legs while I rip through your men one after another," Alex demanded. His cold, focused stare was unsettling. The rage behind it was sinister. He wasn't the image of a brother who had lost a lifelong companion. Not at all. Rather, he looked at her as if she were a thief in the night who'd stolen something he wanted for himself. Envy and rage intermingled, but she had no time to think about why.

When he refused to leave their protection, she raced to join her men, who were holding off the Luxorian troops with all their might. They needed her help. Her soldiers could handle three Luxorians apiece with the wide swings they took with their swords, but the Luxorians still grossly outnumbered them. Her chance to kill Marcus would come, but not now.

"You, gather the troops to contain this breach! The rest of you, with me!"

She heard Marcus call out for her. He would soon make the mistake of coming after her. She just needed to wait him out. For now, she set herself to cutting away at his men, one after another. None of them could stop her.

Finally, she spotted a wink from fate. Tied to a tent stake was a riderless horse. She jumped into the saddle with a single, smooth motion. Here was her only real chance to succeed! Finally feeling optimistic, she turned to see an infantryman with a spear lunge forward and thrust his blade up into the throat of her steed before she could break away. She tried to dismount, but fell with the horse instead, her foot trapped in the stirrup. The massive stallion had nowhere to collapse but was right on top of her, its weight too much for her to push away.

She cut down the soldier who had thought he could claim her life, and as the battle raged around her, she lay unnoticed. No one saw her there, covered in blood, muck, shit, and tears. Alex desperately tried to wriggle out of the sinking mud pit the slaughtered horse trapped her in, but it was impossible to free herself. Her muscles trembled from exertion and adrenaline. She was nearly free, but then a careless soldier kicked her helmeted skull. Stunned and pinned, she could only listen to the sounds of her men dying around her. She was useless.

When the ringing in her ears finally cleared, she heard men in the final throes of death amidst an otherwise silent camp. She longed to be among those whom death took into his pocket, but he had no interest in her for now. Instead, she lay pinned in the middle of the camp, bathed in horse blood, barely able to breathe but not permitted to die.

As Alex struggled to take even the smallest puffs of air into her lungs, the world around her was becoming blurry. Her mind drifted, and she reflected on the events that led to this battle. They seemed scrambled and too difficult to comprehend now. One incomprehensible memory would float by, only for another to take its place. Faster. Shallower. Faster. Shallower. Faster. The speed at which this happened was nauseating, but if she retched now, she'd surely choke.

She could no longer distinguish friend from foe; gruff Artorian groans and strident Luxorian grunts all sounded the same. All she had left to consider was if this was the actual voice of death, whose face she already knew all too well. Indiscriminate and soft.

Her slowing heartbeat flooded her ears and a numbing tingle began its ascent up her body, when suddenly, her eyes locked onto Marcus as he surveyed the carnage. His stride was predatory and his form loomed. He stopped in front of the fallen steed that had trapped her in the mud and removed his helmet. His powerful jaw and stubble-dusted cheeks drew tightly into a stoic expression. His cool, icy blue eyes held none of the bloodthirsty pleasure she would have seen there had he been his brother.

She could only watch helplessly as he withdrew his blade. Would it be honorable to die this way? She could tell that he didn't see her and had only planned to end the struggling horse's suffering. He lifted his blade, which glinted with the blood of her brethren, when his muscles suddenly clenched and all motion stopped. He saw her.

With a look of disbelief, he crouched down and encircled his muscular arms around the horse's underbelly to pull it off her. She tried to push up, but they were both too weak. His praetorians swarmed toward their prince to aid his effort, revealing her broken and bloodied form beneath. She could hear them whispering as she gasped for air.

'Is she really the princess?' She could hear the men whispering.

Marcus studied her carefully, and her vision faltered. His face filled her last moments of consciousness with the sight of him frowning down at her with an indecisive look creasing his bloodstained brow. This was it, she thought. She was never to wake again. The war was over. This was a good day.

'I'm going home.' She thought with a broken smile.

"Disarm her. Put her in the tent next to mine and have the physicians see to her. I must write a letter to the emperor to let him know what she did to his eldest son."

The praetorians lifted her out of the dirt, and Marcus turned away. He needed to arrange for someone to transport his brother home.

CHAPTER 2

Nearly a full day after they had dragged her into this tent unconscious and barely breathing, Alex's swollen eyes cracked open. The first indicator that she was still of this world struck her like a stone. Pain radiated from the top of her scalp all the way to the curl of her toenails, making her grind her teeth so hard that she felt her jaw pop. There wasn't a breath she took now that didn't make her wince, but what was more alarming was her confinement.

She tried to move - to sit up, roll over, anything - only to find that her hands were securely bound to the legs of the cot. The torn cloth bindings were so tight that it surprised her that her hands hadn't turned blue. They had captured her, but she wasn't dead yet.

A few tears of frustration slipped down the side of her face, and she realized what must have happened.

"Damn horse," she cursed under her breath. Her mind was still foggy, and she struggled to make sense of her surroundings.

She was alone in an undoubtedly guarded tent, strapped to a wood-framed field cott. At the foot of her bed, there was a closed cedar chest. There was a tin pot filled with water on top of it. In the far corner was a small bathing tub. In the middle of the tent was a tall, metal support beam, and beside her cot was a table littered with her bloodstained armor and tattered garments.

Wincing, she lifted her head and whistled a soft tune into the bleak silence, hoping to hear a reply. The stillness of the midnight air momentarily dampened her hopes that any of her men might be as lucky as she was to be alive.

She felt so vulnerable, which was infuriating. To her relief, they hadn't bathed her, nor had they given the cut on her arm more than a quick stitch job. A scratchy gray blanket covered her lower half, though it did nothing to conceal her broken body that was so easily visible beneath a thin, dirty shift. She squirmed a little to wriggle the blanket up higher, but it was no use. She'd have to settle for what she had or risk losing the small piece of modesty they'd given her altogether. A thought occurred to her and brought a spark of hope: if she could break her cot, she could free herself from her bonds and slip away unnoticed to find her men. Even if they couldn't hear her, surely some of them were still alive.

Maybe Kaden...

At the thought of seeing her redheaded giant again, she fought a little harder against her restraints. The approach of heavy footsteps nearly made her stop breathing. What should she do? What could she do? At the last moment, she threw her head to the side, so her muddied tresses covered her eyes. Perhaps her captors would be foolish enough to loosen her bonds and tend to her while she appeared to be sleeping. They would surely carry a weapon, even if it was a low-ranked guard or healer.

She heard his steps come to a halt just in front of her. He folded the blanket down several times, just as someone who'd needed to inspect her wounds might do.

She believed her ruse was working until...

"I know you're awake, you barbaric sow. I heard your call," the intruder sneered in a quiet voice, right before heaving icy river water on her with a loud splash.

Alex seized, gasping in surprise as the chill of the frigid water rushed across her body and rendered her gown practically transparent where it wasn't already deep red. In fury, she fought against her binds with all her might, ripping her arms and legs to no avail. He exposed her to the greedy eye of a laughing stranger and she was powerless to stop him.

Before her stood a Luxorian commander. With dark brown hair cut too close to the scalp, he stood as tall as the tent. The sight of her filled his hard brown eyes with an icy rage that momentarily stilled Alex's defiant tongue. There were lines around his mouth and eyes that suggested a ready smile, but his face was more befitting a hangman. His glare offered cold, harsh judgment without even a glint of mercy or compassion, not that she expected to find any.

"Now then, why don't we get acquainted? I am Prevak Rustionage, son of Senator Rustionage. I am the man who will pry from your lips every secret you've ever kept until I know you better than your own mother did."

The man's voice was grating, each word pushed out of a chest, heaving with emotion and past a clenched jaw. He paused deliberately when he threw the bucket away so he could admire her soaked figure.

Then, with a grin, he unsheathed a small dagger from his boot and lifted her chin with the blade to look into her eyes until his face fell once more.

"You are the woman who killed my friend, Antonius Evandrus. Think for a moment about what that means for you," he commanded, his deep brown eyes boring into hers with an intense scorn.

She couldn't help it—a contented grin curled across her lips. Even though he was threatening her with his blade, she couldn't resist wearing her pride on her lips. She had done it. She had killed the heir to the throne of the Luxorian Empire. This would surely appease her cousin, and all would be well.

Finally, when Prevak's red face looked ready to pop, she spoke up.

"I am Alexandra Monica Raybrandt, the sole daughter of Jiordan and Victoria Raybrandt, Princess of Artoria. What you think awaits me is irrelevant," she sighed and met his arrogant gaze with her own war-weary eyes.

"You think that killing the heir to the throne of the Luxorian Empire is a light matter? You have no comprehension of the pain that will I will inflict upon you," he promised. Without warning, he grabbed the collar of her shift and brought the tip of his knife down on her windpipe until he drew blood.

"What a charmer you are. You must have an entire camp of women pining for you," Alex wheezed, her upper lip twitching as she called his bluff. If he had the authority to slice her throat open, she'd be dead already. She just needed to wait him out, or so she hoped.

"Keep your filthy mouth shut," Prevak snarled as he released her gown and backhanded her across the mouth so hard that her lower lip split open. Violently, his hand then snaked through her hair and gripped it by the roots, pulling her head back to reveal more of her throat. "Unlike the unwashed animals you rutted with for all these years, I know where a woman belongs and the duties she is fit for."

"What duties would those be? To clean your war wounds? There's only one problem: you don't seem to have any. Afraid to get your hands dirty, Commander?" she taunted through clenched teeth.

"Peasants and fools collect wounds, just like you." He was so engrossed by trying to frighten her he didn't even notice the tent flaps open, admitting the only man still alive who was fit to bear the armor of the imperial house of Luxor.

A silent, lithe praetorian whose hand draped over the hilt of his sword, and whose pale gray eyes averted away from her as soon as he followed him inside. What struck Alexandra was his hair. It matched hers in length and color almost exactly. Naturally, he kept his tied back out of his youthful face, but Alex couldn't help but to wonder if having a personal guard as young and as thin as him might be a mistake she could use to her advantage.

"Ah, Commander Rustionage. I thought I made myself quite clear. She is mine to interrogate. You may leave us now," Marcus announced with an affected air of indifference.

"Yes, Your Highness," Prevak mumbled with a bob of his head. He turned to glare at her once more to make it clear this was far from over. Finally, propriety forced him to leave. Rank bested him, for now.

Alex remained silent, admittedly unnerved, as she watched him leave. Tonight, he had approached her with only a small dagger. Tomorrow, would he use a cursed artifact against her? She was at their mercy. A harrowing notion that elicited violent images of the twisted death that surely awaited her.

Movement out of the corner of her eye made her head snap away from the entrance. What cruelty did this prince have in store for her? She watched him retrieve the discarded blanket and gently drape it back over her from foot to neck.

She could see he was trying to hide the pity he felt for her. What remained of her life would be difficult and degrading. They both knew it. She'd be lucky to survive a year in his father's court as an abused servant who'd they would work to the bone until her body broke. A fate worse than death for a warrior.

"There is no point in catching a chill. I may even allow you to change, if you can answer a few questions for me," Marcus suggested in a soft, leading voice.

"Was that a commander of yours? Impressive. It takes quite an admirable amount of skill to attack the bound and injured like that," she scowled, glaring in the direction Prevak had gone. She ignored his promise of dry clothes. It was an obvious lie.

"What room do you have to speak with men known as Vexor the Butcher and Hector the Skinner in your camp?" Marcus asked her with a raised brow. He pulled up a chair and calmly sat two feet away from her. This was the closest that the Luxorian and Artorian royal families had been to each other in over a hundred years. It was a monumental victory for his family, to be sure, yet she didn't see the expected joy in his eyes.

"Did you see them among the dead or the captured? Please do me a favor if that is the case. If they're dead, let the crows pick out their eyes. Or, if they're captured, have their fingers ripped off with hot tongs so they might never use them again," Alex remarked darkly, pleased to see Marcus show surprise at her suggestion.

"You call for the dismemberment of the men loyal enough to follow you into death?" Marcus balked. "What am I to make of that?"

"Make of it what you will, but they were never my men. My father gave them power. When I sought to put an end to their liberal abuse of it, they turned their blades on my subjects," she explained, her pride urging her to defend herself.

"And who do they serve now?" Marcus asked with a sigh, as though he'd already lost interest. This was a tactic to push her into giving him all that he wanted to know in one sitting by acting as if none of it even mattered. It mattered. It mattered a lot.

"Themselves, I expect, as they always did," she replied, tactically avoiding his actual question.

Who was in charge now, if not she? So far, this conversation had been going well for her captor, she realized. He had confirmed a fracture in the Artorian forces. She needed to shut her mouth. Just because he wasn't the worst of her enemies didn't mean he was her ally.

"Princess Alexandra, I must ask: why a suicide raid? Your maybe twenty surviving men confirmed who you are, but not why you led them into a bloodbath. Until now, your strategies have always been abundantly cautious, but this raid doesn't fit the pattern at all. Help me understand why."

"Help you? Why should I help you?" Alex asked, with a hint of suspicion creeping into her voice. Did he really think she had forgotten that he was her enemy?

"Because if you do, I can make your imprisonment a comfortable one, and will afford you the privileges of a princess to the best..."

"Do not treat me as if I am a scared little woman who has never felt the chill of an icy blade pressed against her neck before! I am no princess you have ever known," she snapped. There was a wisp of a connection that she felt looking into his eyes. He was reaching out to her, from one warrior to another. It made her especially uneasy that a tiny piece of her wanted to reach back out in return. She needed to break that fragile thread as if it were a spider's web with frantic fury.

She wasn't sure what she expected his next move to be, but he did not prepare her for him to reach down and pull a small blade from his boot. Her brow creased, and she immediately began testing the restraints again.

"Relax. I need your cooperation, not your life," he murmured in annoyance. He cut the binding to release her left arm before moving to her right.

Out of the corner of her eye, she could see that the young praetorian who had accompanied the prince was on edge. He unsheathed his sword a couple of inches, just in case she put up a fight that his master couldn't handle. What did he think she could do in her present condition?

They were the ones with the magic, after all.

Besides, unlike Prevak, Marcus was calm. Attempting to disarm and overpower him with arms and legs gone numb from lack of circulation would not end well for her.

"Victus, go find me some manacles, a collar, and a long chain," Marcus whispered to the willowy guard who nodded dutifully and left.

Alex strained to sit up, hissing when the pain became too great. She could feel the consequences of that horse falling on top of her all the way to her pelvic bone. Damn it all.

"Why are you letting me sit up?" she asked quietly, unsure of his intentions when he moved to free her legs.

"I couldn't know for certain when or if you were going to wake up. Keeping you like that wasn't ideal, but I only have one prison and it's currently full of your men. I didn't need a second attack today. From the looks of it, though, my concerns were almost entirely unfounded. You look like you can hardly hold your own head up, let alone execute a deadly plot, so I'm giving you a minute to stretch before I leave you for the night," he sighed with a shake of his head. With her limbs freed, he pushed his blade back into his boot and took his seat across from her once more.

"I'd like to hold your head up," she muttered under her breath. Ever so slowly, she eased her legs over the side of the bed and drew the blanket up around her shoulders to keep herself covered. It was all she could do not to sob from the pain.

"What about my men? You said twenty survived," Alex pressed delicately. Her heart overflowed at the potential that Kaden might be among them.

"I said maybe twenty. Not all of your surviving men were doing well enough when I saw them to even speak on your behalf. I might sooner count them among the dead than I would the living. What I want to know is: Why? Why did you bring them here to die like this?" Marcus asked. He sounded disgusted.

"I told them to leave," she snapped. "I told them to let me do this on my own, but they refused. Each of them chose this fate. I don't know why. Go ask them."

Alex shook her head, not caring to divulge any more details of her failure to the man whose family she had fought against her entire life.

"Go ask them? For the sake of the Gods, you are their princess! You answer for their actions, not the other way around. You killed my brother, not them!" Marcus roared, leaning so close that his spit caught her chin and nose.

"You're right. I am their princess and I owe their sacrifice the respect it deserves. That means I will take our kingdom's secrets with me to the grave," she answered, her own unwavering gaze daring to meet his.

The two hot-blooded royals were at a stalemate. She felt Marcus' anger pulsating off him with every controlled breath he took. Perfect. It meant she was digging into a nerve, which could lead him to making a mistake.

"Your fate, for now, is in the hands of the council and my father." He informed her. "They will know you are being held here, and we will arrange terms for your kingdom to surrender. After that, we'll see if I grant you the courtesy of a grave."

She opened her mouth to fire back, but he continued with his verbal assault.

"I never supported this war. I argued against it every time they sought my counsel. When speaking of terms of surrender, I was the voice calling for gentle terms to speed the healing. You've ruined that opportunity, you wretch, and you refuse to even tell me why!" Marcus screamed and balled his fists. His rage took Alex aback this time, but her uneasiness seemed to only excite him more. He seemed intent on destroying any fragments of pride she had left to cling to.

She knew he could snap her neck from where he stood, if he truly wished. For the first time, Alex was sincerely afraid he might display his strength.

Thankfully, before his will to keep her alive eroded any further, the young praetorian named Victus walked in with the shackles Marcus had requested. Shaking his head in disgust, he scoffed and grabbed the meat of her arm. With a violent wrench that made her cry out, Marcus pinned her against the central support beam of the tent. She lurched forward to fight, but Victus gave her no time to muster an attack. He was behind her and caught her free wrist before she could swing her fist.

"Let me go!" Alex screamed, twisting and struggling to no avail. Even her most impassioned attempts to break away were no match for two uninjured men who had a firm grip on her. She had counted on Marcus making a mistake, but she was the one who'd let her guard down first. She was a fool.

Once they secured her, Marcus attached her chains to the pole and clasped the shackles around her wrists. With that done, he pulled the bindings tight and forced her arms excruciatingly high above her head. With a sliced bicep freshly sewn shut and at least a bruised rib, the pain alone was enough to blind her. Alex felt her teeth grind against one another once again, and the sound of her jaw popping filled the tent. The pain stole her breath completely. Were they really going to leave her like this?!

Victus knelt down and put pressure on either side of her jaw with one hand until he forced her mouth open. Then, he quickly wedged a sodden cloth between her teeth. "Valerian root and ale. It will at least keep you from breaking all of your teeth." He explained quietly.

Alex bit into the soaked rag begrudgingly. Fire erupted across her busted lips, but it began working the moment the odorous remedy slipped down her throat. She was a sniffling, quivering mess, but at least she was breathing again.

Finally, Marcus retrieved the collar Victus had set aside, closed it around her neck, and connected it to the manacles. The design was so that if she pulled against her arm restraints, she would choke herself out before she caused any trouble.

"Enjoy your rest, princess, and reflect on how you'll answer my questions in the morning." Marcus stormed out of the tent, leaving her to wonder what tomorrow would bring. Victus glanced back at her only once before following his master.

He seemed to be uncomfortable with what he saw, but all he said was, "Spit it out when the pain stops."

CHAPTER 3

They would not deter her with a leash and a threat. She had to get out of there. She had to see who she had left in this world and how they were doing. Killing her outright didn't seem to be Marcus' intention, but there was no telling if his mind might change come morning.

Testing the collar and chain that bound her yielded conclusive results: the collar rammed straight up into her windpipe. She coughed and gagged violently, but no one came to her aid. Too bad. The soaked rag dislodged from her mouth, but already the agony was much less than before. Just a persistent, but manageable, throb.

What am I going to do?

"Think. Breathe. Be calm. There we go." She told herself between slow breaths and took in her surroundings for almost an hour. During this exercise, she laid her eyes on two thin, scarcely visible pins that must have fallen during the construction of this tent. Stretching her foot out, she touched the ends of the pins with the tip of her big toe before abruptly scooting them back toward her. She clasped the metal pins in her toes and brought her toes up to meet her restrained hands. Her saving grace was their fault. She'd have to remember to thank them someday for removing her armor and leaving her nearly bare, or this would have been impossible.

Once she had her trembling fingers wrapped around the pins, the rest was easy. She jammed the pins into the lock and worked with it for a solid five minutes. CLICK. The manacles burst open, allowing her arms to fall freely down to her sides. Alex didn't waste a second. Unlatching herself from the collar, she dragged herself to her feet and tiptoed silently toward the tent flap.

Aside from two guards positioned outside her tent, the coast was clear. She needed more relief from the pain. The rag was filthy now, but she didn't care; she bit into it again and again. She sucked on the root juice greedily with a pained groan while she considered her next move.

Suddenly, a heavy pair of boots approached, and her heart dropped. Fearing it was Marcus, she threw the blanket over the cot so the edges of it met the ground and scrambled under it. Better that he fear she was missing and go on a frantic search for her, than fasten her to that post again, or worse. From her hiding place, she listened quietly and planted her right ear on the cold, hard ground.

"I am here to free the captive. Stand aside." It was Prevak, but now he sounded three sheets to the wind and was being driven wild by his intoxication. Alex had nowhere to hide if he pushed his way past the guards. She didn't have a prayer of finding a discarded weapon in here, either. Her silent prayer was that Prevak was so inebriated that he'd either be compliant enough to walk away when told to or easy enough to evade if need be.

"No, Commander Rustionage! The Prince said no one was to enter. Please stand down!" cried a guard, who was clearly shouting loudly to get it through his thick, alcohol-washed brain and draw the attention of other praetorians who may be nearby.

The sound of a blade being drawn filled the night air, far louder than the not-so-distant sounds of drunken merriment.

"No, Commander Rustionage! Put the blade away!" the apprehensive guards pleaded.

"Get out of my way or die with her!" Rustionage slurred and charged into the tent like a blind bull. He smashed right into the beam they had secured her to and collapsed the entire tent on top of himself. She saw her chance. She had to escape now or risk getting caught by his blade in one of the wild swings he was taking to cut his way out of the thick, animal-hide canvas.

In a desperate clamber, she rolled out of the back side of the cot and crawled through the muck. She left her rag behind, but in exchange, she took the blanket with her. The attention of all the nearby guards shot to the chaos unfolding under the collapsed tent, so no one even noticed when she ran away at full speed to hide behind another nearby tent.

There, she caught her breath and watched Prevak make a drunken ass out of himself while legionnaires danced around him like fools, trying to secure his blade without hurting him. She wrapped her scratchy blanket tightly around her shoulders and tiptoed over to the other side of the tent she was hiding behind.

Could she make it to the next set of shadows undetected?

A moment's pause, then she flung the scratchy material over her head and curled herself into an unassuming ball of cloth as five legionnaires hurriedly passed her by.

"She's missing! Find the princess!" she heard Marcus shouting, scattering the men who had gathered to subdue the raging commander. Thinking fast, she tucked herself under the canvas of the tent she'd been hiding behind. In the candlelight, she saw that the only occupant was an elderly man who was sound asleep.

She dove beneath his cot and held her breath. When the guards burst in to look for her, just like she knew they would, they saw the sleeping man and hastily withdrew.

The marks on the uniform that hung over his mirror told Alex that he was likely just a scribe. He was also too old to be bothered with the inexperience of the young right now. She waited for the sound of heavy footsteps outside to fade before making her move. Aside from the contented snoring of the undisturbed scholar, there was only silence left in their wake. In the darkness, doubt flickered to life.

With men like Prevak out there looking for her, would it be better if she just sought Marcus and his protection? No. No, she needed to find her men. She needed Kaden.

With her priorities firmly established once again, she wriggled out from underneath the old man's cot and quietly slipped away into the darkness. With a small dip and a silent breath, she was back in the cool night air where she could hear the chirps of crickets mix with the ruckus of merry men. It appeared not all the soldiers knew that a half-naked fugitive princess was amongst them. That would change if she waited too long. She had to go.

Heading away from the sounds of revelry, she cautiously navigated her way through camp, scurrying from shadow to shadow. At first, she hid herself easily enough. She gave campfires and the hungry men crowded around them a wide berth, but as she neared the edge of camp in search of the prison, the shelter became sparser and her knees wobbled from exertion. Her head felt as light as vapor and her legs may as well have been encased in lead. She couldn't feel her bare toes curling into the bitter cold dirt. The valerian root had made her forget about the pain and was now overtaking the other sensations she needed. Like touch.

Her cheeks burned when she heard the high-pitched cries of passion and light-hearted giggles of camp followers in the tent next to her. Cautiously, she peeked out and saw Marcus across the camp, standing over the drunken Prevak with a drawn sword.

"Let this be a lesson to everyone! No rank or order shall ever overrule mine!" He thundered. His praetorians pushed the noble to his knees and forced him to bow with his hands outstretched on the ground before him.

While Prevak was subdued, Marcus' boot shot out and crushed the commander's right thumb with a loud crunch that even she could hear. A cry of shocked pain reverberated through the camp. Until it healed, even attempting to wield a sword would be incredibly painful, but it was the brutal swiftness of it all that shocked Alex. If this is what he did to his own commanders, what would he do to her if he found her?

"When you disobey me and attempt to murder my prisoner, you lose the right to use the part of yourself that caused the offense. You should be thankful you didn't intend to rape her."

He pushed past the healers, who were racing toward the shameful cries of agony.

"Get him out of my sight!"

Rustionage's retinue whipped into a frenzy to collect their lord before he could do more damage to himself or his reputation. The crowd dissipated and the search for the missing princess quickly reached a feverish pitch. It wouldn't be long before they thought of searching the prison. She had to find it now.

"Won't get anywhere by standing here and shivering," she thought to herself, calling on her courage to move on when a massive, burly arm wrapped around her waist and tugged her inside of a large tent.

Alex stumbled and almost lost her balance as they hurled her into a pit of men. She was ready to fight the praetorians who had caught the runaway princess, but what she found was a group of emboldened legionnaires who were ready to celebrate.

"Oh ho! We got a live one, boys!" chimed her captor with a hot chortle.

"Calm down now, wench. We got you first, fair and square. Don't act shy! We pay well!" another said as he ripped away her blanket, revealing her soaked shift.

"Touch me again and I'll kill you," Alex swore, but really, how threatening could she look? She was soaked from head to toe, had mud caked on her face and brandished no weapon. She couldn't fault the men for mistaking her for a camp-following whore, but she'd be damned if she'd let their mistake stand uncorrected.

She turned on her heel to leave, but one of them smacked her on her nearly exposed ass cheek, sending a loud crack echoing into the night.

"Oooh, she's firm, boys. Mind if I go first?" the largest man asked with a giddy smile.

"Nah, let's make a game of this! Let her choose!" a man who reached out to run his index finger up the back of her inner thigh until it caught on the hem of her shift suggested. Slowly, he guided it up over her left cheek until she whipped around to snatch it back down.

Wide-eyed, she scanned their faces for the person who had touched her, but before she could identify him, another hand whipped around from behind to give her breast a knee-buckling squeeze.

"LET ME GO!" she screamed and spun to knee him in the groin. He collapsed to the ground with a strangled cry and cradled his wounded member as if it were a priceless jewel. In that instant, the mood of the room changed from barbaric taunting of a disoriented woman to outrage.

"You fucking whore!" their leader barked. With a massive fist, he backhanded her so hard across the cheek that she spun around and landed face-first in the dirt.

She was trapped and suddenly pinned. One man was leaning down on her back. Another split open her thighs while resting his weight on the backs of her knees. Her heart was like a hammer against cloth and her muscles quivered, but no matter how hard she tried, she couldn't fight them off. She couldn't overpower them, and she had nowhere to run. In that moment, she wished for the swift death that Marcus had denied her.

What no one saw was Victus silently entering the tent behind them. With a grim face, his gloved hand lashed out like a hammer, delivering a punishing blow to her attacker's head. He instantly knocked the legionnaire unconscious, without even the time to cry out in surprise. Her savior didn't stop there. Without a word, he lashed out with his left foot, snapping the nose of the man holding her thigh, then taking out another with an elbow to his temple. He moved with precision and speed.

"This prisoner belongs to Prince Marcus. Remove your hands from her royal flesh before I peel yours off," Victus commanded in a cold, hard voice. None of the soldiers dared to disobey him. In fact, they tripped over one another to leave her exposed to the frosty night air. None of them dared to allow their shadows to even touch her skin now.

Who exactly was Victus?

"Get up."

He didn't move to help her. After such cruel treatment from the soldiers, she had expected him to at least take the chance to grab her violently, but he gave her space and time to secure her footing. Her shift, if it could still be called that anymore, was not doing much for her dignity. The scuffle had torn it in several places and sliding down her shoulders, forcing her to hold it up to keep from flashing her bruised breast.

Once she was steady, Victus removed his thick, blue cloak from his shoulders and draped it around her. He removed his hands as soon as it was secure and again waited to make sure she wouldn't fall over. She didn't understand why he was granting her this measure of modesty. What was he trying to prove?

She realized quickly that she was relieved by the tiniest bit of kindness this praetorian had shown her, and for that, she softly whispered, "Thank you." Victus didn't answer. He just silently escorted her outside.

Alex's expression suddenly soured when she saw Marcus standing there with a proud grin on his face.

"There is no escaping my camp, Princess, though I see we will need better restraints. I hope we won't need to waste any more of Victus' evening to maintain your honor. You ought to apologize to him."

"Apologize? Why? Your commander attacked me. I had to run, or he would have killed me!" she cried, storming past Victus, who picked up his pace to keep her within arm's reach.

Her overzealousness annoyed him. What did he think she was going to do with a tent full of frustrated men at her heels who would eagerly snatch her back up to show themselves a good time? They bested her for now, so she followed as Marcus led her back into the heart of the camp.

"If you hadn't attacked our camp in the first place, you wouldn't be in this position. You did this to yourself, Princess," Victus reminded her curtly.

"Where are my men?" Alex demanded. Her desperate blue eyes scanned Marcus for a spark of hope. She could find none. It was like staring into chips of ice on the banks of a frozen river.

He said nothing. Finally, they neared a group of men scrapping the tent where Commander Rustionage would have run her through if she had not outsmarted her captors, but they kept walking.

"What are you doing? That's my tent." She dug her heels into the dirt, forcing Victus to push her along until her knees gave out.

Stumbling to the ground, Alex's eyes caught the glint of a silver blade handle sticking out of Victus' boot. Her mind raced with the possibilities this presented. She had a hope of escape, if she could only pluck away Marcus' watchful gaze long enough to grab it.

"On your feet!" Victus barked. Alex obliged, carefully palming the blade out of its sheath and concealing it in the folds of the cloak he had given her.

"I said, where are you taking me?" she said with a new undertone of iron in her voice that might have betrayed her confidence if they'd been paying attention.

"If you can't even recognize my family's crest, then your wits are nowhere near as keen as they led me to believe," Marcus remarked wryly over his shoulder before he entered his tent ahead of her.

Once inside, she quickly realized that he didn't care for extravagant shows of wealth or power. With only a desk, a wooden chair, a couple of chests, and a simple cot making up the furnishings, she wouldn't have even known that a prince slept here had it not been for the imperial crest. The cot was perhaps wider than they issued the average soldier, but it certainly was not the four-posted bed her spies told her that his brother ordered his men to cart around for him.

"I allowed Victus to spare your modesty on the walk here, but now I'll thank you for returning his cloak and kneel beside the pole there. I still have questions, and you're going to give me answers," Marcus ordered coldly, his intense, startling blue eyes commanding her to oblige. Having her kneel on the ground was an obvious power-play, and she did not appreciate it.

Alex had two choices laid out before her. She could either try to kill these two men and take her chances outside the tent, or she could confess about the knife she was holding. Carefully, she ran her thumb along the edge of the hidden blade. It was disappointingly dull. It seemed she had found his cooking knife. Better for spreading butter than slitting throats.

Slowly, she rolled her left shoulder out of the cloak and then she flung it into Victus' face. She needed to disorient him just long enough to toss the blade into the ground right between Marcus' legs. It was a pity. It had been such a clean shot. Unfortunately, it would have hurt her more if she'd tried to take it.

With a cocky grin, she walked past them and dropped to her knees with her hands clasped loosely behind her back.

"It seems I'm not the only one around here you should accuse of being duller than expected. Your guard over there is too easy to get one over on," she taunted, and leaned her bruised face up against the pole.

The moment she looked up into his eyes, she realized she'd made another catastrophic mistake. She didn't care. He'd obviously expected her to muster an escape attempt, but she could tell that her effort to slip a weapon was something completely different. His brows drew down in an angry glare, and he reached behind the desk, drawing out several lengths of chain and leather bindings. Yet again, no artifacts. No magic. Perhaps the legends weren't true after all?

"I will give you something to rebel against, just you wait and see," he promised in a dangerously smooth tone. Before she could even try to back away, he had her chin in one hand and was attaching a new collar about her neck to the other.

He then used the collar to jerk her head to one side and directed her gaze to a steaming tub of water in the far corner of the tent. "Yes, you are a clever, dangerous opponent, but you could have had a warm bath behind a privacy screen and clean, dry clothes, had you simply been a tolerable one as well. Instead, you can sleep in your damp, torn rags while strapped to this pole for the rest of the night."

She should have kept the damn cooking knife, as useless as it was; maybe if she had actually made an attempt on his life with it, she could have provoked him into ending this. Instead, she would languish here with the frigid night air biting at her bare legs while her knees throbbed under the pain of her own weight.

It would have been better if he had stripped her naked. The damp cloth that clung to her skin made chills run straight down to her bones. She took another longing peek at the steamy tub, but she was careful to be quick about it. For all he knew, she'd endured much worse at hands that were much larger than his.

"Leave us, Victus," Marcus ordered, tossing the knife back to his stunned praetorian.

"So, you think denying me a bath and some dry clothes is going to persuade me to betray my men? You didn't have many real friends growing up, did you?" she scoffed, his behavior reminding her of a spoiled child who punished his peers and pets with his temper when he didn't get his way. She was trying to convince herself that he was merely annoying, not threatening. Maybe if she could make herself believe it, she'd only be shaking from cold, and not fear as well.

"No, I'm showing you what it costs to be a fool who tries to escape and fails. If you don't answer my questions, that will have its own consequences." He sat down on his cot a couple of feet away from her.

"You mean to say that if the roles were reversed, you'd be a meek, obedient little prisoner? You're a hypocrite." She glared at him from her place on the ground as though she stood five feet taller than him.

"I am the victor. Now, I am going to give you one more chance to cooperate before I go to sleep and leave you in that condition until morning. Answer just one question and you can have your bath and clean clothing." His eyes connected with hers, unyielding. "What was the purpose of today's raid?"

Running her tongue over her teeth, she gave careful thought to his question. Then she answered, perhaps a little too bluntly. "What is the purpose of any raid? To kill."

She shrugged and looked away. She had answered his question with the absolute truth, even if it lacked the detail they both knew he sought.

Marcus stood with a disheartened shake of his head. The next thing she knew, he seized her jaw, and despite her violent, writhing complaints, he jammed a dry, dirty rag between her teeth.

"Remember what I said? Failing to answer my questions has its own consequences. If you can't give me a true and complete answer, you can sit there in silence and think about what you've cost yourself." He stood and blew out the lantern that hung above her.

He threw the entire tent into darkness. The rustle of clothing and the clanking of armor filled broke tense silence. She saw a sliver of light as Victus opened the tent flap to leave. She assumed Marcus was undressing for bed. He confirmed this when she heard the cot creak from accepting his weight. She sat there fuming, enraged at her treatment.

Her rage burned hotter when she heard his pleased voice hum to her from the darkness. "Sleep well, Princess."

Her rest was far from restful. Alex did not sleep at all. Each time her head drooped forward, the collar would choke her. Every time she leaned back, the bindings on her elbows made her arms feel as though they might snap. To find any comfort, she had to sit perfectly still, but even that came with the pain of being forced to sit with her back arched and her knees bent for hours on end, no matter what crawled over her bare toes.

Perhaps the worst of it was the dry cloth gag. It was way too big for her mouth, further cracking her busted lips. Within minutes, her tongue was devoid of any moisture and her throat was unbearably dry. Thirst, hunger, and exhaustion stole her savour for the honour of denying Marcus the whole truth.

Alex refused to give in. Only once the rising sun illuminated the edges of the tent flaps did she dare to hope her torment was almost over. The first thing she wanted her captor to see when he opened his eyes was the same glare fixed on her face as the night before. She had to make him believe he had not broken her. She willed herself to stay vigilant, but soon, even her furrowed eyebrows ached.

If it hadn't been for the roaring fire of rage and pride in her belly, she would have wept from the exhaustion alone. What she didn't expect was the way he looked back at her the moment he woke.

His eyes were grainy and tired. His body was slick with sweat. For just a moment, she saw a tormented soul behind his normally steely visage. His face cried out in fear, loss, and sorrow. Then he closed his eyes, and when he opened them, they hardened once more.

"Good morning. I hope you enjoyed your rest," he remarked in a rough, gravelly voice. When he slipped out of his blankets, she learned he slept nude. She wrenched her head away, much at the cost of her own throat; he could tell that his nakedness bothered her and he chuckled. She didn't look again until there was a rustle of clothing. When she saw him next, she saw he'd dressed himself in simple attire, lacking armor. Another slap to the face. He slipped the gag from her mouth and sat on his cot with an unruffled expression on his rested face.

"I am about to tell my guard to go retrieve my breakfast. If you answer my question from last night, you can join me and get some food in your belly. If you choose to let stubborn pride hold your tongue, you can continue to rest there and watch me eat. Now, what was the purpose of that suicidal raid of yours? What were your objectives? None of it makes sense," he said in that same calm, deliberate manner, his eyes locked onto hers.

Alex worked her mouth while he spoke, trying to see if she could work up even a drop of saliva. Nothing. It felt like he still had the gag wedged between her teeth. The only word she wheezed out was, "Water..."

He wanted her to give a long-winded explanation of her motivations for the raid? Well, first he was going to have to hydrate her shriveled husk of a tongue. She waited for him to agree or resume with her punishment, but either way, he wasn't ever going to get the answer he wanted without a bit of water to sweeten the deal.

Luckily, he seemed to understand. With a sigh, he stood and walked to the small desk on the other side of the tent. He picked up a pitcher of clean water, filled up a cup fashioned out of a steer's horn, and returned to her.

"Drink up." He pressed the chalice to her lips and tilted it back. She wanted to refuse and to spit at his face. She wished she could force herself to protest, but she desperately needed this. So, she contented herself with glaring angrily at him from over the rim of the horn and guzzled down every drop of water he slowly poured into her mouth.

"Now, give a more complete answer to the question I asked last night," he whispered. "Please."

Alex rolled her eyes, swished the last mouthful of water around, and loudly gulped it down. It was such a relief to soothe her aching throat, but it was hardly enough. Licking her cracked lips, she tilted her head back against the pole.

"I gave you the truth last night, but you didn't like the answer. You want details, but you should just embrace your ignorance. It's easier that way," Alex croaked.

She was unwilling to admit, especially to him, how much control she had lost over her life, let alone her kingdom. Cursed be her sex. Sensing he was about to get up and order his breakfast without her, she shifted her gaze a little and continued.

"Look, the whole point of the raid was to kill. Kill you, your brother, and whoever else our swords could slice through before we met our ends. There was no other reason than that. I'm not sure what you're hoping to hear," she protested, desperate to make him understand while giving as little actual information as possible.

Her confession revealed that she knew her end was to be met, or at least that had been the plan. It made her look pathetic, but she'd sooner appear weak than actually become it by blubbering about the details of her exile.

"You expect me to believe that Princess Alexandra Monica Raybrandt, the most feared battlefield commander in Artoria, decided that a suicidal run with a skeleton crew into the heart of our camp was worth the miniscule chance you'd reach me or my brother? You're too cunning for that. I don't know if you are lying to me to conceal some deeper, ongoing plot, or if you have some other reason for this deception, but I am not satisfied," he told her in a low, sincere tone.

Without another word, he marched over to the bathtub that he'd offered her last night and filled the hollow steer's horn with cold water. He callously dumped the water over her head and marched out of the tent to claim his breakfast.

Alex wanted to scream. She wanted to just blurt out the truth. The whole truth. Of course, he didn't understand. A few weeks ago, this outcome would never have crossed her mind. How could she expect him to understand a path she still wasn't sure how she found herself on?

Before long, Marcus returned with a plate full of food that made Alex's eyes as wide as his dish: eggs, sausage, bread, fresh rabbit, and an apple, along with a goblet of wine. Alex's entire body was dying for a bite. He sat across from her and took slow bites of a plump piece of rabbit that made him hum with pleasure.

"So, tell me. Are you always this viciously stubborn? If so, it's no wonder your father's armies left you to die." Marcus bit into the juicy, red apple with a crisp crunch. Her eyes were heavy and her mouth fell open as though she hoped to catch a taste of his breakfast by just breathing through her mouth. No such luck.

"I'd like to think myself amiable in the right company," Alex replied, leaning forward despite the pain it caused her to catch a stronger whiff of his breakfast. The smell was clouding her judgment and she could feel her will slowly erode.

"Well, that's a relief. How about this, then? I swear to the Gods that I will let you see your men as soon as you are clean, fed, and rested if you'll tell me the name of the person your family's army now follows."

"Will you swear on your mother's name?" Alex asked quietly, desperation pooling in her eyes. He silently nodded in agreement. She raked her teeth over her lower lip and then relinquished a name. "My cousin, Nicholas Raybrandt. He is who they've pledged themselves to."

Alex breathed deeply, eager to get out of her chains so she could do as he promised and go see her men.

"Nicholas Raybrandt. Is it solely because he is a man, or is there something more?" Marcus asked. He took his piece of bread and kneeled before her while he waited for her answer.

"That wasn't the deal. I gave you his name and now I want to see my men," Alex hissed, addressing the crumbly loaf of bread in his hand.

"Ah, but the bargain is not yet complete. I said that you could see your men after you were clean, fed, and rested. You've still yet to meet even one of those requirements. Answer my next three questions, however, and you just might before nightfall." He reached into his pocket with his free hand and fetched the key so he could unbind her.

Alex hissed between the grit of her teeth. How had she allowed herself to be lured in by something so obvious? She was just so impatient to see who she had left to her in this world. How could she not oblige when she felt so close to seeing them? A little food, a wet cloth, a quick nap, and she'd be with them again. Simple enough.

"They follow him because he is, in every way, more like my father than I am. I banned the brutalities my father encouraged after his death. What you see before you are the consequences of that choice," Alex explained quietly, as though fearful she feared someone would overhear her hushed whisper.

Marcus mulled this over for a moment and then pushed the loaf of bread to her lips. Alex wasted no time in devouring it wholeheartedly, soft moans of relief and all. He waited for her to finish and poured her a glass of wine. Anything to keep her lips loose and her mind open while he pressed on with his inquisition, she supposed.

"So then, how long ago did this happen?" His brow quirked, his gaze much softer now.

"About three months now. My small band of loyalists and I have been trying to regroup ever since until..." Alex caught herself and quickly took another sip of wine. She'd answered all that was required of his question. "That's two. You have one more."

"What were you going to say just now, before your wits caught your tongue?" Marcus reached up to unfasten her collar so she could finally sit normally without choking herself.

"Until..." Alex paused again. She didn't know what talking to Marcus so frankly would mean. Was she an unredeemable traitor, a pitiable prisoner, or just a defeated monarch? Did it even matter? This was his third question, and a deal was a deal. "Until he sent word that he would burn an Artorian village for every week that we made him wait. He wanted us to attack your camp. He wanted me, you, and your brother dead."

"And you went along with this madness?" he asked cynically, even as he reached out to take her hands to help her to her feet. The process was agonizingly slow. Her quaking knees nearly caused her to crumble to the ground more than once, but Marcus was gentle in his persistence. He waited until she stood without a grimace or gasp of pain, then led her over to the table where she could have her fill.

"Not at first, no. About a week ago, we came across a village that had clearly met the traitors from my family's army. The men had their entrails cut out, and they filled their guts with coals. And the children..." The images of the burned corpses flooded through her mind, preventing her from even lifting a fork for this feast. "They flayed the children and hanged them from the trees before being set ablaze. And I found their mothers without a trace of cloth to cover their blackened bodies. They laid them on their backs with their ankles tied behind their heads in a grotesque contortion as a message to me."

"Because you're a woman?" Marcus asked softly, encouraging her to go on while he chained her ankles together.

"Because their revolt started the day that I stopped one of my commanders from raping a Luxorian woman."

CHAPTER 4

In a tent in the center of camp, Marcus had just finished explaining Alexandra's side of the story to a gathering of mostly entitled but important men.

The woman she had saved was from Yenus, a Luxorian border town that the Artorians had invaded to gain ground. These towns suffered constantly from changing leadership and laws, which led to mounting frustrations that one woman could apparently no longer abide. Her outrage made her an easy target, and Alex stepped in to protect her.

"So she says, but what proof is there? Her tale seems convenient. I would urge Your Highness not to allow yourself to be manipulated by our enemy so easily," remarked LaClair representative.

Each of the five noble families had sent their envoys, and each of them had a simple ambition: they needed to be heard. From their mouths sprouted the tongues of their masters, though in this case, none of them really knew what to say. Some had a responsibility to remain neutral and simply gather information until they received word about how their masters wished to respond, while others were more bold with their opinions.

"We ought to chop off her head for what she did to our prince, your brother, Your Highness," suggested a representative from the Shievre house. They were perhaps the closest in power to the mighty Rustionage house, but they still lacked the land, titles, and heritage to give them broad influence. They leaned a little too heavily on the security the Rustionage name brought, and it often put them on the wrong side of battles they could not later avoid. Marcus, for one, had not forgotten their ruling on his marriage to his murdered wife.

"So, we are to be Artorians in this matter? Without procedure, we are to just lop off her head? Are the proceedings of the council not what gives your masters their power? Why should you so quickly wish me to usurp it?" Marcus locked his eyes onto the Shievre representative, making him squirm and struggle to form a cohesive answer.

Rustionage's envoy chuckled sarcastically. "Ah! We are Luxorian once more? What a relief, Your Highness. Last night, we all feared you had forgotten your honor when you broke Commander Rustionage's thumb without so much as an informal hearing. If I might ask on behalf of my master, where were the procedures then, Your Highness?"

"You may tell your masters this: I have not and will not tolerate the sort of spectacle Commander

Rustionage showed yesterday. He has established that he is a danger to my prisoners and to my men. By stripping him of his sword and sparing his life, I did what needed to be done to ensure peace. Whatever the council has to say about this case is of little consequence, for Prevak is a commander in my army and is therefore subject to my rulings." Marcus slowly rose from his seat at the head of a massive oak table that had laid out on top of it a detailed map of Artoria and Luxor.

He forced the Rustionage representative's obnoxiously smug gaze to land where it never had before: on him. He was to rule an empire now, though few had counted on such a twist of fate. They had not considered Antonius' death likely, and they were still reeling.

"What of the Artorian captive you keep in your tent? Has she not proven to be a threat to herself, your men, and all of us?" the Rustionage representative pressed, his nose curled as if he smelled something that had spoiled.

"She is a prisoner who I detained moments before death. In her current state, she is not a threat. She is also not a member of my army, and therefore, it will be up to the Emperor and the Council to decide her fate. My role in this matter is to bring her to Valencius, where she will face justice according to our laws," Marcus replied calmly, his eyes not leaving the Rustionage representative until the Alvarado representative spoke up to redirect the conversation.

"While I think most of us respect Your Highness for following proper protocol, this raises the question of the princess's word. Likely, it is this very story that will determine her fate at trial. Is there a way to test her honesty?" the representative inquired, a demure tilt of his lips and squint of his eye betraying his own skepticism.

"I should think so. She has named the village of Damnad, to the west of here, as the village she found razed and her subjects slaughtered." Marcus pierced the massive map with his dagger to where the fallen city of Damnad was. It was a two-day ride, at most. Fortunately, they could afford to investigate her claim and wait to see if more troops would fall in from Artoria in the meantime. "I will have each of you send a proxy to this village and report back their findings to me. If she telling the truth, your proxies will find a few dozen unmarked graves in the center of a scorched village. Now, go."

He dismissed them with instructions, but approached the Estradian representative before he could leave and placed a hand on his shoulder. "Wait just a moment. You didn't voice your opinion on the matter. I have to admit that I was eager to hear what you might say about all of this."

The older man turned, cleaned his glasses, and bowed his head politely. "Your Highness, my master would not have me speak my mind unless I was certain, and I am not. I apologize for the disappointment this has caused you, but I would be remiss if I did not assure you of my master's fealty."

"Of course, and I didn't mean to imply any doubt about that." Marcus bowed his head, quirking a brow when the Estradian representative didn't turn to leave. "Is there something else?"

"I'm curious. Why Damnad and not Yenus?"

"War breeds atrocities like rape far too often for us to trace her claim quickly. An Artorian town that's decimated like she described is less common. We don't have time to search the minds of traumatized townspeople, but a mass Artorian grave we didn't dig is simple to investigate. Either it's there or it's not."

"I applaud your logic and feel that my master would agree. That being said, I will dispatch two proxies, with Your Highness' permission. One to investigate Damnad, as you command, and the other to seek information on what exactly happened in Yenus. Trust my men to find the truth and I will have a report for you hopefully within the week, provided fair weather."

"Very well. Thank you and please thank Senator Estradian for me." Marcus smiled and walked out of the tent, the burden that this was turning into hunching his shoulders a bit.

It had been nearly six hours since he'd left her sleeping. He wished he could simply allocate two of his praetorians to stand guard just outside the tent and give her a little privacy, but last night had proven to be an impossible expectation. He would not allow a rogue vigilante the opportunity to strike. Besides, Victus felt he had something to prove.

"Anything to report?" Marcus murmured quietly as he pushed into the tent, his eyes landing first on the resting prisoner and then on his attentive praetorian.

"She talks in her sleep," Victus muttered resentfully.

"Anything interesting?" Marcus chuckled, patting Victus on the back to get him to loosen his hold on the brooding anger he held for the woman. It was one thing to be enraged while she was awake. Quite another to be foaming at the mouth while she slept.

"No, nothing. The sounds she makes are more like the snorts of a fat pig." He raised his voice just enough to rouse her.

"You're a loud breather," Alex groaned, her eyes landing on Victus and his bruised pride. Then, with a charming grin plastered onto her face, she added: "It may be because your nose is bent. I think a woman may have gotten the better of you more than once before. Am I right?"

Victus spared his honor and turned his back on the fallen monarch without so much as a sound, and Marcus allowed it. Their time in each other's world would be short. There was no need to make it unbearable for his right hand by asking him to shake hers.

"Do you often make enemies so nonchalantly?"

"Hmm. I hadn't really thought about making amends to poor Victus for stealing his knife. I suppose if it matters that much to him, I could work in an apology the next time that I see him." Alex rolled onto her side, her arm now awkwardly suspended by the chain Victus had used to bind her after she'd finished her breakfast.

"I think that would be very gracious of you." Marcus smiled and dug through his chest in search of something more appropriate for her to wear. Her bare shoulders and rosy cheeks were telling enough signs that she was uncomfortable. If she could play nice, so could he.

"Grace? What would I know of that?" Alex snorted with a grin. She was watching him from the corner of her eye, tracking his every move. There was a lightness to the way she spoke he found contagious. When was the last time he spoke with a woman who didn't harbor false pretences?

Marcus' chuckle seemed to make Alex's smile broaden all the more. It was the first time he had seen it, truly, and it brought forth a pulse of joy that squeezed his heart. "Probably about as much as Victus knows about women."

They broke out into quiet snickers, and the alarming sight of tears filling Alex's eyes gave Marcus pause.

"Ow, ow. Stop. You're making me laugh. It hurts," she complained breathlessly. She pulled her arms down as close to her sides as she could with a soft groan. Then she bent over and exposed her scarred back to him again. Only this time, he had a moment to take it in. Scars and burns mostly littered her back. It appeared as though there were very few battles from which she had walked away unscathed, much like himself.

Marcus understood then why her men had followed her into the abyss: she was one of them. He sat in a chair right in front of her, waiting for her to recover.

"My apologies, Princess." His softening gaze settled on her poor, abused face. He could tell that beneath the bruising, blood, and swelling, she was a great beauty. He regretted being the one responsible for some of her pain.

"Never mind it. Tell me, have you ever stolen before?" Alex asked, the moment between them passing abruptly, much to his relief.

"Maybe once or twice when I was just a child, but I wasn't fond of it. There wasn't a thrill in it for me. My brother was far more comfortable with the idea, and was clever about it too," Marcus remarked with an angry scowl that led Alex deeper into the conversation.

"Oh? Did he steal something from you?"

Marcus wasn't sure how to answer, so he didn't. He knew that she'd switched topics to spare herself the pain of her new reality and to fill the otherwise silent void with noise. She didn't care. So instead of answering, he walked over and unchained her. While she delicately eased herself off the stiff cot, he returned to his chest and fished around for something for her to wear.

"Put this on," he instructed when he finally tossed her a white tunic and a thick brown belt he hoped would fit her. It wasn't much, but it would be enough to cover her until they got to the next town. "You can either wear this or I can ask a camp follower to spare an outfit."

"I'll take my chances with this, thank you."

Satisfied, he turned around for a moment to allow her to slip into the tunic unobserved. He couldn't permit her the time it would take to locate a blade, so the instant the rustling of clothes stopped, he turned back around and shackled her wrists once more.

"What of my men? Please. I want to see them," Alex asked. He felt a twinge of pain that was born of the hurt inside of her voice. It was time that he came clean.

"Princess, we have already moved your men to our base camp in Tripsburgh, nearly a day's ride from here. We will pack up camp tomorrow morning so we can set base there until it's decided what is to be done with the lot of you." He tried his best to stay passive as waves of devastation rolled over her face. As much as he would have liked to, he didn't relish it.

"You lied to me?"

"No, I didn't. You will see your men, I promise. A trusted commander of mine moved them for their protection. Mostly to keep the rowdiest of my men from making sport of them before you even woke up," Marcus explained, a forceful, stony expression on his face that he was struggling to maintain.

"I don't believe you! Are any of my men even alive?" Alex shrieked, jumping to her feet in outrage. She had been dangerous before he had given her rest and food.

Now that she had both, she was more than capable of continuing her campaign against him. He needed to distract her.

"Yes, but I'm afraid that for now, you're going to have to do something you won't like very much." Marcus spoke calmly and put his hands on her shoulders to keep her still.

"And what exactly would you dare ask of me now?" Alex shot back with a curled lip as though she were preparing to rip his throat out with her canines.

"Trust me. I promise you will see your men in Tripsburgh, but I must ask for your patience. Can you do that?" he asked with a raised brow. He expected resistance, but knew all along that he would accept nothing but her full compliance.

"Fine. I guess you can go," she muttered under her breath and jutted her chin toward the exit.

With a grimace, Marcus extended his hand. If only she'd accept. "Would you like to join me for a walk around the camp? I will, at the very least, let you say goodbye to the men we must leave behind."

"All right," Alex replied solemnly after a few tense seconds of silent contemplation. She walked past him into the sunset that shone as red as blood, with streaks of purple and blue clinging to the outer edges of the sun's rays.

Victus was waiting just outside the tent, his eyes fixed on the ground. Once Marcus passed him, Victus was up on his feet. Marcus knew that if Victus thought even for a moment that she was going for a weapon, he wouldn't hesitate to slice off the offending hand.

"And just what is your problem?" Alex turned on her heel, facing off with his loyal and armed guard without even a hint of fear when he grabbed her shoulder for getting too close. Marcus admired that about her, not that he'd ever admit it.

"You are, you barbarian-bred nuisance," Victus snarled, showing a side of himself that Marcus had never seen. He was so often a quiet, dutiful servant, and he'd never seen the fire in his eyes that was now burning him alive.

The look in his eye even seemed to take Alex aback, but it was only a moment before she lurched forward to counterstrike. If he let them, they'd go for each other's throats, and at that moment, Marcus wasn't sure who'd win.

"Stop it," Marcus barked at them both. He grabbed Alex by the scruff of her tunic and pushed Victus back a step, causing him to fall submissively onto one knee.

"I expect more from you, Victus. If you're going to continue to act as my personal guard, you'll do so without antagonizing her unnecessarily. As for you, eyes forward. You're not in control here, Princess. Accept that." He violently grabbed the meat of her left arm and dragged her along after she spit at the feet of his shamed praetorian. He'd seen enough.

Marcus waited for her attention to focus on the sights of the surrounding camp before he let go of her arm: the small fires, the white, crisp tents, the iron armor plates, the swords, the jovial men who either fell silent as she passed them or mocked her with open taunts that were cut short by Marcus' scornful gaze. He knew this walk wasn't easy for her, but the fresh air and stretching were necessary. He could tell from her strained gait she was going to need a carriage to ride in tomorrow, which was just as well, he supposed. The more he could keep her out of everyone's way, the better it would be for all.

Alex interrupted his thoughts with a quiet voice. "Marcus, I have a question. You must have known I was the commander for quite some time, as did your men. What stories or legends did you all dream up about me?"

They passed a group of men who said a quick prayer before rushing into their tent. Their reactions were mixed and strange to her. She wasn't used to being treated like a proper princess, but she also wasn't accustomed to being regarded as a plague.

"Well, there are quite a few stories that the men pass around. The most popular one is that the reason your soldiers are so faithful and determined to protect you in battle is because you reward heroism with sexual favors. Whichever soldier shows the greatest heroism is your bedmate until another surpasses him." Marcus couldn't help but smirk as she turned her head away to conceal the blush staining her cheeks. Quickly, he thought of the next story.

"Others say you were originally a man, which is why you are so gifted with a blade, but a witch cursed you and transformed you into a woman. Others insist that you have studied swordplay from birth and lead a virgin life of chastity akin to that of a priestess. Their general perception is that you are a bloodthirsty warrior with no honor, that you led your men into war, but are only willing to strike when the spirits are out and the stars are in your favor. I've had to whip the sense back into many men who thought your presence on the battlefield meant they would surely die. It took several victories for me to shake that tale out of circulation."

"So, the women of Luxor don't fight?"

"Not with swords, no, but they can be just as devastatingly effective with their charms. The women of our nobility are masters of manipulation, and honestly, I don't know who I'd fear more: them or you." He laughed, surprising himself at how easy it was to talk to her so openly.

"What are the women of your kingdom like? It's hard to imagine them in anything but leather and armor with swords at their hips, considering your culture is, well…"

"Oh, stop dancing around it. I know what you really think. Your guard dog back there made it pretty clear. I don't really know. I ran away from my home when I was nine or ten." Alex wouldn't meet his eyes.

"Why would you do that?" Marcus' curiosity was growing by the minute.

"I saw something that frightened me. It was something I couldn't change. I ran away with a man named Kaden. Kaden had been by my side since I was born as my personal guard, and was my most trusted friend. We joined a small and rather unimportant squadron of my father's army. They raised me along the war-torn border towns where we fought against...you for as long as I can remember."

"Well, what did you see?" Marcus asked, the curiosity eating at him. As a child, he occasionally begged his nurses to tell him scary stories at bedtime. Artorians were often the antagonists of those stories because of their barbaric torture methods, but this was his first opportunity to find out if there was any truth to it.

"If I tell you, will you tell me if you perhaps noticed that man among the injured? He is quite memorable." If she couldn't confirm for herself that Kaden was still alive, asking Marcus was the next best thing.

"You have a deal," Marcus nodded, hopeful he could really keep his end of the bargain this time and not disappoint her again.

"There is a reason your men make jokes about the barbarian blood running through my veins. I know it better than anyone. One night, right before dinner, they caught a servant stealing a necklace from my mother. They brought her and her two small children to our great dining hall, where all the noble families ate together with my family. At one end of the hall was a monstrous brass bear that I had always assumed was just a decoration. That night, I saw the servant and her children being stuffed inside it through a small door on its back, after being stripped naked in front of the room full of guests."

Marcus watched as her eyes took on a ghostly, trance-like quality that made his heart beat faster. Whatever she was describing, she could clearly see in her mind's eye, and it was causing her pain. He considered telling her to stop, but his curiosity got the better of him. He wanted to know what could have driven her from the comforts of a palace and into the life of a lowly foot soldier at such a young age.

"They sealed the door shut, and a fire was lit beneath the bear's belly. It turned gold in the heat after a while, and their screams sounded like loud roars bursting through horns sticking out of the bear's mouth. Suddenly, the meaning of my kingdom's colors became clear to me: fire and blood."

Marcus' face lost all its color. Silently, he listened and envisioned the scene as she described it, his breath catching in his throat at just the thought of being so helplessly terrified.

"Everyone was glad that mother and her children were being cooked alive. Laughter filled the hall every time the bear rocked or there was a loud roar. This carried on until all that remained were ashes and bone. I laid awake that night thinking about how they died. I was afraid that if I didn't leave, I would become one of the many smiling faces in that hall, laughing at the misery of others. So, I ran. I quickly found out that the real people of Artoria aren't what you fear them to be. They are good, kind people who are just innocent victims. I wanted to defeat your armies for them and restore my family's honor. Unfortunately, my cousin seems to have picked up my family's bloody legacy and has their support. So, here I am."

Marcus knew that his silence was making Alexandra nervous, but he was at a loss for words. He'd never heard of something so horrendous. Even the ghost stories his nurses had told him paled in comparison, but this was no tale. This was her life, and for a moment, he felt a surge of sympathy for her.

"Now you need to answer my question. He has flaming red hair, stands well over six and a half feet tall, has arms as thick as oak branches, and is... well... a giant of a man, really. Oh. Brown eyes, too. You couldn't miss him. Is he one of your prisoners?" Her eyes brimmed with hope he knew he would have to dash.

"It seems we both have cause to hate each other. This red-haired man you're describing is the reason my brother died. As I came upon the battle, he faced off against me, truly quite skilled with a blade. I couldn't get past him. When you killed my brother, I slipped my blade in and cut the man down. I don't know if I killed or only wounded him." Marcus explained empathetically. He didn't feel any better about his position with her, but to his surprise, her response wasn't the emotional tirade he'd expected.

Instead, she matched his gaze for a moment to search for the truth she clearly hoped wasn't there. When she found it, she just shook her head. "No, I have no reason to hate you for that. By my command, my guardian, mentor, and friend may now be dead. I pray he is among the injured, but I know better than to hope for such an outcome," she admitted, still clearly reluctant to unveil the full extent of her guilt to him.

He led her outside the camp where dead Artorian and Luxorian men alike were resting in lines of ten on pyres. He dared not anger their spirits by placing them beside their enemies, but they were all there. A line of ten Artorian men with their heads held up proudly, as they should be. Further up, with their feet a scant inch from scraping the tips of the Artorians' scalps, was another row of ten. This went on for almost twelve rows. All accounted for, a hundred and twenty lives lost. Three Luxorians for every Artorian.

At the end of each line, they had assigned a guard to shoo away the crows and buzzards who were eager for an easy meal. He'd have none of that. Marcus had too much honor to leave their bodies to rot out here. Friend or foe, these men were warriors who'd sacrificed everything for their beliefs. They didn't deserve to be ripped apart by animals.

The only casualty not present was his brother. An envoy took him away earlier that morning. They would deliver Antonius to his father for a proper burial in the catacombs.

Marcus had looked into the face of death many a time, but never for so long or so silently. They'd light their way to paradise by the glow of a massive, collective pyre, but not before she saw them, not before she said goodbye. To her credit, she did not shy away from the horrifying sight or curl her nose in disgust at the hair-raising smell. Her knees shook and her head fell at the sight of their sacrifice, but she refused to give in to the desire to cry in front of the enemy. He knew she wanted to ask if her Kaden was among the fallen, but it seemed disrespectful to even consider looking for him. So many of the bodies were so mangled that she didn't know which banner they'd stood beneath. She didn't know which side they had died for.

After a few moments of silence, he gave the signal. A man stood at each corner of the pyre, with their torches ready to ignite a trail that would engulf each man with his own coffin of flames. Within two hours, they were all overcome by fire, and the heat would soon turn their bodies into ashes that would become food for a field of wildflowers.

The flames stretched toward the heavens, devouring the loyal, brave men. He could see Alex battling silently with the fact that every living man was staring at her. She wasn't free to cry without the scrutiny of his men, but slowly, small, salty rivers found their way down her cheeks all the same.

"Follow me," he whispered and gently led her away as the heat became so intense that his face felt like it would blister. This was a place for only the dead, and Alexandra could no longer stand among them.

Once they were free of the crowd, he turned and stopped her melancholy march in silent regard to her lamentation. He didn't know what to say. He couldn't really imagine how she felt and nothing he could say felt right, so they kept walking. When they returned to the tent, it surprised him when she broke the silence.

"I'm sorry about your brother. I'm sorry I took him from you." She was rubbing her arm with the pathetic, downtrodden look of someone who would hang from the gallows come morning. No, it was worse than that. She looked resigned to it. Even like she wanted it. He couldn't know what was going through her mind, but perhaps a glimpse into his own might help her see that she wasn't all alone in her pain.

With a sigh, Marcus leaned his head back and recalled a painful memory. "You asked me before if Antonius had ever stolen anything from me. While I was campaigning in the south one day, we needed shelter. I was leading a small patrol and came upon a farmhouse out in the middle of nowhere. There was a woman there, Meridian. Her hair was long, curly, and darker than a raven's wing, and she had a body made by the Gods to be pleasing to any man's eyes. She sheltered us there with her son. Someone had recently killed her husband in a raid, leaving her and the boy to run the farm alone. I made the farmhouse our base of operations, paying her gold for the inconvenience. It was the only way they made it through the oncoming winter."

Marcus went to a sideboard, taking out a decanter of wine and a pair of glasses. He filled them, handing one to Alex and drinking deeply from his own.

"I fell in love that winter. My Meridian. I kept her a secret from my father and brother. I brought her gifts, helped her keep the farm, and raised her boy as much as I could. Then my brother found out about it, and he told my father." He took another deep drink of his wine, trying to steel himself for the rest of his story.

"They deemed her unfit for a prince. As a widow, she was a power-hungry harlot, at least in the eyes of the Council. My father gave her a purse of gold; enough to keep her comfortable for years to come if she used it wisely. Then he forbade me from seeing her again. My brother spoke as though he had sympathy for my plight. He offered to distract the guards so I could go see her one last time to say goodbye." Marcus could feel his throat closing, but he couldn't stop now. He only had to recount what he saw. She'd had to live with it, even if only for a brief time.

"I slipped away when he told me, and I reached her farm. The first thing I saw when I pushed the door open so eagerly, so desperately, for this last sight of my Meridian, was my brother and his legionnaires raping her. They had enchanted her with a forbidden artifact to keep her from resisting. When he saw me, my brother calmly said that they had warned her that if I returned, it would be her death. He killed my Meridian then, right in front of me. Her boy as well."

Marcus stood and sat his empty glass down on his desk and returned to his chair.

"He was mine to kill, Princess. I had it planned out. He may have stolen her from me, but you took away my vengeance. You robbed me of my chance to let the last thing he heard be her name. Instead, he died in combat.

He died with honor. They will erect memorials in his name for his valiant battle with the warrior princess of our most hated foe."

Marcus rubbed his hand across his gloomy face and leveled his gaze at her once more to await her cynical laugh. What he saw shocked him. Those weren't the shallow tears of a prisoner. This was actual emotion. She looked horrified.

"Marcus, I don't know what to say. Why are you telling me all of this?"

Tears coursed freely down her stricken face, making him regret laying the blame of his cowardice at her feet. He'd had years to exact revenge for his loss, but he worried that if he acted without the right alliances in place, he'd be digging his own grave instead of Antonius'. Under the press of a knife, she had done what he was too afraid to do.

"Maybe because I just needed someone to know, and because I don't want you to carry the burden of having murdered a good prince who would have done well by his people. I can see that the weight of your station weighing down your heart. You would do well to cut away those strings now. Nothing good will come of it." He took a deep breath to clear his head and stood up once more.

"I'm going to give you some time to yourself before dinner. Give me your wrists and know my guards will be just outside. Use this time to mourn and then let the dead go."

Pinching his lower lip with his tooth, he turned to impart a small warning to his fractured prisoner. He hoped she'd be wise enough to take it for what it was worth. "I trust you'll remember that there are some men in this camp who wouldn't think twice about stealing from you what they took from Meridian. There are even more who would be happy to see you join your men in a pyre. Please ensure that you don't cross your path with theirs."

With those warning imparted, he stepped out of the tent and instructed a guard to stand watch. As much as he'd like to see what she'd do if left completely unguarded, he didn't want to see how men like Prevak would use the opportunity, so he had no choice. He would give her as much privacy as he could allow, but he would not carry the weight of her coffin on his back as he had Meridian's all these years.

CHAPTER 5

Sometimes, only a truly deep, soul-wrenching cry can wash away the stain of such a terrible loss. After releasing the depths of her despair into a soft blanket of furs, Alex emerged refreshed and prepared to consider her next move.

What should she do now that she had earned this precious sliver of Marcus' trust? Should she wield that weapon against him and finish the task Nicholas had laid out for her, or would she accept the risk that her people might continue to suffer raids from Artorian soldiers?

Rubbing her sore, red eyes, she momentarily considered taking Marcus' life and then her own. Their deaths would save the lives of many. That's what she thought right before charging into the camp. As a leader of men, wasn't it her duty to prioritize the greater good over her own selfish desires? Then again, was Nicholas really the man who would give her people the peace and unity they so desperately sought, or would his ambitions prolong this bloody war? The doubt in her heart made her chest swell. What was she going to do?

She walked over to Marcus' desk, which was covered by an extensive map of the Artorian and Luxorian border, where most of their skirmishes and battles had taken place. They had marked lands lost and gained on this map, as well as presumed locations of the Artorian strongholds, but he had it all wrong. He failed to identify the border towns they'd invaded in recent months, nor did it seem that he was aware of a handful of other strongholds they had built up under her father's reign.

This information was outdated, and if this was what they were working with, Nicholas' victory on the field was very much assured.

The sudden rustling of tent flaps made her take a quick step back from the table, her inquisitive blue eyes landing on a well-dressed man in robes of green and silver with thick spectacles covering his honey brown eyes. He was a turtle of a man with a very unassuming face, but he wore a confident and warm smile that made Alex feel nauseas.

"Ah, Princess Alexandra, is it? My, what a pleasure." The charming fellow approached, making Alex take an uneasy step back. Instinctively, she twisted her body and her right hand went to her hip, but there wasn't a hilt to be found. Damn it. Her eyes darted around the tent, but there wasn't a weapon in sight. The prince's trust in her only went so deep, and rightfully so.

"I doubt very much that this is a pleasure for you. What do you want?" she asked, looking past his shoulder at the back of the guard who had let him in here. Was he sleeping or was there something else going on?

"Ah! A bit on the nose there, but that's just as well. There isn't much time to waste. Here." The man offered her a small purple vial tethered to a necklace. "Use this in the prince's food or drink. It is odorless and he'll be dead before he can even concern himself with the taste. Do this favor for my master, and we will release you, along with the other prisoners, in Tripsburgh."

Alex was stunned, unsure of how much of this was true or what she was going to do about it. Why would his master want Marcus dead? Who did this man represent? She could dream up a few scandalous theories, but why would he entrust such a delicate task to someone like her?

Schemes like this reminded her of a game that gamblers used to play in markets across Artoria: for the price of what they had in their pockets, the poor could reach their bare hands into a burlap sack that contained both a precious gemstone and a venomous viper. They may walk away with the gemstone, but they often walked away bitten. Even worse was the fact that sometimes the stone was just a rock meant to trick the hopeless. Gamblers with more money in their pockets would bet how many steps that hopeless peasant would take before dropping dead. The only winner was usually the snake and its owner.

Was she desperate enough to stick her hand into that sack to see what she might draw out? This man and his master were likely counting on her to take the bait, but she wanted no part of it. She wasn't a cowardly woman who would hide behind the strength of an assassin's dirty tricks. If she wanted Marcus dead, she'd run her blade through his gut!

"Look, I don't know who you are, but you need to leave. If you don't, I'll scream," Alex threatened, taking a defiant step forward. Maybe he secretly feared her supposed mystical powers, like some men in this camp apparently did. So she puffed her chest up and tried to look intimidating. It accomplished nothing.

"Scream if you like, but I am one of the prince's most trusted advisors. Cause a scene and it wouldn't be very hard for me to put your pretty little neck in a noose, young lady. All I'd have to do is explain how I found you poised to poison the prince's decanter, and that when I moved to stop you, you screamed out of fright." He shrugged nonchalantly, as if she were a shiny red beetle beneath his boot that he could squash at his discretion.

"Marcus wouldn't believe you! He's seen me..." Alex paused, a blush consuming her cheeks as she weighed her next words. "He's seen me without very much on. Where would I have hidden it all this time? Your scheme will be as transparent as you are," she snarled, imagining all the ways she could break his jaw with her clenched fists.

"Oh? Were you not just outside, where an Artorian mole might have slipped this into your hand while you pretended to grieve? How about for the past hour? This canvas has weak spots, as you well know. It would be easy to slip it under the right spot. He can't have his eyes on you at all times, Princess, and that little seed of doubt is all I would need to convince him that this barbaric trinket is yours." He methodically ripped apart her logic while dangling the vial in between them. It felt like he was taunting her. Egging her on to take it.

"Why are you doing this?" Alex asked, her voice broken as she witnessed the very illness that destroyed empires spawn right before her eyes.

"Does it really matter? I'll leave this with you. Take care to see it done before we reach Tripsburgh if you ever want to be a free woman again."

With a swift bow, the mysterious messenger disappeared, leaving her alone with the necklace he'd set at the foot of the cot. She didn't want to even look at it, let alone touch it.

What had just happened? Alex felt like she needed to be slapped to bring her back down to the ground. She couldn't stay locked up like this for long. Rushing forward, she took the necklace and wrapped the leather cord around her wrist and rolled it until it was tight around her bicep and snug against her armpit. She only stopped once her sleeve hid it.

Nicholas might send his army on another murderous rampage at any moment, and the thought was eating her alive. The possibility of Artorian victory combined with the obvious division within the Luxorian court made the choice look rather simple on the surface. But what would happen when the seemingly oblivious prince's superiors faced off against Nicholas, who intended to rule them all? Peace might never follow.

Alex labored on these thoughts all night until she gave herself a searing headache. Alex was grateful to eat her dinner alone, and she made sure it looked like she was asleep long before Marcus turned in for the night. She wished she didn't feel this way. She prayed to all the Gods to give her a dream, a sign, or a reason to choose one path over the other, but nothing came to her that night other than the gentle hums Marcus occasionally unleashed in his sleep.

Were the Gods punishing her for shirking her responsibilities for the entirety of her youth? No doubt she would have mastered intrigue had she worn the crown like a dutiful princess, but she had insisted on having that damned ornament melted down and made into a fine dagger. The decision she now had to make without its keen edge almost made her regret all the choices that led her here.

The lackluster breakfast of a single apple the next morning told Alex that they were to leave sooner rather than later, and she was relieved. Marcus informed her that their journey to Tripsburgh wouldn't be on horseback but within the confines of a carriage, where he'd force her to look at him. Talk to him. Laugh with him like before. The man they expected her to murder in cold blood. She felt that apple unsettle her stomach and threaten to ooze back up her throat, but with the frayed willpower she had left, she forced herself to keep it down.

She just wanted more time alone to think, and she hoped Marcus was observant enough to pick up on that. He wasn't.

"I can handle myself. I don't need your protection," Alex muttered softly, disinterested in his company. She had the passing thought that maybe he would deny her the chance to poison him if she acted distant. The attempt was fleeting and futile.

Gently and without warning, he collapsed her knees with his forearm so that she fell back into his arms with a small bounce. He used that momentum to hoist her onto his shoulder, making it clear to all that she was his prisoner.

"Sorry, but embers and even blades have a way of finding themselves unattended during a camp breakdown. I won't have you unnecessarily harmed under my watch." Marcus smiled, clearly trying to ease her out of her dark depression with a bit of faux chivalry, the likes of which surprised even her.

Alex squirmed to pull her tunic down as far as she could to keep her bum covered before he could walk through the entire camp. She wasn't confident that it covered her completely until his own hand came up to pull the tunic down and hold it for her. She wanted off of his shoulder, but he obviously wasn't willing to risk her health for the sake of her pride.

Alex craned her neck to see where he was taking her and spotted the magnificent accommodation he had requested waiting across the field. "I had some sandals brought for you to wear, but they are in the carriage."

He carried her past his men, like a sack of potatoes, toward the edge of camp where the luxurious carriage of silver and sapphire awaited. Some of his men gawked in surprise at the sight of her, while others simply grinned perversely. Imagining their thoughts made Alex itch. Just who did they think she was?

He planted her at the foot of the carriage steps, where a pair of tan leather sandals waited for her.

"So, yours or your brother's?" Alex asked about the gaudy spectacle that was this palace on wheels.

"My brother's, isn't it obvious? I knew many of his traits, but humility was never among them," Marcus grumbled softly. He might not have been one of Antonius' admirers, but he knew well enough that many of the men in this camp were, so he watched his tongue.

Once she was sitting inside the coach, Marcus broke away to speak to one of his commanders in a hushed voice. The message was simple: they would ride ahead of the rest of the men to keep the temptation of rebellion to a minimum. Many of the men in this camp had strong opinions about what should happen to Alex, but none of those opinions mattered as far as Marcus was concerned. Whose opinion did matter to him?

He plopped down in the seat across from her with a tired groan and called out for the driver to move along. A sigh passed his lips as the stress of caring for a royal captive clearly weighed on his mind. If she were any other prisoner, his men wouldn't give a flying rat's ass about her, of that she was sure. Then again, neither would he.

"Let me help you," Marcus said, seizing the left sandal Alex was fiddling with. "These require you to bend and your ribs must still be sore,"

He lifted his head to look her in the eye, putting the rest of the world out of her mind for the moment. When she didn't resist, he gripped her leg by the calf and lifted it to his lap. Setting the sole of the sandal upon her foot, he started winding the cords around and up her slender leg.

"Thank you..." she whispered solemnly as she leaned back to give her aching ribs some relief.

Alex felt sick that she was really considering killing a man who'd been kind to her, but what choice did she have? Surely, that mysterious man would just frame her for any attempt he made on his own, or worse.

The thought was too heavy a burden for now, and she could feel the beginnings of another headache throbbing just behind her eyes. So, she abandoned it in favor of a much lighter topic, hoping to clear her mind.

"Tell me, future Emperor Marcus Evandrus, what kind of travel games do you like to play?"

Marcus looked up from the leg she left resting in his lap and shrugged. "I fear I have no games to suggest. You'll have to make one up."

He made her suck in her breath when he ran his fingertips over her tight calf muscles before she snatched her leg away, forcing him to move on to the next shoeless foot.

"Can't say that I can recall one, either. You'd better find some way to entertain me, and fast. I get sick in these things if I notice the bumps too much," she warned with a grimace. His light, warm touch had distracted her from the motion of the carriage, but she knew if silence took hold, she'd have nothing else to focus on but the nauseating thought of him choking to death on his own bile.

"All right then, we'll ask each other questions one at a time. First person to ask a question the other refuses to answer loses. I'll start by asking you a question I've been wondering for quite some time. The only things I know of you are what I have seen on the battlefield, that tent, and the few tidbits of gossip the villagers in our occupied towns have said. Your love life remains a mystery. Why is that?" he asked gently before he dug a knuckle into her sore calf. She'd failed to notice that he'd finished with her second sandal some time ago. Now that he was massaging away some of the tension, it felt like a crime to pull her leg away.

"That's probably because I've never loved. I am yet a maid, so I suppose some of those legends your men believed prove true," Alex admitted in a hushed whisper. She wasn't willing to look at him when she said this. Instead, she watched the landscape move past her window, only to think better of it and snatch the curtain shut.

"Never loved? Come now, your mother and father would be sad to hear you say such a thing." Marcus faked a pout as he popped her left knee, jarring her out of her staring contest with the back of her eyelids.

Alex snorted and grinned. "They hated each other and me most of all. I was just a pawn destined to carry on the family name when my mother couldn't have more children."

"And you never...? Not once?" His thumb worked its way a little higher up her thigh.

"Never," Alex shot back, unable to contain the bloom of crimson that was slowly creeping up her chest. She didn't know why he was doing this or why she didn't stop him. She wondered if he knew what his touch was doing to her.

"That's a hard thing to imagine about a beautiful woman who has lived in war camps with soldiers. Passions run high after victories or close escapes, passions that soldiers look to vent whenever they have the chance. But you say that in nineteen years of life, you have yet to feel the touch of a man? Curious." Marcus smiled devilishly.

Alex shivered when he let his nails rake her inner thigh. He gave her goosebumps. He had to know she felt it, but she was trying so hard not to acknowledge it.

"Well, it's the truth, not that I care if you believe it." She disregarded his chuckle. It was her turn to ask a question, and she had thought of a good one.

"So, what were you like when you were young? It might shock you, but I was probably a lot like your brother–I only cared about making myself happy. My people suffered more than they should have because I didn't take the weight of my crown seriously enough."

"Sounds like you were like every other child in the kingdom. The difference between you and my brother is that you matured. You woke up and realized you weren't the only one who matters. He only ever acknowledged the needs of his own reflection."

He unexpectedly joggled her leg off his lap. Her face soured, and without a second thought, she threw both her legs back onto his thighs.

"Don't stop doing that," she commanded softly.

"You don't want me to stop doing what?" Marcus asked innocently. He crossed his arms behind his head with a knowing grin.

"Th-that! You know what you're doing." A crimson mask was overtaking her face, but she pressed on. When he refused to give in, she got up from her seat and sat next to him. She didn't understand it, but she was curious about this strange feeling. She didn't want him to stop. Not now.

"Oh, you mean don't stop pleasuring you? Very well, I won't." He motioned for her to turn her back to him so he could work at her shoulders. He swept her golden locks out of the way, giving him room to work. "So, tell me, Princess..."

"I shall not," she chimed and bit back a moan. His hands went lower and her back arched, pulling her tunic away from her cleavage.

"What do you mean, 'you shall not?'" With just a small tilt of his wrists, he made her upper half dance like an exotic dancer.

"It's my turn. You asked your question," she giggled, the last remnants of her fears fading away.

"You mean when I asked what you didn't want me to stop? Oooh, you little sprite," he grumbled with a sour, bratty tone.

"Exactly! Besides, you never answered my first question. That's right, I noticed. Now tell me: what was little Marcus like?" Alex turned her head over her shoulder to look him in the eye for a moment, inadvertently pressing her back against his chest and giving him a much clearer view of her milky peaks.

It surprised her to find a serene sadness there that, in that moment, took her aback. She didn't know what he was going to say, but suddenly, looking him in the eyes while he answered her question had become too painful. She turned her face away and bit her lip. Had she pushed too far?

"Hmph. Afraid, mostly," he admitted. His hands stilled just over her navel so he could rest his head against hers, aligning her delicate ear with his firm, supple lips.

"Afraid of what?" A roll of anxiety crept through her body. Somehow, she already knew the answer. It was something they had in common.

"Everything and everyone," he confessed in a hushed whisper.

His lips brushed softly against the rigid slope of her ear. Alex turned her head slightly to look him in the eye. At that same moment, he was tilting his head down to catch her eye as well. Before either of them could stop, their lips shared the lightest of kisses that made Alex's chest burst open with butterflies.

He didn't dare lean forward for more, nor did she. For a moment, they just shared the same space and breathed the same breath of air. He captured her in his smoldering blue eyes, and she couldn't move. Finally, he leaned in to press the edge of his lips against hers, this time like he meant to do it. That moment sent shock-waves through her entire body she could neither deny nor justify.

When their lips parted, Alex was lightheaded and happy. The glow lasted only for an instant before she remembered that this was wrong. She shouldn't be doing this. Not with him.

"S-stop," she gasped, snatching herself away from his warm embrace.

"What's wrong?"

She pulled as far away from him as she could and fought to choke back a sob. She frantically shook her head and brushed away tears. For a beautiful moment, she'd forgotten that he was her sworn enemy. It was a lovely dream, but she knew it was time to destroy it. Alex snapped the cord from around her arm and she tossed the vial onto the bench between them.

With wide eyes, he stared at the vial, with an aghast recognition. She knew he expected her to say that she had plotted to poison him like a cowardly witch, and he would want to know who had given her the means to do it. This would end badly, but at least it would be over.

"What is this?" Marcus snatched up the tiny container between his thumb and forefinger. His voice thundered. His eyes were as sharp as a blade. Her own voice quaked, and her eyes delicate pools of crystal that he stood on the brink of smashing.

"It's poison." Alex tried desperately to compose herself, but failed. How could she even forgive herself for even considering such an idea? She forgot how badly that man had twisted her arm and focused only on her faults in this. She was wicked and cowardly.

"And who gave it to you?" She hesitated, but he'd have none of that. Slamming his fist into the carriage wall next to her face, he shouted, "WHO GAVE IT TO YOU?"

"A man! Your most trusted advisor, he said. He was wearing a robe of green and silver and he had spectacles and brown eyes. He said you wouldn't believe me if I screamed for help. I didn't want…"

"Stop the carriage," he called, cutting her off mid-sentence. He swung the door open and called over a replacement. "Victus, give me your horse and ride with her. I need some air.".

Marcus fixed Victus with a look that invited no question or objection. When the man assented, Marcus threw himself into the saddle and spurred the horse into a gallop with a swift kick. Meanwhile, Victus loaded himself into the carriage, where he found Alex curled up in the fetal position in the farthest corner. The carriage surged forward, and the pair rode in silence until her sniffles got to him.

"So, out with it, Princess. What did you do?" She was pitiful, but she could tell he didn't pity her. The uncertainty of the situation probably had him on edge. His hand never strayed from the hilt of his blade for even a moment, and he was constantly glancing out the window while he waited for her answer.

When she spoke, it was barely above a whisper. "I betrayed my people because my pride wouldn't allow me to be the coward they needed me to be."

She turned away in shame to lean her head against the glass, hoping the cool surface would extinguish the solitary flame Marcus had left flickering deep within her heart. It wasn't enough, so she suffered in silence.

Perhaps her pain and guilt were apparent enough that Victus spared her any further words of condemnation. Instead, he spent the rest of the ride supplying comfort where he could by sharing funny stories about himself. She finally relaxed enough to share a few of her own stories, and it surprised her to find that they both shared a love and an almost unhealthy craving for spicy meats.

After a few hours, the carriage finally came to a stop just outside the forest town of Tripsburgh. He rose to step outside, but Alex grabbed his sleeve to stop him. She blinked up at him and surprised him with a sad smile. "I might not get another chance to say this, but I am so sorry that I stole your knife and called you dull in front of your prince. Please forgive me."

"You have my forgiveness. I would have done far worse if I had been in your shoes," He said with a respectful bow before a chuckle broke loose..

"What is it?" Alex asked, intent on knowing what she said that could have made him laugh at a time like this. Was it about her?

"Oh, I was just thinking how we probably would have been friends if we had met under different circumstances. I'm not sure why I thought that. I apologize." He seemed unwilling to meet her gaze for the first time since they'd met. Strange.

"Don't apologize," Alex murmured softly. She released his sleeve, shame marring her face more deeply than the bruises. Respect and kinship that was once only for her men was now expanding to others she'd only just met on the battlefield a few days ago. This new sort of bond she shared with her enemy was strange and forged much like a blade. Painfully.

"I should go find Marcus. Stay out of trouble while I'm gone, if you can," he smiled and shut the door behind him, failing to hear her whisper the end of her sentence.

"I feel the same way."

CHAPTER 6

"I would hate to think that this wasn't a foolish test laid out by your master!" Marcus hissed, enraged by the situation that brought him before the Estradian house representative.

Marcus was fuming, but he wasn't irrational. Still, his eyes spoke of murder so pure that even the representative felt a chill. Had the family he trusted all these years truly deceived him, as the princess claimed? If such was not the case, he'd have to transfer her custody to a more hardened veteran who would not be so easy to trick. He threw the vial at the little man's chest and advanced so close to him that five Estradian guards stepped forth from their tables across the tavern, ready to intercede.

"What is this?"

It was eerie how much the guards blended in with the townspeople; their unremarkable features hid unimaginable skill. Marcus eased his stance, careful not to reach for his blade, but only so that he might avoid the sharp poke of a dagger pressed to his own back. The tavern was dimly lit with a crackling fire in the hearth to stave off the cool chill of autumn. It was subdued in both ambiance and company compared to the other taverns in Tripsburgh. No tipsy tavern wenches with their heaving breasts on display, or the enticing sounds of loud music to draw in the men. The curious would poke their head in and quickly leave for a livelier scene. This was a place for the weary to have a respite. For who simply desired a quiet drink, a warm meal, and the company of a crackling fire to keep their spirits alive.

The advisor held up his hand to stop the prince's advance and sipped at his chilled cup of mead. He picked up the elixir from his lap as though he were holding a precious jewel. "This was a test, Your Highness, and she passed. My master will be interested in this, no doubt."

"A test? A fucking test? What if she had slipped that past me? What if..."

The man before him opened the vial to show that the liquid would have dramatically changed colors from purple to green if she had even let the air touch it for the briefest of moments. Without hesitation, he confidently drank from the vial.

"It is an elixir meant to freshen the breath, Your Highness. Nothing more. Quintus Estradian remains your most loyal friend; he wanted only to know the character of this woman while he awaited reports regarding her honesty. For this test, I did pressure the young princess, who rebuffed my efforts to tempt her with promises of freedom for her and her men. She only relented when I told her that if she screamed for you, as she threatened to do, I would convince Your Highness that I had caught her trying to poison you."

Marcus twisted his lips at these revelations, struggling to concentrate on anything but the sinking feeling in the pit of his stomach. He'd been harsh on Alex. The look of fear in her eyes when he'd screamed in her face so soon after having pressed his lips to hers made him want to crawl into a hole. She probably hated him now more than ever. But why should that bother him?

"She still could have told me much sooner. I would have listened."

"Would you? Really? Tell me, Marcus, does my word mean as much as that of a rebel princess? No, it doesn't and it shouldn't. She was wise beyond her years not to panic when I left her with the poison. Instead of dumping, burying, or testing the concoction, she weighed her options carefully. Oh, and what options they were. I have to say, I don't know what I would have done in her place." The Estradian representative calmly pulled out a pipe from his bag and went about stuffing some tobacco into it with his thumb.

"She has a mad usurper cousin, who, if her stories are to be believed, has sent her own armies to burn at least two of her villages to the ground before she came to kill you and your brother. Do you know why he wanted you all dead?"

Marcus quietly pondered the situation as he paced the course of the room, putting himself in Nicholas' shoes as his hand ran across the top of the tavern's oak counter. He stopped in front of the roaring fire, searching for an answer in the flames. What would he do if he was just one maddening step away from the crown that the princess seemed revolted by? Would he simply have her banished, or did she possess the love of the people? If she did, would he have her killed? What if taking it a step further was almost as easy and reaped so much more reward?

Marcus turned to face his advisor once more. "He commanded her to perform a suicide raid so that she would remove the heirs of the Luxorian and Artorian crowns from the equation, leaving him as the only viable option of ascending the Artorian throne. As for Luxor, we'd have only a sickly emperor to oversee an empire already racked by turmoil, both from within and without. His objectives are childishly simple; I can't believe I didn't see it sooner."

He sighed with a tight frown at the nodding advisor who was now happily puffing away at his pipe.

"Yes, I should say that is probably so. His ongoing negotiations with the Yukonian Council might soon conclude and wed him to their sole heir and princess, Isabella Montague. Her mother acts as queen regent for now until they crown the new king. Such an alliance would mean..."

"It means that he isn't seeking to end the war. He's planning an invasion and with the strength of a powerful navy like the Yukonian fleet behind him..." Marcus was terrified of what this could mean for his people, and in that instant, he could only imagine what she must have felt all along. Hopelessness came to mind. Why then? Why was she still fighting as hard as she could when Nicholas clearly had the upper hand?

"Does Princess Alexandra know all of this?" Marcus asked softly. He slumped forward to press his bloody knuckles to his lips, allowing himself to remember how soft her lips had felt against his.

"I do not have all the answers, Your Highness, but I would say that given the time she took just to consider killing you, she probably knows a lot more than she lets on." The representative tapped his pipe on the counter to empty some of the ash onto a small plate. Clearing his throat, he softly said, "I will also say that I glimpsed the truth in that young woman's eyes. I think only death can stop her, and I think Nicholas knows that as well."

Those words clung to Marcus' soul as he walked through the bustling town that was coming to life as the sun fell behind a sheet of low-hanging clouds. There, on the edge of town, was the carriage where he'd left her to lament alone almost two hours ago. It had taken him this long to process the information he'd learned and the emotions surging through his heart. She wasn't a vindictive, cowardly witch who resorted to cheap tricks to see her mark dead. She was a woman under immense pressure to do one thing: to kill him.

Honor was a tricky thing. On one hand, he was honor-bound to keep this strange, fascinating woman as his prisoner and wring her for information in the emperor's name. On the other, more personal side of honor, he had doubted her intentions without giving her time to explain them, and he had drawn false conclusions. He may have been justified in those conclusions, perhaps even in his reaction, but at the very least, he felt he owed her an apology. He'd allowed his unexpected feelings for her to blind him when he thought that her feelings for him had all been an act. That wasn't fair.

"She fears you see her as a coward and that she is going to die for it, Marcus. Any news to the contrary would be of great comfort to her, I'm sure," Victus encouraged when the tenth minute passed, with Marcus still frozen at the edge of the clearing that housed the carriage. Uncertainty paralyzed him. He hated he had ruined the strange sense of harmony that had they had found, and he wanted to make it up to her. He wanted her to trust him again, but for the life of him, he didn't know how he could convince her he was worthy. And through all of it, she was still his enemy, still the woman whose family his kingdom had battled for generations. How could he reconcile the hatred this war had taught him to feel with the powerful emotions brewing deep within him for her?

Finally, he steeled his courage and approached the carriage. One deep breath was all it took before he slowly turned the handle. He stepped cautiously into the darkness with an apology burning on his lips. He hoped she would listen and that above all; it wasn't too late.

"So, it seems you weren't lying after all," Marcus began awkwardly. He eased onto the seat across from Alex, closing the door behind him.

"Oh? So, you haven't come to kill me?" she asked, her voice dripping with the venom she'd refused to lace his drink with. He watched her dip her nose into a glass of whiskey she'd found in his snack chamber and made no move to stop her. Her voice was smoky and hot with ire.

"I still have no interest in killing you, especially now that I'm learning how much more complicated all of this truly is," Marcus replied softly as he poured himself his own snifter of whiskey. "There are many secrets wrapped around you, Princess, plots and plans made by those who would work me like a puppet. Unfortunately for them, I will not be another man's plaything, and I won't do their dirty work for them."

"Then you'll release me to relieve yourself of that burden? If you don't, you will find your strings being pulled eventually, and my head rolling at your feet. I used to claim I would be no man's fool, that I would navigate my path in this life and this war. Look how well that ended for me."

"Unlike you, I have no shadowy cousin waiting in the wings to swoop in and throw me out of power. I am the sole remaining heir to Luxor. Alex, I promise you, I will not just kill you to appease the will of your cousin. I want answers to the puzzles that keep popping up around you, and I won't be able to find them if I kill you. Aside from that, I respect you and I promise that whatever may come, I will be an advocate for you," he swore, passionate and self-assured. His eyes leveled to meet hers, hoping to see some sign of the respect, and perhaps more, that had been kindling between them.

"No, not a shadowy cousin to step on your toes, but a gathering of men I know little about and care even less for. You feared me when I had that vial because I told you one of them had slipped it into my hand. After all, why would you leave to confront the man I described if he didn't exist? Stop trying to act like you're so much better than me when you have your own shadows to fear," she shot back, damning his hopes for a compassionate reply. Her guard was up, and this seemed to do nothing to help. No matter. He wasn't ready to give up.

"I am not necessarily better than you, Princess, but our circumstances are different. Yes, there are dangerous corridors in the court of my empire. Those troubled waters can be murky and difficult to navigate. I have enemies alongside me that claim to serve my interests. Yet these are waters I have tread all my life. I will wager you didn't spend your entire life fearing this strange cousin." Marcus would let her take her swings if she needed to, but he already missed the woman he had been talking to on their journey to Tripsburgh.

"I left to see if there was an actual threat, and I learned that there was not. Because of that, I learned a little more about you. I learned you weren't willing to kill me with that poison. I had hoped that by now you would have learned to trust my word as well."

"I can't trust your word until I see my men. You promised me I would see them if I answered your questions and I still havn't seen anyone. When can I see them?"

"I made a vow, and I will see it fulfilled. In the morning, when you don't have the scent of expensive spirits on your breath."

"Hmph. This? This is nothing stronger than rose water. I'm fine. I used to drink with my men all the time and I want to see them now." Her voice turned hoarse and demanding.

"Then take the bottle and bring it with you, but you won't be seeing your men until morning. Unless you think that men who endured a cross-country march with injuries from battle will think fondly of their leader, who rode in a carriage sipping whiskey with the enemy?" He stepped out of the carriage and held out his hand to help her step out.

Alex had nothing to say, though he noted with relief that she left the bottle behind. She took his hand and worked her way down the steps with an uneasy sway that wasn't apparent enough to him until it was too late. With an abrupt spin, she smacked her hand against the side of the carriage and heaved up the evidence of an almost two-hour binge. It was only then that he saw the bottle's seal discarded on the seat next to where she sat. The bottle had seemed relatively half-full before, but now that he realized she'd consumed it all herself, he realized how dangerously half-empty it actually was.

He gently eased an arm around her waist to support her, but kept his hands well clear of any territory that might lead to an accusation of improper intentions.

"Just lean on me and we'll get you to a soft bed and a good night's rest. In the morning, we will visit with your men. You have my word." He guided her toward the inn where he had established his headquarters.

"Am I going to die?" Alex croaked from between her trembling fingers. She was undoubtedly reeling from the rush of pain that accompanied such a vast expulsion of alcohol. It was a wonder she was still standing, given how much she'd obviously consumed.

"No, but you may wish for death by morning. Of course, as an experienced drinker, I'm certain you'll know how to handle it."

In a private room with a single bed, he eased her beneath several blankets. There wasn't much else to the room, really. Just a bed and a small elk-skin rug. Nothing for him to worry about. He turned for the door, but she stopped him by lightly tugging on his trouser leg.

"I forgive you," she slurred before falling into a deep, troubled slumber. Once her breathing slowed and she was peacefully asleep, he shut the door behind him and fully encased her in a soothing sheet of darkness.

"Am I insane?" Marcus asked Victus quietly as he walked out into the hall.

"Probably, but for the record, I don't want to see her suffer anymore, either."

Marcus shrugged and then settled into the room next to hers to rest for a few minutes. Victus admired his prince, not only because he gave her dignity and privacy when and where he could, but also because every hour, Marcus went to check on Alex to make sure she was all right. Only after the worst of her nausea had passed did he and Victus turn in for an all-too-short night.

CHAPTER 7

"You should have killed me," Alex groaned when Marcus came in to check on her the next morning. She had finally awoken long after dawn with a pounding headache.

"But you used to drink with your men all the time, right? Come on. Just have a bite," Marcus chimed with a punishing grin. He tried to push a forkful of fresh scrambled eggs to her lips, but she twisted away, her stomach roiling at the thought of food.

"It was a lie, all right? I just didn't want to feel the pain if you were going to kill me." She groaned and rolled over, pulling her blankets along with her to shield herself from the smell of those rotten eggs.

"I'm sorry I made you feel that way, but Alex, I want to ask you something. You told me your motivation behind the suicide raid when I promised to let you see your men. Then you told me about the poison. Why? Was it because I..."

"Look, I don't want to talk about this. I just want to see my men." She had nothing more to say to him.

She'd made her choice and now her people would suffer for it. A more reckless princess had never lived, for her fragments of hope, as few and precious as they were, had fallen right into the palm of his hand.

Marcus reluctantly seemed to take the hint. He was lucky to have gotten what he already had from her. If he hoped to ask her about Nicholas' plans, he needed to deliver on his end of the deal.

"All right. I'll take you to them right now. I'll be out in the hall when you're ready." He stepped outside to allow her to prepare herself at her own pace.

Once she combed her hair, brushed her teeth, and straightened her tunic a bit, she stepped out into the bright afternoon light with a groan. The sun felt like it was trying to pierce her brain with its searing light, but she forced herself to push past the pain for the sake of her men. They must be worried sick. What had they been told? Did they even know she was alive?

Marcus and Alex walked through the hustle and bustle of the market to a secluded part of town. It was unoccupied, except for a few Luxorian soldiers who were milling about, waiting to hear where their next orders would take them. The Luxorians who didn't have enough money to spend on an inn had made themselves at home here. As she passed by the tents, small fires, and camp followers, she felt like they'd never left the battlefield, save for one ominous structure. She knew her men were waiting for her there.

"Princess, this is our prison camp. Your men are the only prisoners presently held here." His arm swept toward the outpost that was guarded on all sides by alert legionnaires.

"Very well," she murmured, fearful about what she was going to find. The closer to the door she came, the more images of Kaden's pale, ghastly white face littered her mind, making her knees feel weak. How could she live if he was dead?

"I'll give you some time alone with your men while I speak with some of my commanders in that tent over there. Call for me if you need me, Princess," Marcus whispered in a soft, caring tone. He turned on his heel and marched off.

It was a shame he had to leave, for she felt her men could benefit from meeting him as the man she was coming to know, not the monster they feared. Swallowing hard, she slipped through the door and the smell of rot immediately slapped her across the face. Clasping her hand over her mouth for a brief second, she silently made her way into the room where the wounded and dying lay on bloodied cots, and those well enough to do so sat beside them to offer comfort. A collective gasp filled the room when her men realized their princess was among them. Those who were able gathered around her and took a knee.

"Princess, how did you find us? You're alive, are you not? Is this your ghost come to bid us farewell?" a wounded soldier named Vallen asked.

She smiled, shook her head, and took his hand in hers. "No, Vallen. I am not dead. I am here because the Prince of Luxor allowed me to be, but I cannot stay long." She needed to sway their hearts toward Marcus. She'd soon be gone, and the sooner they could come to peace with that, the more likely they'd be to live on through this ordeal. Perhaps they could even continue their lives as warriors, if she could persuade them to wear blue instead of red.

"Where is Kaden? Is he...?"

A wiry young man grabbed her hand. "This way. Please. He's been waiting." Her men parted and made a path for her to the ailing Kaden, who sounded like he was mere breaths away from letting loose the horrid sounds of a death rattle. Marcus' blade had torn his ashen face in half, and his chest was practically wide open. He hadn't received medical care. None of them had.

"Oh, Kaden," she breathed, tears pooling in her eyes. Maggots wriggled in his open wounds and he looked paler than she thought any living creature could. While she had snubbed attempts to make herself more comfortable, he had been suffering immensely.

"Ah, there's my princess. I promised, didn't I? I'll never leave your side without your permission," the giant rumbled softly. He spoke slowly and deliberately, every breath a tremendous effort. He cupped Alex's grief-stricken face with his massive, quivering paw and there she tenderly held it until his eyelids fluttered.

Recoiling away from him as though a specter had touched her, she pushed her way through the gathering group of hollowed men to the front of the warehouse. "Why was he left like this? Why were they all just left here to die?" she demanded of the legionnaires charged with guarding the warehouse. They shrugged and refused to answer her. He was a lost cause in the eyes of the healers, but not to those who loved him.

Their silence infuriated her, but not enough to blind her. She needed Marcus, and she could see the tent he had gone to. "Fine. I'll just see what the prince thinks about this. MARCUS! Ahhh!" She tried to march forward, but they shoved her back inside violently. They'd heard their prince, but Alex was still a prisoner and they had their orders. No prisoner was to be let outside without an escort, and they weren't about to walk her through the town.

"The prince will return for you in his own time. Until then, you're not going anywhere," one of them snarled. He slammed the warehouse door shut, damning her hopes of securing any relief for Kaden for now.

Crestfallen, she turned back toward her men and returned to her mentor's side, feeling as though she had no more power than a speck of dirt. She had done nothing but develop an affection for the man who had done this to him while he lay here in agony. "Kaden, oh my sweet Kaden. I'll save you. Just you wait. I promise. Just stay with me a little longer. I'm so sorry." She squeezed his hand tight, noting the way the skin around his wounds seemed to shimmer and squirm.

"Shhhhh. Your voice is so loud in a poor old man's ears," he quietly complained. He closed his eyes and exhaled deeply, as though he were about to go to sleep. Alex slapped him back awake with all her might, sending a ringing SMACK through the warehouse.

"Silence, Kaden! You will live and I'll hear no more about it!" she insisted through her tears. She tore her eyes away from his when his festering wound grabbed her attention once more. Maggots were burrowing deep within the gash where a grown man's fingers couldn't reach. She wasn't sure that she could get them all, but if these could be his last moments, she could at least try to make them a bit more dignified.

"Stay with me," she commanded, and gently caressed his pale cheek. Softly, with eyes sparkling with hope, he nodded his head, and she darkly said, "Hold him down."

Kaden's screams echoed through the cavernous space for a full hour. The burning sensation of those disgusting bugs trying to eat their way into his flesh finally abated, thanks to her. "The maggots are mostly out and I've stitched you closed," she breathed, tears of hopelessness pooling in her eyes. She had done all there was to do. Now they could only sit and wait for someone to bring help. She dared to hope that Marcus would actually help him, but if she was wrong and Marcus tried to pull her away now that she could see the life in her old friend's eyes again, she'd run him through.

• • •

Marcus hurried to his headquarters across the street, the cool afternoon air feeling good on his skin. He hated the uncertainty churning within him. He couldn't deny what he felt when he looked into her eyes. There was something there. At the very least, a mutual respect was growing between them and it wasn't something he was ready to surrender just yet. He would fight for her, just as he would for his own people. He would make things right.

He stormed into the command tent, ignoring the guards as he passed them along the way. Inside were the commanders of his legions, ten men including a subdued Prevak. "Report," Marcus said, and went to a sideboard to retrieve a glass of wine. He then stood at the head of the table, sipping the wine and examining the map spread before him while he awaited their answer.

"My prince, the legions have taken up defensive positions along the border, as commanded. We have halted all advances and council representatives have sent their envoys. There is, however, one command we couldn't reach: a cavalry cohort sent behind enemy lines to harass Artorian supply lines. I sent a scout to find them, but their orders were to stay hidden. They will be difficult to locate," Commander Hardin stated.

He was the commanding officer of Marcus' personal legion and his right-hand man in this group. He'd been the only one Marcus could trust to oversee the prisoners' transport without fearing that he might turn his men loose on them for sport.

Marcus nodded, and then Commander Maximus spoke up. "I think we would all like to know why we are retreating from the border when we ought to take advantage of the opportunity. We have them on the run and there are at least five enemy villages nearby that we could easily pillage. My men are eager for companionship," he said with a dirty laugh. He was the brawniest of his brother's commanders and infamously dedicated himself to butchering Artorians. Hatred brimmed in his deceitful green eyes for the barbaric Artorians that he'd known his whole life needed to be put in their place. Now that he had the chance, he wasn't keen to just turn away.

"We are falling back because those are the orders I am giving you. You will keep your men here until further notice. If they want to dip their spears somewhere warm, tell them to spend some of their wages and get a whore," Marcus replied with a voice as cold as winter, refusing to pay him even the smallest respect of a glance. Luxor had a narrow coastline that might make fending off advancing troops easy, but the same bottleneck that defended them could also condemn them. An embargo would be easy enough to enforce, crippling their economy and eventually starving them into submission. That was his concern.

"Oh, and did you pay for your little playmate? Rumors say animals raised her; she probably fucks like one too, eh?" the commander guffawed, slapping his knee. "Come on, Marcus, what harm is there really? It wouldn't take long to sack a couple of villages."

"My orders are simple! We may have a chance for peace if we are wise enough to seize this opportunity. I am waiting to hear if we have that long-sought peace in our grasp, or if the war shall continue with a new Yukonian and Artorian alliance. Until then, I will not terrorize the people who may soon be our brethren." He finally lifted his head and walked over to the foolish, slovenly commander who should have forfeited his post long ago. "As for the Princess Alexandra, allow me to remind you she is a princess, even if she is our prisoner. You WILL show royalty the respect it is due! You may start by calling me 'Your Highness.'"

"Yes, Your Highness," Maximus murmured with barely veiled disdain. He turned his head away from him and his fellow commanders who, mostly, were glowering at him for his obscene outburst that had nothing to do with the purpose of their gathering. Maximus was lucky that his friend's father was a powerful councilman, or many of them would have had the mind to do what Marcus could not.

The meeting concluded without further incident. They covered reports on injuries, total prisoner counts, troop settlements, and suspected enemy locations with precision. Even Prevak was silent, though he was incapable of hiding his glare, which Marcus regarded as little more than a troublesome itch. Once his commanders were up to speed on the next steps, Marcus dismissed the group and headed back to the prison camp.

A flurry of activity surprised him when he entered. His praetorians placed their hands on their blades, expecting trouble, but none of her men seemed to even regard their presence. Marcus kept moving forward with a dismissive wave of his hand, telling them to stand down. Every mobile prisoner was in one corner of the warehouse, hunched over something. He heard the princess softly crying over the man he'd cut down. Nothing seemed too out of the ordinary until he realized that most of the wounded prisoners bore no evidence of medical treatment at all. The blood rose to his face as he saw how the prisoners were being treated against his orders. He silently motioned to one of his praetorians.

"Bring me the head healer. Now," Marcus growled in a low voice. The prisoners were so focused on the actions of their princess that they still hadn't noticed his presence. It took several minutes for a man wearing the white robes of a mystic to arrive, looking very out of sorts and disgruntled for being summoned so abruptly.

"Why did you drag me down here?" the man sighed, as though this was a complete waste of his time.

"Why aren't these prisoners being treated for their wounds?" Marcus asked in a deceptively calm voice, his eyes still focused on the princess.

"They aren't being treated by the decree of Prince Antonius. All prisoners are to be kept in the condition in which we receive them. We feed them, but no wounds are to be treated, and no medicines administered. He deemed it too costly for the empire to heal prisoners of war," the healer replied defensively. "All prisoners are under the rule of summary execution, only to be held long enough for the executioner to write their names and ranks before beheading them. Tending their wounds would have been a waste of resources."

"I see. Prince Antonius is dead, and I am the heir to the throne. Is there no way for me to countermand that order?" Marcus asked, still not looking at the man, his eyes fixed on the one named Kaden.

"Not without becoming a traitor," the healer replied, barely able to keep the accusatory edge out of his voice.

"And what of refugees? Is it too costly for us to tend to their wounds as well?" Marcus inquired, his eyes lifting to meet the mystic's.

"Well, no. He gave no orders concerning refugees."

"Then I would like to know why these refugees have not had their wounds tended."

"Refugees? But you just said they are prisoners of war!" the healer exclaimed, confused and annoyed.

"Are you questioning my word? I am telling you there are no prisoners, save the princess. All enemy combatants are dead or fled. We brought back a band of refugees, however, that were caught in the crossfire, and I expect you to treat them." Marcus finally turned to glare at the small man to shrink him all the more.

The man shivered in fear and scrambled to leave the room. "My... my things are outside. I will tend to them immediately and I'll also send for more healers! I'm sorry, Your Highness."

Marcus realized that Commander Hardin had followed the mystic in, and he motioned him closer. "Hardin, when they are strong enough to move, I want these men released. They are refugees, not prisoners of war," Marcus said, staring his commander in the eye. He needed to see for himself just how loyal this man was.

Commander Hardin just sighed deeply and rubbed his brow. "Your Highness, if word of this decision gets out, things could go poorly for you with your father."

"I don't give a damn. These men deserve our respect, not a bug-infested grave. Offer the men the chance to leave, under the sole condition that they swear an oath to never lift a blade against a man, woman, or child of Luxor again. If they refuse..." Marcus paused and looked down at Alex.

"Then I will execute them." She said it loud enough for her men to hear. The war was over. They were never again to lift a blade against Luxor and if they couldn't swear to that, then it was clear to Marcus that, as her irrevocable last act as their princess, she was ready to drench her hands in their blood. Better theirs than the blood of innocence she claimed to protect, he supposed.

With that assurance in place, he dismissed his commander and turned his attention to the princess. The newly appointed refugees noted his approach, his air of command wrapped about him like a sharp suit of armor that seemed to part them like waves before the keel of a ship.

"Princess, this is the best healer in my camp. He is going to tend to the wounds of these refugees before we send them on their way. I apologize he thought they were prisoners of war, bound for summary execution by order of my late brother. I have corrected his mistake. We must leave so the talented healer can get to work without interference. I will give you a moment with your old friends."

His gaze snagged onto the barely conscious eyes of Kaden, and he nodded regarding the man's prowess. Marcus had been the one to deliver the nearly fatal blows, but it had been one of the most arduous battles of the prince's life. He turned and marched away from the prisoners, giving her a few more moments of privacy before he'd have to lead her away. She was still his prisoner, after all.

"Alex, I think I'm in excellent hands now. Thank you," Kaden breathed, drawing her concentration back before she could argue for why she should stay by his side.

"But Kaden, I don't trust him. Not with you. I don't want to leave," she whimpered defiantly, planting her head on his giant fist she held so tight.

"Then don't, but know that you risk Marcus' patience. I know you have been working quite hard for us to be given such a favor. Will you let it be for nothing?" Vallen rumbled from behind.

"It was nothing like that! Kaden, I can't..." How could she admit to what she had told Marcus and what she had been doing with him while her loyal friend lay dying on this forsaken cot? It was shameful to even think about. Her men may never forgive her. She didn't deserve their forgiveness!

"Shh. Know of my devotion to you, no matter what you do," he said, nudging her away gently with a wink. Taking one last look at Kaden and the rest of her men, she took a deep breath and walked away.

"I'll see you all again soon. Have your wounds treated and don't cause any trouble. Please."

Drawing deep breaths of fresh air, she closed her eyes and staved off the desire to cry. Through teary eyes, she could see Marcus standing there, but she couldn't speak. "I was..." She had almost been too late for a man who had saved her life more than once at the cost of his happiness and independence. It shook her to the core to see what they had done to such a proud, powerful man. "Thank you," she choked out through her hiccups, though confusion still curled her brows.

Marcus knew why. He was a prince, and he was supposed to lead his people and to care only for them. He was the commander of an army and he was supposed to fight bravely for his empire. Yet he just ordered a group of enemy soldiers to be healed and released on the condition they would never lift a blade against a Luxorian again.

Was he doing it because he had compassion for the princess? Because he believed her? No, he believed in honor, and killing a wounded prisoner with neglect contradicted that principle. He would not be party to that, no matter the repercussions. He did what he did because it was right, for no other reason.

He examined the face of his only prisoner, tears coursing down her face as she leaned against the wall for support. His face softened the longer he looked at her. Alex was like a mother bird, crying out and fluffing her feathers to protect her hatchlings, even though a storm had already knocked down her nest. She didn't care that they were dead or dying. She would continue to fight for them as long as there was breath left in her body, but such devotion always came at a cost.

It burned Marcus to see her in so much pain, and so, without another word, he took her hand and led her back to the inn where she could grieve in private. To his surprise, though, she took the lead with a stiffening upper lip that matched her mounting resolve. He was pulling her away from the camp, but she plunged them back into the heart of it. She had a fire in her belly. She marched into his command tent, snatched the quill off his table, and bent herself over a map of the border of Artoria and Luxor.

She stood there for several minutes, scribbling notes while muttering under her breath about the son of a bitch who had done this to her and her men.

Finally, she threw the quill down with a heavy breath. "There! I would rather my people endure the shame of a lost war to an honorable man like you, Marcus, then to spend another moment under the rule of my cousin."

Marcus shook his head in disbelief. He snatched up the map, examining all the Luxorian vulnerabilities she had pointed out that Nicholas could take advantage of. The towns she had marked on this map had been under Luxorian rule for years, but she claimed otherwise. A side note on the map clarified it was all a front.

Artorian forces had slaughtered the invaders and dressed some of her late father's soldiers as Luxorian legionnaires. They did not visit or bother these towns, but when they were, the Artorians made themselves scarce, only appearing for brief meetings where they'd report that nothing was amiss.

She had also marked the strongholds that she knew of, penetrating deep into Artoria and Luxor. Beside each marker was a set of notes detailing the weaponry, the number of men stationed, as well as the terrain.

It was a treasure trove of information, but Marcus was apprehensive to present any of it to his commanders. If he was wrong and it cost the lives of his men, he would go down in history as the biggest fool of a prince that had ever lived. "How do you know all this to be true?" He had to step cautiously, not wanting to seem distrustful, but needing to know the veracity of her claims all the same.

"You should know by now that I was a brilliant strategist who would have fought for my people until my last breath. When I met with Nicholas, I stole a map and copied it over and over. I even checked several of these locations myself to test the validity of his claim that my men had turned to him as a leader," she explained, eyes downcast. Her shame made it unbearably hard for her to even look such a successful leader of men in the eye. Where had she gone wrong? What could she have done differently? These questions were so clearly scribbled across her face. Marcus wished he had the answers.

"He was right. I'm not needed in Artoria anymore, but the kindness you just showed my men has assured me I have made the right choice to aid you in what I suspect will be my last days." Her body quivered as the weight of her earthly burdens fell away, one by one.

"What are you saying? Luxorians do not operate as Artorians do. My father and our Council will not call for your life. You have proven yourself to be an honorable and dignified adversary. Even with the death of his son, he'll have to admit that you acted in the best interests of the many, as any true leader should," he reassured her.

Marcus set the map aside so he could draw her close for a soft embrace that she did not return at first. "Thank you for sharing this with me, for trusting me. You'll find that it's not been in vain," he whispered, a little taken aback when she lifted her head to look into his eyes with a hard, skeptical look that he'd not expected given the tenderness of his vow.

"You think I will survive this? If Nicholas cannot have you or your throne, he can at least have me and mine. He can use many threats against your people and make many promises to anyone he must. He'll do anything for the chance to rule Artoria and I know ambitious men looking to secure favor with other ambitious men run your council," she hissed. She pulled away until his hand reached out to her. He brought her head into his chest, wrapping his powerful arms around her. His grip was loose enough that she could easily have pulled away if she wanted to, but she didn't.

Marcus rested his sad smile on the crown of her head as she pressed herself tighter against him. The bite of her nails made him tense for a moment until he realized she was shaking. He brushed a few golden strands out of her eyes that were still so full of doubt and fear.

"You're going to be okay, I promise. I won't let them kill you. You'll see."

With his solemn oath made, he leaned down to plant an unhurried kiss on the princess's lips without shame. Insistently, his tongue lightly flicked her lower lip until she eased open her mouth to let him in. The sweetness of it made Alex need for more. She pressed herself against him in search of something she'd always denied herself, but now had the freedom to discover, thanks to him.

"Let's get out of here," she whispered, a small spark of excitement lighting her eyes.

Marcus hesitated for a moment, but who was he to deny such a beautiful princess? Seizing her hand, he kissed it softly and brushed the back of it with his stubbled cheek. His softened blue eyes became captivated in hers and he whispered, "I'll lead the way."

CHAPTER 8

She was iron sheathed in silk, and in that moment, she was his. He had spirited her away like a randy teenager to the inn, but once he had her there, he was a little unsure of himself. Every woman he'd ever been with had been more experienced than he was. None of them had reserved their virginity for him, so this was a first for them both. He wanted it to be right.

He took everything at her pace. He didn't want to rush her or make her feel uncertain. So, when she sat on the bed with her legs crossed, he sat behind her with his back pressed against the headboard. He pulled her against him, leaning her onto his chest so he could just hold her.

He liked that every time the tips of his fingers traveled under the collar of her tunic; he got a glimpse of pink nipples that were already rigid with anticipation. It made him hard, and the way she was grinding her firm posterior against him as she tried to get comfortable only made the bulge in his pants more pronounced. His hands slid down her shoulders and began working her tunic down. He paused whenever it made her squirm, and he was quick to plant tender kisses along her neck to soothe her anxieties.

When she finally looked back at him to whisper, "I'm ready," a devilish grin spread across his face. Without warning, he ripped her tunic down, rubbing the cloth over her erect little buds and making her shiver against him. He drew her close when she gasped and pulled her back against him while she adjusted to the cool evening air.

"Now may I ask a question?" he purred softly, his eyes locking with hers.

"I suppose." Her leg twitched as his hand traveled down to the valley between her thighs, his fingers brushing against the lips of her glistening sex.

"Well, since you've kept your virginity, how have you dealt with your desires until now? It's obvious that your passions run as hot as any warrior's. Was it self-pleasure, or did you have a lucky servant to aid you?"

While he waited for her answer, he ran the very tip of his index finger up the length of her hot slit, smiling, when she let out a breathy moan. There was a reason behind his question, though he doubted she would deduce it. Experience did not seem to be on her side. He wanted to know if she even knew what brought her pleasure. It would make things so much sweeter for him if she knew and could direct him to her tender spots.

When she arched in response to a second pass of his finger, his pronounced grin made her slap his leg in retaliation. "How am I supposed to answer when you keep doing that?"

Marcus just laughed, the blow worth the discovery that she was dripping wet. When she leaned back once more, he took that as permission to continue and gripped one of her thighs so he could spread her legs and pull her completely into his lap. Watching her wrestle with herself was a treat, but time was up. He planted a soft, wet kiss on the back of her ear and allowed his soft whisper to both tickle and urge her to hurry. "I'm still waiting for an answer."

"Fine. I've taken care of my own needs since I was fifteen. A whore who followed our camp taught me. She caught me watching her every move one night; she charmed every one of my men, and it even captivated me. Jayne was her name, I think. She came to my tent later that night to teach me about the secret places on my body and what I could do to satisfy them. It was a lesson without demonstration, of course."

So, she had known for the last seven years what a man could do for her and had remained celibate? Did she really want this? Was he reading her wrong? He had to be sure. "I have just one more question, then. What do you want to do right now, Princess? Not what do you think we should do, but what exactly do you want us to do at this very moment?" His eyes were lit with desire, but his body remained still. This was her choice, and she needed to feel as little pressure from him as possible.

With a grin of her own, she pulled herself off his lap and turned to face him. Though her scars that might never fade marred her skin, she was an exquisite beauty that any man would be lucky to have in his bed. Her eyes alone enthralled him.

"If you really have to ask that, then you are terrible at reading women." She crawled back over into his lap, facing him this time, so her healed lips could tenderly lock with his. Their tongues danced as though they had been kissing for a lifetime. Gently, she ran her fingers through his hair and sat up on her knees to position herself over his shaft. She tentatively pressed down on him, making him groan with pleasure.

"Do you think you can be gentle?" she asked. Her lips parted from his, hesitation in her voice.

"I can be gentle," he assured and kissed her once more. This time, he drew his head back with her lower lip fixed between his teeth. "But for that, I need to be the one on top." Marcus shifted his weight a little and pressed his rough hand against her spine so he could swivel around. With her lying on the cushions beneath them, he could have more control over what she experienced. He intended to make her trust in him worth her while.

With his new position established without protest, Marcus began by exploring Alex's naked body. With a tender caress, he brushed her hair off her face and let his fingers slide down her cheek and neck until they reached her chest. There, he rested his entire palm on her left breast, where he pushed his hand up and around her supple flesh. He took care to tease each nipple to rigid attention before abandoning his mountainous goals for another treasure buried much further south.

His expedition continued with the rake of his fingers down her abdomen in a slow, delicate stroke until he brushed his fingertips over the top of her silky mound. Without reservation, he dipped his fingers deep into her warm depths and dropped his head to distract her with another kiss.

While he lost her momentarily in the depths of his kiss, he moved his fingers over her sex in rhythm with her quiet breaths. Once he found the spot that made her arch, he rubbed, massage, and tease her with many repetitive strokes that he hoped would drive her wild with desire. Marcus happily noted everything that made her body quiver and tense. Dutifully, he memorized the pleasure he could inflict on Alex's body until he was sure they were both ready for more.

"Are you ready for me, Alex?"

Her cheeks were as scarlet as a rose, yet in her eyes was a serene peace that made him want to keep giving in to her. He wanted to see her happy. She gave the smallest of nods, ready for what came next. He carefully rolled his hips forward once they were both ready until her body put up a natural resistance.

He watched her face for signs of pain. Then, pausing for just a moment, he savored the feeling as one would if they were standing on the edge of a cliff. Vulnerable and wild, Marcus felt his heart pounding in his chest when he looked down into her loving eyes that continued to seek his leadership in this endeavor. He would not fail her.

His entire body pulsed with need as he slowly continued to push into her. His genuine struggle was that he didn't want to be slow or careful about this. He wanted to slam into her. He wanted to use her seductive, perfect body to pleasure himself, and forcefully drive her to an enthralling world of passion. But she had never had this experience before–he had to take it slow.

This was really happening. In awe, he smiled when Alex looked into his eyes. A haze of pleasure simmering there that reassured him when their hips finally met. To his delight, this didn't seem to agonize her, perhaps because he was going slow. The pressure was incredibly satisfying.

He held his body above her and gazed down at her perfect form to allow her time to adjust. It was so intimate. She lifted her head, kissing what felt more like his soul than his lips. The instant he felt the magnitude of that kiss ripple through his body, he knew she was alright, and so slowly, he slid his shaft in and out of her. Every thrust worked him just a little deeper into her tight sheath.

He moaned into her lips; the sensation of her gripping his entire length so tight had his body quivering with pleasure. He was straining to hold himself back from the recklessness that he craved. He trailed his kisses down her neck to her breasts. She was so tight that at first it felt like she was trying to hold him inside her, fighting against his attempts to pull out, and then when he tried to return, he had to push against her just to squeeze himself back in. Without thinking, he bit her breast and let out a soft, primal growl. He needed the release. He needed to be fierce with her somehow.

Her passionate cry that followed only urged him on. He ravenously suckled on her defenseless peak, needing to be a little rougher with her. She met his thrusts with little ones of her own. He gasped and arched against her when she raked her fingers through his hair, gently dragging her nails along his scalp as he pressed his lips tighter against her breast. Soon, they found their rhythm together, and she no longer needed his supportive kisses or lingering looks. She was free to enjoy her first time with a man, and she made no secret of her pleasure once it materialized.

"Marcus, don't stop," she moaned. Her breasts rocked gently to the rhythm of their thrusts as he picked up the pace just a little, driving her to the edge of that dangerously high cliff so quickly that she lost her breath.

For a virgin, she was quite the minx. Marcus was still holding back, still being gentle, still forcing himself to use slow, long thrusts. His mouth attacked her collarbone, covering her with slight bruises to mark her as his for the world to see. Every bruise would be a source of both pride and shame for Alex in the coming days, but for now, their creation just added to the mix of sensations that threatened to overwhelm her in a maelstrom. Marcus moaned with glee against her neck, the feel of her hips grinding against his, her hands squeezing him, petting him, desperately trying to feel all his flesh. It all made him mad with desire.

He switched positions now, confident he could do so without hurting her. He laid her out beneath him and adoringly stroked the side of her face. This new position allowed him to access her depths in such a way that he filled her completely. Her wet lap smacked against his with every thrust, her tits bouncing every which way. With one powerful thrust, he hit a spot deep within her that made her toes curl and abandon all inhibition.

So, he stopped being gentle. He took her.

His hips sped up, hammering his cock into her tight, hungry sex as fast as he could. His body was glistening with sweat as he levered himself up and kneeled upright on the bed. Grabbing her arm, he pulled her up with him, one hand upon her ass and the other on her shoulder, as he braced her on his kneeling thighs. His face level with her heaving breasts, he craned his neck up to nibble and kiss at her throat and the line of her jaw. He needed to taste all of her.

"Marcus!" she cried out when she discovered the pleasure of being found by grinding her clit into his pelvis every time his hips met hers. Ultimately, Marcus made sure she could do nothing but take it as he slammed into her again and again, making her cry out from the intensity of such a ride.

Marcus enjoyed the noises she made. They weren't the practiced moans of a whore or the bored outbursts of someone just trying to save a man's ego. This was a woman feeling something, experiencing something that she just couldn't restrain. Every moan, every shudder of her body let him know he was truly pleasing her. In that moment, she was more beautiful than she had ever been to him before.

Then it happened. Her body stiffened and her sex tightened to where he could feel her slick walls trying to force him out, but there he stayed. Gods, he relished every second of her release: his hands manipulated and controlled her body, his mouth bit into every supple piece of flesh he could sink his teeth into, marking her as his, and his cock delivered blow after blow to her sweet cunt.

"You're so tight," he groaned. She clenched her womanhood around his length, almost painfully so, squeezing and convulsing until she fell against him, almost entirely limp. The sensations were quickly sending him over the edge.

So, as soon as she loosened her grip on him, he gently laid her back and started his thrusts anew. His cock was so firm and full that it didn't take long. With a heartfelt groan, he quickly pulled out of her and ground himself against her. His orgasm rolled from the tips of his toes up the curve of his spine. He claimed her, his seed spraying out across her belly, breasts, and a few stray shots at her cheeks. His body shook with the force of his orgasm, but when he slumped forward, he caught his weight just above her.

"That was glorious," he rumbled with a chuckle, staring down at her face, waiting to see her reaction once she came down off her orgasmic high.

Moaning at the warmth lost and gained, he watched her savor the moment for as long as she could. She let escape an occasional twitch or convulsion and her eyes looked droopy, but her smirk was prideful. He was proud of her, too. She had seized something she wanted.

"You're a piece of work," she informed him before grabbing his pants to clean herself up. She didn't even recognize the mess she had made on his own lap.

"Well, I'm glad my services satisfied you, Your Highness," he mused with a tired chuckle. The thought that she may become a toy for his father or the Council was truly bothering him. He might never know why she had given him such a gift, but he certainly would not risk her temper to ask. He fell back and pulled the blanket up over them, prepared to rest for a bit when a burning question passed her lips.

"So, who in this whole wide world will you marry, Marcus Evandrus? Your father, sad to say, is ailing and not likely to make it through the summer. You'll soon be emperor, and then your Council will all but hound you to decide. You must have your eye on some lucky princess from a neighboring kingdom who'd like to align herself with the champions of this war." Alex didn't sound bitter or jealous when she asked her question, only curious.

"Whom would I marry? Until now, it wasn't a concern. Aside from being told not to marry another common widow, they left me alone. I won't lie. Meridian's death scarred me. I had planned to live the rest of my life alone because of it," he admitted quietly. "I have met princesses and the daughters of nobility in my homeland and from far-off places. Most were as wanton as the rest of the capital. That's not what I'm after. In all honesty, the only princess I've met whom I respect is you. So, I guess I will have to wait and see what happens."

Marcus laid out his heart in the same spirit of complete honesty that she had shown him. He would hide nothing from her. While he assured her they wouldn't execute her, because he honestly believed it, he couldn't deny that the chance existed. She was, however, a courageous woman and she deserved for the days of her captivity to be spent with someone who respected her. The least he could do was give her that.

"Ah, you've mistaken love as a requirement for marriage. It's not. Take my advice and marry someone with a large army, and soon. It'll protect your heart and the lives of your people." She smiled sagely.

"That's where you're wrong, Princess. Love is the only requirement. I give my life for my empire, but I refuse to surrender control of my heart to them as well. If a woman is going to share my life and my bed, I must care for her," Marcus said quietly, before a passing thought stuck in his mind. What did Alex want? "So, what would you want to do if I released you from my custody?" Marcus sighed, hoping, on some level, to hear her say that she would stay. He wanted her to stay by his side to fix what their families had done to the world, but even he knew that was asking too much.

"Hmm. If the war was over, I would go somewhere quiet, off to the west where the weather is relatively warm year-round and you always have a chance of smelling the coast if the breeze is just right." Her eyes fell shut as she dared to imagine that world for just a moment. "I'd use what money I had left to open an inn and assume a completely new identity. Maybe I could have a couple of babies if I found a man I could love. I'd never set foot inside another castle or on a battlefield ever again," she said with a whimsical sigh, not denying that her thoughts drifted toward that hilltop inn of her dreams more than once a day.

Then her eyes eased open to meet his stare with a soft smile. "But of course, the war is not over, and at this rate, it may never be. If I could, I would make Luxor my home until we could resolve everything for my people and yours. This war is as much my family's fault as it is yours, and you shouldn't have to carry this burden all alone."

The difference between the dream she entertained and the reality she would choose to face left Marcus stunned. She wanted to escape, that much was obvious, but that didn't mean she was ready to abandon him. That thought made his heart swell and his eyes squeeze shut. He relished the feeling of holding her tight for a moment longer until he gradually loosened his grip so she could be free.

"You're a remarkable woman, Alexandra, and I think I'd like to release you."

CHAPTER 9

"I'm sorry to bring this news to you so unannounced, but I think you need to read this, Your Highness," the Estradian representative explained quietly as he entered the command tent where Marcus had spent hours hunched over scrolls and maps. He worked to strategize the next decisive moves he should make under Alex's notes. His commanders had been by his side for the past two days, helping him work through every possibility, and he was confident now that his plan of attack was foolproof.

They were going to take back the border towns Alex had tagged once and for all. Then, with a team of soldiers posted in every town, they would close the border. As a united front, they would push their way up and cluster around the Artorian strongholds until they fell, one by one. The terrain, the political climate, and the notes Alex had given him had determined how many men he should send, what kind of weaponry they should carry, and the timing with which he would dispatch them on their missions. Now he just had to hope the formula was right.

"Have a seat," Marcus sighed and pinched the bridge of his nose to ease some pressure. He sat back in his late brother's plush blue leather chair. His commanders were all off refilling their goblets, their stomachs, and their spirits by now, even Hardin. It had been a trying day of opinions, and Marcus was feeling the strain his brother must have felt. It was becoming clearer by the moment why Alex had pushed aside her own crown for so much of her youth, but with her help, he hoped his head might not hang so low.

"Where is the princess?" the Estradian representative inquired as he took a seat to Marcus' right and tapped his scroll on his knee to release a bit of pent-up anxiety.

"She is in the prison camp, where she has spent every waking moment for the past two days. She knows she will need to say goodbye to her men as soon as we leave Tripsburgh."

"So, all of them are to be left behind?" the advisor asked as he took a sip of his wine. To his delight, it was a red. He enjoyed the musky, unsweetened taste of a true red grape.

"Well, I've made an exception and will allow her to bring two of her own personal guards. She's named Vallen and Kaden as her guardians. She values their service as her surrogate family more than she has ever treasured the swing of their blades, plus her choice does little to upset our men. One of her guardians is now half blind, and the other can barely lift his head, let alone a broadsword. It will be a long time before either can be of proper service to her, but she'll be fine until we reach the capital. My men will step in. They'll keep her safe."

"Your Highness, I believe that the level of protection around the princess is not sufficient. Please read this," the advisor urged, and held out the scroll for Marcus.

He took the missive and skimmed through it, his face hardening as he absorbed Estradian's warning. He was at a loss for words. Alex had been right all along, and he didn't know what to do about it. "So, Nicholas has suckered my father and most of the council into calling for her head without even a proper trial?"

"It would seem that way. By my estimate, we have just a few days to decide on a course of action before the official edict will arrive and they'll leave you with no choice. They will force you to execute her if fate doesn't intervene..." the envoy warned ominously.

After some silent consideration, he continued, "She could flee, or she could become untouchable by our laws to all but the emperor, who would need to deliver the verdict in person."

"I'm not sure what bush you're dancing around, so just get to the point," Marcus growled, and he threw the scroll across the table with a disheartened sigh. He'd gained the trust and care of a woman he was going to be ordered to murder. Alternatively, he could let her escape and forever risk losing the trust of his men, which would ultimately lead to his own demise. There were no good options. He felt crippled by this news, but Estradian's puppet sat there with a calm smile as he watched Marcus' face pale. He already knew what needed to be done, and he knew Marcus would do it.

"You'll need to marry her, my prince, if you want to save her life." Casually, he swirled the wine in his goblet and took one last gulp while Marcus collected his jaw.

"Marry her? What are you saying? I've known her for four, no, three weeks," Marcus snapped a little too loudly. The false pretense of genuine help irritated him.

"You have known each other for longer than an hour? How fortunate for you both! Most royal couples may know only the other's premarital name and perhaps see their portrait, and you will not have to know the pain they must endure." The advisor huffed and leaned back in his seat, irritatingly self-assured and certain of his plan.

Marcus was speechless. To say he was wrong would have made him sound like an ignorant, petulant child, but he was wrong! Marriage was a sacred bond shared between two souls that were close enough that they'd gladly swear their eternal servitude. The kinship Marcus shared with Alex was a welcomed relief, but it wasn't enough for him to surrender his heart and happiness to her, was it?

But that wasn't his only consideration. What if he married her, and she met with the same fate Meridian had? She was royal, yes, but she would be far from safe if the senators poisoned her or the majority voted her onto the chopping block. Could he live with that? Could he ever look at himself in the mirror again, knowing he had saved her life only so that the council families could butcher her themselves?

These weren't questions he could answer right now. It wasn't a reality he could face. The thought of failing to protect a woman who swore solemnly to care for him and who he might grow to adore was gnawing at his soul.

"You are my prince. I would never advise this if I did not think it would benefit both you and the people of Luxor. Think calmly for a moment. Would your people be better off under the rule of a man so crazed that he would slaughter entire villages of his own people in a push for power?"

"Have your men returned? Did they validate her stories?"

"Yes, he burned villages and tortured his subjects. The last moments of those women and children would have been horrific. Also, the agent I sent to Yenus to investigate what truly fractured the army's bond with their princess has returned just last night. He stayed in towns along the Artorian side of the border every night of his journey and reports that one thing is clear: her people love her. Legends of her kindness and bravery were close to my agent's ear as word of her capture spread. It devastated her people to learn we had captured her." The advisor reached into his pocket to reveal a small, weathered scroll that had arrived at the foot of a falcon of the only family that seemed to keep theirs from being ripped down from the sky.

Marcus unraveled it carefully, reading the names of towns he had stayed in and comparing those names to his newly improved map. His agent had avoided all the false banner towns and had written a note at the bottom regarding Alex's character that made his heart surge with a pulse of energy he thought only possible to find in the euphoria of battle's end when all went quiet and he was still alive.

They say she was the shooting star of Artoria. It is said that to look upon her was to feel a moment of hope that someday the crown and all who wore it would not only hear the cries of their people, but would selflessly dedicate themselves to their resolution. In their gloomy taverns, they confided they wished they could have helped her as she had helped them, and that they feared for their future under her cousin's rule.

"So, she is beloved by the people of Artoria and they are the ones who this war has struck the hardest," he murmured thoughtfully and leaned his head against the back of his seat in contemplation. "If they can love her despite the horrors the Raybrandt family has inflicted against their own people, so too could Luxor. Is that what you're telling me?"

"Yes, my prince. In time, they will see what her own people do, and what I think you see too. Make no mistake, Your Highness. You are still at war. Nicholas Raybrandt conspires not only for her death, he seeks the destruction of your empire as well. He promised my master the lands of every house who opposes his rule over a new and unified Yukonian Empire, should Senator Estradian help make his dream a reality. He cannot achieve his dream while you live, Marcus."

Drawing a deep breath, Marcus raked his fingers through his hair. His fears were becoming realized. He might die before ever accomplishing anything of true value for his people, and yet, as a princess in exile, Alex had already accomplished great things that had earned her the reputation as a heavenly sign of hope. What had he done that was so great? He had blindly followed the orders of his father and brother, and nothing more. He feared his subjects would not even recognize his face for how little they knew of him.

He needed that infectious smile she had. He needed her compassion, her strength, and her resilience as much as she needed his protection to keep breathing. So, maybe that was what their marriage could be: a partnership, an alliance. He could reserve his heart for his actual wife, and she could shield hers, too. Together, with the support of the people at Alex's back and the strength of Marcus' army at his, they could build a powerful union that would unite their two kingdoms under the rule of two monarchs who would cherish and defend their subjects.

After a few more moments of silent reflection, Marcus bowed his head into his hands with a heavy, soul-abandoning sigh. "I understand what I have to do. Let us hope she will, too."

Hours later, after they drew the revised battle lines, and they brought every Artorian town they could safely reach under the protection of the Luxorian crown, Marcus emerged from the tent as a battered man. His worn face looked like it desperately needed just a few moments of relaxation that he felt he didn't deserve. He was about to ask his enemy for her hand in marriage. Was this actually going to work?

So many uncertainties plagued him he felt like he might choke on his own tongue when he called for Alex to emerge from the depths of that warehouse. When he saw her warm and grateful smile, something inside him knew that this was right. In a wave of relief, the tightness in his chest washed away because she reached out to take his hand and gave it a light squeeze. He couldn't let this woman die.

"Ready to go?" she asked in a soft, almost soothing voice that exposed the inner peace she had somehow found in what she still thought were her last days alive. She had already let go of so much, but maybe that wasn't what this serene look in her eyes was about. Maybe she was also happy that her man, Kaden, was making a quick recovery. If the healers were to be believed, he'd be back on his feet in just a couple of days.

"Yes. Let's get back to the inn. I'd like to change out of this heavy armor and there is something we need to discuss." His voice spoke of serious implications while remaining calm enough not to alarm her. He wore the same armor he'd worn when he met her on the battlefield. It suited this all-but-abandoned side of town that still felt so much like a war-zone. But for what he needed to say, he wanted to be sure she saw him above all else. Not the glimmer of his armor, the edge of his blade, or the crest of his family's name–just him. Maybe then she might say yes.

They arrived back at the inn, hand in hand. He expected that the townspeople who knew Alex would stare at them, but do little else. There was no harm in that. The innkeeper, his wife, and daughter had been kind, but what he didn't know was that every meal they spent apart, she'd spent in the company of their family, picking their brains about what it was like to run an inn. Alex seemed to fascinate her, and quickly, their six-year-old daughter grew to trust her.

In exchange for their wealth of knowledge, she would tell grand, enrapturing tales of adventure that thrilled and inspired, until eventually Marcus would come back to bring her to her men. The innkeeper's wife was happy for the distraction that let her breeze through her morning chores, but she still kept a close ear on the conversations they had. It pleased her that the princess had entertained her daughter for hours while still being careful to keep some of the more gruesome details of the war with herself.

The innkeeper's wife shared what she had seen and heard with several of the other mothers in town, who had wondered why their children couldn't say enough about the captured princess. So, imagine Marcus' surprise when they encountered a small gathering of men, women, and children standing outside of the inn, waiting for her to return. He felt Alex tense at the sight of the gathered crowd and looked down to see her face. She was nervous. Had she said or brought an angry mob down on herself?

"It's the princess!" A small, redheaded girl broke out of the crowd, freckles dancing upon her cheerful face as her warm, brown eyes sought her new friend. She ran forward, her forest green dress with gold embroidery floating about her, until she crashed into Alex with a light-hearted laugh. "How are your friends, Princess? Are they feeling better today?"

Alex just cracked a bit of a nervous smile and gently stroked the girl's unruly red hair while the girl hugged her legs. "They are feeling much better today, Ceilia. Thank you for asking. What is all this? I hope I'm not in trouble."

"No, Princess! You're not in trouble. Come over here." The little girl pulled on Alex's hand insistently with all her might. Alex stepped toward the waiting crowd, and more children came rushing forward, each wanting her attention. The parents smiled at the sight of their joyful children and the foreign princess who had captured their hearts.

"Princess, it's a pleasure to meet you. My Ceilia here just can't get enough of you, but I also wanted to introduce myself properly and thank you on behalf of my cousins who live in Jenaus. They say that although you invaded the town, not a drop of Luxorian blood fell. You brought medicines, gold, and food to that poor town and left it better than you found it," the redheaded woman recounted to her as though she hadn't been there.

"Yes, I remember Jenaus, a very humble town filled with warm, kind people. I could not have wanted for better company while I was there." Alex smiled and gradually melded into the crowd. Marcus could only stand off to the side and watch the scene unfold. More men and women came forward, each with their own stories of how they knew of her. Each of them wanted her recognition and time, as though she were already their princess, too.

Finally, the innkeeper's daughter piped up. "Princess! We want you to see the Harvest Festival with us!" Her little brown head bounced up and down as she giggled, having been the one to reveal the surprise.

"Oh? It's the harvest moon tonight, is it? And how does your town celebrate that?" Alex asked, and she kneeled in front of the fair-faced little girl, who just grinned while she twirled in her yellow dress.

"Yes, yes, yes! We eat a whole pig, sing around a gigantic fire, and chase fireflies when the moon gets really high! Will you come?" she begged, taking both of Alex's hands into hers and encouraging Alex to bounce with her.

"Well, I don't know."

One man in the crowd stepped forward. "Princess, if we may. We came here to welcome you to the town's Harvest Festival. We want you to know that you would be there as our guest, not an intruder. Of course, the decision is ultimately up to you and our prince, but know that we want you there." The rest of the crowd offered nods of affirmation.

Alex turned to look at Marcus, who gave a very subtle nod and a light, approving smile. She turned back to the crowd and said, "I'd love to come."

The children cheered and ran around the legs of the adults, who all basked in the moment's warmth. None of them had really believed the tales that had circulated around the border towns until now. There was a commonality about her that made her more approachable than even their own prince, and a light shone from deep within her eyes that no one could ignore, least of all Marcus.

Marcus stepped forward and gently placed a gloved hand on her shoulder to give it a small squeeze. It was a gentle reminder he was still there and needed to speak with her when she was ready. She had not forgotten, so when the children asked her if she would play with them, she had to decline. "My sincere apologies, but I need some time to get ready for this evening's festivities. I can't go dressed like this!" They all sank back with dejected sighs, so she said, "Give me a couple of hours and I'll meet you all downstairs. I'll help you catch so many fireflies that our jars will shine as brightly as the sun!"

With that dream planted in their heads, they rushed off, with their parents following behind. Alex turned back to Marcus, took his hand once more, and led him inside. Once in the privacy of their room, she swept aside the sheets that their passion had tangled and took a seat on the bed. "There. I bought you some time to tell me whatever it is you need to tell me. Just promise me that no matter what it is, I can still go to that festival. It sounds like a lot of fun."

Marcus saw then what she kept so brilliantly hidden beneath the surface in front of everyone else: he saw how frightened she truly was. It was worrisome. If he could see it, the senators and their wives would see it, too. They were nothing like these simple townsfolk. Their aspirations were high, and their methods were going to be unlike anything she'd ever experienced. Rather than using brute force to break her, as her family would have, his council would use venom that would be maddeningly untraceable. She wouldn't know where to swing her sword, and nothing he could tell her would do her any good. The people loved her for the same reason his father and the council would hate her: she was honest. He wasn't about to ask her to change the thing he most liked about her.

"I promise. Is it true that Kaden's condition is improving? I'm glad to hear that." He smiled and began removing his shoulder plates while she washed her face at the water basin.

"He's eager to return to my side," she chuckled as she piled her hair high atop her head. Alex slipped out of her tunic and put on a silvery blue dress she'd bought in town the night before. She realized this was the first Luxorian blue garment she'd ever worn. It looked beautiful on her, capturing the glow in her eyes, whereas her old garments only seemed to mirror the blood on her hands.

"How do I look? I can't disappoint the children tonight." She dropped her hair over her shoulders so she could size herself up in a mirror. Not regal, but mature. She could certainly live with that.

"You look stunning, Alex." He smiled and wrapped his arms tightly around her from behind, pulling her close. Alex loved this feeling more than anything, and he could tell she did by the way her eyes eased shut as she leaned into him with a soft exhale that left her almost limp.

With a soft kiss pressed to her cheek, he resisted the call of the bed and gently set her straight again. When they stepped into the town square together, polished and draped in their fineries, there was no doubt in anyone's mind who the most attractive couple in town was. She complemented him in every way. Before anyone noticed her or demanded her attention, he led her out the back of the inn toward a pond that glistened in the setting sun.

Once he was there, he felt a moment of panic. He didn't know how to say any of this. He'd given himself no time to prepare. Everything was so rushed, but that's how it had to be. They were almost out of time! The woman that he admired was in danger, and this was the only way he could save her now.

"It's okay, Marcus." Alex's soft voice cut through the miasma of doubt that had threatened to engulf them. "I know you've brought me here to tell me I'm going to die. That's why you're acting so strangely, isn't it? That's why you're so quiet. You didn't even bring Victus, so I know it must be bad." Alex's voice caught in her throat.

Before she could completely dissolve into tears, Marcus reached out to cup her cheeks and lower his face to hers so she'd hear him when he soothingly whispered, "No, Alex, no. I didn't bring Victus because I didn't want him to be here when I asked you to be my wife."

"Wh-what?" Alex stammered as she blinked away tears and tried to concentrate on the nonsensical words that had passed through his lips.

"You heard me. As forward and odd as my proposal may seem, it's the only solution I can find that will allow you to walk out of this town alive. Marry me before I receive the imperial edict commanding me to kill you. Our union will make you a princess of the Luxorian Empire, and when my father dies, you will rule by my side as queen. We can work together to stop the bloodshed and end the war once and for all." Marcus looked deep into her eyes, watching the sunset within them. "Or I can smuggle you out of town with your men, and you can just disappear. I will tell your cousin that you died in an escape attempt and we threw your body into the river. You can have your freedom and even go open that inn you spoke of, while I try to make peace with the new King of Artoria, if I can. It's your choice, Alexandra. What do you want to do?"

"Wait, wait, wait. Slow down. Hang on." She tried to process his proposal, but could barely make sense of the words. A blush had blossomed over her cheeks as she thought of being married to him. "I just need a minute. Are you sure? You've known me for your whole life as I have known you. Marcus, you were the shadow of my night. I was the curse on your blade. We have only come to some level of civility with each other in the past few days, and it has not been without tests that I would argue have pushed us, or at the very least, me, to the brink. Are you saying you want to spend the rest of your life married to me?"

Marcus smiled. "I told you before, if I ever truly marry again, it will be for love. I can't claim to love you, but I hold a deep respect for you. Even when you were my enemy, you were an honorable one. So, I propose we buy ourselves some time, and with this marriage, begin walking together down the long road to mending the fracture between our two lands." Marcus rubbed one hand along his jaw and chuckled nervously. He could tell she was hesitant to trust him. Could he blame her? Not for a moment.

"I know this is not a romantic or ideal situation, and it's probably not the way you envisioned a proposal of marriage. You would marry a man you don't really know, one who was far from kind to you just a few days ago, but I think you should at least have a proper proposal." Marcus slipped his fingers into the pouch on his belt and withdrew a woman's wedding ring. They made it of iron, the band intricately carved to resemble leaves. A Luxorian blue sapphire set upon the band, the center of which seemed to shine with inner radiance.

"I had the blacksmith fashion the band from a piece of my armor. Know that if you choose to wear this, I will protect you as my wife. Princess Alexandra Monica Raybrandt, I offer you the protection of my home, the comfort of my arms, and the wisdom of my counsel. I promise to be as kind as I can be and to always act with honor. Alex, will you marry me?"

"Marcus, I will marry you." She lifted her left hand to look a little closer at the ring he had given her. "I will try to be a dutiful wife, who will hold her heart in one hand and her sword in the other. Both will be at your command," she proclaimed proudly as the last rays of the setting sun danced across her face.

CHAPTER 10

The festival was everything Alex and Marcus hoped it could be. It was a moment in time where their place of birth didn't dictate who despised them or who loved them. They even opened the warehouse doors, allowing Alex's men a moment of reprieve and fresh air in the moonlight. Though still under close guard, they could drink their fill of mead, eat sweet pork, and even teach the crowd one of their favorite songs about a powerful priestess who traveled the world, finding enchantments and charms all across the kingdom as she went to from the lowliest stables to the emperor's court. By the end of the night, many men were chanting it while the women sang the chorus.

Though they had forged a strange sort of harmony, there were a few faces notably absent from the festivities, especially Prevak and the legionnaires loyal to his family's name. It set Marcus on edge, but with the entire town here, what real trouble could they make? Tonight, almost all the town was happy to be alive under the harvest moon, while those who couldn't stomach the concept of an Artorian and Luxorian alliance stewed in the shadows.

Alex concealed her ring from those without the keenest of eyes, but sometimes those with sharp eyes have even sharper tongues. Hushed rumors spread throughout the evening and into the early morning hours, and Alex felt exceptionally unprepared for the eventual fallout. Morning came without incident, leaving them both breathless and bare underneath the crisp white sheets that cocooned them. They'd emerge soon enough from their early morning escapades, but Alex wanted to know what would come next.

"So, who do you trust to handle the ceremony? To witness it? This is sure to cause quite a distasteful reaction from some of your men, and your father will be livid. Are you so sure you are ready to risk that?" she asked quietly as she lay there, her bare legs tangled with his as the predawn light crept into their bedroom. They likely had only a day or so to perform the ceremony before word would come down from the council calling for her head. If they were to go through with his plan, it would have to be tonight.

Marcus just grinned roguishly. "My father has been having distasteful reactions to me for a long time. As for my men, the core legions would follow me into the abyss without blinking. The only trouble could come from my brother's old legions, and I have already taken steps to have them contained." Marcus winked and took her chin in his hand.

"As for witnesses, a couple of my commanders will serve, and you may pick a few of your men so that your people know this has happened of your free will. I know a priest here in town. I know I can trust him. He owes me a favor; I stopped my brother from crucifying him when we took the town."

"Wait. A priest? An actual priest who can perform rituals?" Alex sat up suddenly and looked down at him in shock. How could there be any such individuals left in the world? Had the war not lay waste to their culture and their practices? She knew they had all but vanished from Artoria over sixty years ago.

"Yes, there are a few remaining in Luxor. We didn't take as hard a stance with priests and priestesses as Artoria did, though quite a few went into hiding from people like my brother, who would seek to punish them for refusing to fight." Marcus tried to gauge her reaction to the news that there was still some magic left in the world. If this surprised her, he wondered how she would handle the revelation that many in his court still used forbidden artifacts to put themselves ahead of the other houses. It wasn't a conversation for this moment, but they would need to have it soon. He knew very well how fidgety artifacts made the Artorians, but since they required time and precise actions by the victim, they rarely used them in battle.

"Wow! I'm excited to meet him! I never imagined I would ever meet a real priest. Do you think he will hold it against me, the Burnings of Sacratan?" Guilt seeped into her voice.

"No, of course not. You weren't even alive back then. I've spoken to him and he is as ready as we are to see an end to this war. He volunteered to perform the ceremony. Trust me, I won't let anything bad happen." He pressed his lips softly against hers, relinquishing some of his strength to comfort her and make her happy.

A few more minutes of tender discovery passed before his men summoned away Marcus from their bed. He left her in Victus' temporary care, with orders to bring Vallen to her side before the ceremony. As a symbol of their unification, one Artorian guard and one Luxorian guard for the ceremony would accompany her, and then Vallen would take charge from there. If she said that Vallen was ready to raise his bow for her once more, then that was enough for Marcus.

Both Marcus and Alex went about their days with butterflies in their stomachs until late afternoon, when it was time to get ready. Tensions had climbed so high during the day that both felt the instinctive urge to run away. Marcus knew that if he was feeling the ice on his feet, hers froze solid sometime ago. Glancing up at her window, he wondered how she was holding up.

• • •

Breathe out. Now breathe in. Slow, measured breaths. She ran a comb through her golden tresses, hissing in pain when she hit a snag. With a quivering hand, she tossed her comb aside and dabbed a cloth in the water basin to clean up her face. She nearly knocked over the bowl when a soft knock summoned her to the door.

What's the matter with you? Calm down. Cautiously, she cracked open the door and saw Vallen holding a silk gown in his paw, with a bewildered look on his face. "They called for three of us to come to your wedding? Alex, what's happening?" His voice was barely above a whisper, as though the words that passed his lips were blasphemous.

Motioning him in, she took the dress and gestured for him to sit at the table. "Victus, please wait outside the door. I need to speak with Vallen alone for a few minutes." There was nothing for Victus to fear from her old friend if she said there wasn't, so he trusted her judgment. However, if anything went wrong, if the man she'd known her entire life turned on her for any reason, a measly wooden door would not stop him from getting to her in time. Alex knew that.

Once they were alone, she walked into the bathroom and got dressed behind the security of a door. "Do you remember what Nicholas said? The kingdom will burn if I die. I've thought of a way to fight back and to live. All I want to do is what's best for the people of Artoria, and Marcus convinced me that my death isn't best for anyone but Nicholas."

"Is it true? What his men are saying? That you have been warming his bed like a common whore these past several days?" Vallen asked with more than just a little hurt in his voice. Convincing Vallen of her plan would be no effortless task, that much she knew, but his support was crucial. She needed him and Kaden by her side now more than ever.

"You're still breathing right now, aren't you? Free of a death sentence? If you want to keep it that way, you'll take care of how you speak to me," Alex warned as she slipped into the dress. It was a nice fit. The silk left very little to the imagination, and while she thought it could do with another layer of material, it was still beautiful.

"You'll excuse my accusatory tone. I use it only because you've sent so many of your men to their deaths, and…" Vallen laid into her, but Alex would have none of it.

"You mean the man that Marcus fought and then saved? You don't need to remind me of him, either. I'm well aware of what is at stake," she warned, her tone dipping even lower now as she swung open the bathroom door. "This evening, you are to bear witness to the joining of a kingdom and an empire for peace in the realm, and you will do so in silence. If that is too difficult a task for you, I will call for another. Am I understood? I'm desperately sick of death. Aren't you?" She slowly approached him, all but backing him against the wall.

"My apologies, Princess Alexandra. Yes," he hastily replied with a swift bow of his head. He'd forgotten himself, and in his haste to pass judgment, he'd forgotten her, too. "I am sorry. I shouldn't have assumed this has been any easier for you than it has been for the rest of us."

"It's all right. You've done nothing but speak your mind. Now, wait for me in the hall, please. I need to finish getting ready, and I'd like a few more moments to myself as an unwed woman."

Taking a deep, labored breath, he bowed and left her alone with her thoughts. Tomorrow, she would have to sit down for a long conversation with her men. She knew Vallen wouldn't be the only one who felt betrayed, and she needed to ensure that they understood her reasons. They needed to know that she still loved them and that she stood by them, but that this glimmer of hope was bigger than the blood feud that fueled this war.

The innkeeper's wife came and ushered Alex to the garden and then handed her a bouquet of white flowers she had tied together with some soft straw. They were lilies she had grown in her garden, and despite the few clumps of dirt on the bottom, Alex thought they looked quite sweet. They softened her mood considerably, and by the time she walked out into the garden, she didn't look so fierce. She looked genuinely happy as she walked toward Marcus and their marriage.

Though this union wasn't for love, she knew it wasn't a mistake. She could be happy with Marcus, and at the very least, she believed she would be safe. Taking her place by his side, she smiled up at him. "You look very handsome. And surprised."

He wore black leggings, a white silk shirt, a golden vest, and a navy-blue doublet with golden studs. It was more ostentatious than what he preferred to wear; he was a soldier, not a peacock, but he supposed the occasion called for some formality. On his brow was a simple golden circlet, the sign of his royal blood. He had left his blades inside, refusing to wear them for the ceremony.

"I half expected to see you crawling down the drainpipe and fleeing into the forest. The anxiety was killing me all day. I can only imagine how it has been for you." He chuckled nervously, extending his arm for her to take when she was ready.

Alex broke into a wide smile at the thought of herself shimmying down the drainpipe in this dress for all eyes to see. "I promised, didn't I? I am to be your wife." She took his arm and followed his lead to the small arbor.

"You look positively angelic this evening. The dress becomes you." Her face bloomed with color at the compliment. She thought it fit well in all the right places. She realized she'd never been called that before, angelic. It made her hold her head just a little higher.

"Thank you. You look very colorful. I quite like it." A quake resonated through her whole body and made her realize she was very nervous. Why was she so afraid? Her heart was fluttering like the wings of a trapped bird. Why did everything she said sound stupid to her own ears? Cursing herself for her poor wording, she had only meant to say that he looked very handsome. She had always thought so, even when she didn't wish to.

They took their places before the arbor, their witnesses aligned behind them. The priest, an old gentleman, stood under the arbor, ready to begin the ceremony. He had a fresh scar across one cheek, the result of his conflict with Marcus' brother, but other than that, he was the picture of health for his age. The priest wore a white robe that draped off a body that looked like a bundle of bones wrapped in old leather. Despite walking with a stoop and a cane, the old man had a lively spark in his eyes. He emanated an intelligence and wisdom that no doubt reassured his congregation.

"Since this is a covert ceremony, I will skip the preaching and scolding that normally comes with such events. I think you both know your responsibilities and your rewards, which will only come from a healthy partnership," Father Brenar said in a deep, rolling voice that seemed too big for his frail body. It was full of humor and understanding and immediately calmed most who heard it.

"While this marriage is political in means, I urge you both to seek wisdom and solace in each other. Prince Marcus, I know you to be a man of honor. Princess Alexandra is a woman of passion and kindness. I pray that your union will spell an end to the bloodshed and will allow the seeds of peace to sprout from the war-torn hearts of your people."

The sage's voice put Alex at ease. She followed his gentle instruction and pressed her left palm against

Marcus', squeezing it gently as the priest tied a thin, simple white cloth around their wrists.

"Honor these vows you make to each other always." The cloth suddenly began binding their hands and seemed to pulse in time with their heartbeats as he spoke. "Marcus Evandrus, Prince of Luxor, General of the Luxorian army, and heir to the Luxorian throne, do you swear to honor and protect this woman for all of your years?"

"I do," Marcus said simply, looking at Alex with a smile. The hand wrap took on a blue tone as he spoke, tendrils of color swirling around the white, springing from his hand to bind them together.

"Alexandra Monica Raybrandt, Princess of Artoria, Commander of the Artorian army, and heir to the Artorian throne. Do you swear to honor and protect this man for all of your years?"

A bright red light materialized and twirled around the white and blue luminescent lights, consuming their hands. In awe of the magic unfolding before her, she said, "I do so swear." It was clean and passionate. There was no doubt in that instant that she meant those words. Neither of them could vow love to the other, but she could honor and protect him to the best of her ability.

"Then, with my blessing, this union is complete. Marcus, you may kiss your bride." He gave a kind smile and took a step back to allow the newlyweds to enjoy their first kiss as husband and wife. Tilting her head ever so slightly, she embraced his passionate kiss and met it with her own. Their lips locked beneath the full moon in a union that none could have ever foreseen.

By the time the kiss broke, her men had already turned to walk back to the warehouse. They would tell everyone what they had witnessed: that Alex had married their sworn enemy of her own volition, even when given the chance to escape. Two nights ago, they had been freemen with a princess who was passionately against Luxorian rule. Now, she was one of them. They probably couldn't understand what she had just done or why, but in time, perhaps they could grow to accept it.

Squeezing Marcus' hand, she gave him a small, sad smile for the work remaining to be done. The war would not end tonight, but they had taken a very important step toward making that dream possible. If Alex could learn to forgive Marcus, her people could do the same, but if she allowed Nicholas to come to power, the hatred would only fester and grow. It would consume them all in a blaze that would leave nothing but ash and bone. She couldn't allow that to be the future for Artoria or Luxo and the time to act was now.

• • •

When Marcus took her to bed that night, he kept her awake for hours before finally falling asleep in a sweaty, tangled heap of limbs, their bodies pressed together and their hearts beating as one.

He awoke to the feel of her lips on his, telling him to open his eyes. With a growl, he swept her against his chest, squeezing a delighted giggle out of his bride.

"Wake up. I'm hungry," she insisted playfully while nipping at his lips.

"I thought I satisfied your appetite last night. I suppose we should get up, as much as I would rather stay in bed and make you scream for mercy."

Alex shivered. "Mercy? Why would I scream for something you are perpetually lacking in bed?" she grinned, knowing he'd understand her little quip. He had ridden her hard last night, just as he would have a woman with years of experience, but Alex had kept up. She clearly loved it all. They waged sweaty battles beneath the sheets, where they declared whoever lost composure first the loser. With his years of experience he could call on, he was almost always the victor. But she'd put up a fight for as long as she could until she was writhing in ecstasy.

With a chuckle and a final, heated kiss, Marcus rolled out of bed. He retrieved some sensible leather clothing, in black and navy blues. It was the clothing he typically wore beneath his armor and when walking among his soldiers.

"Stay in bed if you wish. Some of my commanders need to speak with me. To make sure no one forgets your status, I will have Victus escort you to see your men. I asked my praetorians to find you some clothing; I will have it sent up, along with your chaperone."

The idea of staying in bed was a temptation Alex couldn't quietly pass up. "Very well, I'll let you spoil me, but only for a little while. I have to speak with my men. Many of them probably still have outrageous claims that I will have to address." She wore her troubles plainly on her face for a moment before he kneeled to wipe them away with a shower of kisses that left her giggling instead of crying.

With no further delays, he left the room. Before facing her men, he thought she would enjoy a little time to herself. He paused in the common room long enough to order breakfast and clothing to be sent up, and then he stepped out into the fresh morning air. He closed his eyes and felt the sun on his face and the breeze on his skin, just enjoying the silence.

A harsh voice that made his skin crawl and his lips curl into the same firm snarl Commander Prevak was wearing shattered the serenity of the moment. "You married the whore Princess of Artoria? Gods, my prince, I know the rumors say you have been celibate awhile, but was she that good? You know what the Council and your father will have to say about this, don't you? This is treason against Luxor!" Commander Prevak bellowed in a loud, carrying voice. He wore full armor and was still wearing his useless sword at his side. However, five of his men who did not have broken thumbs were at his back.

Mutiny?

"Commander, are you aware that speaking in that manner to the heir of the empire is an offense that carries a sentence of death? My brother enacted that law and I am considering making use of it," Marcus replied in a voice colder than ice but pitched to carry clear across the square. "I have married the Princess of Artoria, bringing her kingdom and ours together, in a step toward ending this ridiculous war. And that is as much justification as I am going to give a sniveling child like you. Now, you can either drop to your knees and beg my forgiveness, or you can draw your sword and learn what I do to those who make me their enemy."

"I believe you have betrayed the Empire of Luxor, my prince, and I command you to release your prisoner to my care!" Commander Prevak roared, drawing his blade awkwardly with his left hand. His grip was clearly uncertain, but his rage was unwavering. All five of his men drew steel as well.

"Coward." Marcus drew his own sword and waved his rapidly approaching praetorians away. "Stand down. Allow me to remind you all why I lead this army."

And with that, Marcus was moving. His left hand dipped into his boot and withdrew a thin throwing knife. With a flip of his wrist, it hurtled through the air and slammed into the throat of one of Prevak's soldiers. One down, five to go. He darted to his left and ran to meet the two other soldiers on that side. His blade whistled through the air, weaving an intricate web of steel, blocking and parrying each attack. In a matter of seconds, he had moved past the two soldiers, leaving them barely alive behind him. Prevak and his last two soldiers rushed to encircle him. With a grin, Marcus drew a dueling dagger with his left hand and stood waiting. The square was hushed, lined with citizens and soldiers who watched this fatal confrontation with bated breath. No one even dared to whisper.

Prevak made a slight gesture, and all three of them moved in. Marcus was moving in an instant. He spun toward one soldier and struck their sword with his dagger. He used that leverage to knock the soldier's arm out of position and thrust his dagger into the soldier's ribs. With a grunt, he pivoted and swung the soldier's body around to intercept his friend's sword. He brought his knife up and cut open the soldier's throat.

He stepped back to let both soldiers fall into a heap on the ground at his feet, and then locked his eyes on Prevak. Prevak stood alone, his sword held loosely in his weak grip, sweat rolling down his face as he looked frantically for a way out. Marcus didn't give him one. With a feral growl, he darted forward, and with a single, effortless swing, he knocked the sword from Prevak's grip. Reversing the grip on his dagger, he slammed the pommel into his temple and knocked the senator's son to the ground beside his dead men.

"He is to be manacled and sent home to his father. Make certain the good senator is aware of his son's attempt to murder the crown prince. My mercy won't fall on his house again." Marcus turned away in disgust and left to take care of other matters as his men swarmed the treasonous worm. "Victus, see that you bring my wife safely to say goodbye to her men," Marcus commanded. "I'm late for a war council meeting."

His knock woke her from the nap she had slipped into while sprawled across the bed as naked as the day she was born. She jolted to life when she heard the doorknob turn. "Princess? Are you awake?"

"Don't come in! Just a moment!" With a blush plastered on her face, she grabbed the sheets to pull around herself faster than she had ever drawn a sword.

Going to the door, she opened it just enough to take hold of the clothes he carried under his arm for her. "Give me five minutes and then you can join me for breakfast." She smiled and slipped away, locking the door behind her. Five minutes later, she emerged in a simple violet gown that was made of a material that billowed whenever she took a step. Finally, she felt covered by the inquisitive eyes of the rest of the camp with a dress that came down to her ankles and sleeves that covered her shoulders. White ruffles flowered out of the neck and hem of the dress, complementing her in a very refined way. Tightening the corset a bit, she tugged a comb through her hair and invited Victus in.

He gave a gentle smile and bobbed his head approvingly. "I thought purple might suit you, especially now that you and Marcus joined the houses of red and blue as one. I'm glad to see I wasn't wrong."

He looked proud of himself for having picked out such a lovely dress for her.

"You picked this out? Well, you have a better sense for these sorts of things than Kaden does. I'll give you that." Tentatively, she gave the dress a quick twirl. It looked innocent enough, but her face was hard. She was looking for any embarrassing rips in the fabric she may have missed. She wouldn't put it past Victus to get in a good laugh with his men at her expense, but if he was plotting a trap, this wasn't it. The dress was flawless.

"Am I proven innocent?" Victus mused as he folded his arms over his armored chest and leaned against the doorframe to take some of the weight off his tired feet.

"Are you coming in or not?" Alex sighed, reluctant to admit to her mischaracterization of him.

"No, Your Highness, you're coming out. The innkeeper and his wife have breakfast ready downstairs. It's rabbit."

Alex could never turn down a rabbit and so, without another word, she bounced down the hall towards the smell of succulent meat spiced with apple.

After a quick breakfast, she walked outside and felt dozens of eyes on her, though she acted as if she hadn't noticed. Best not to give anyone reason to pounce. Fiddling with the ring on her finger, she held her head high and puffed out her chest proudly. She was now their princess, too. She should have nothing to fear.

"Victus, stop for a moment. You have been kind to watch me so diligently, but I must ask a favor. As your princess, I am commanding you to take a respite. Trust Vallen to watch over me," she commanded as they turned the corner to the quiet street where they were holding her men.

A concerned look shot across his face, but she was quick to ease his troubled mind. "I am going to see the men who raised me. They need to understand that I have married Marcus not out of desperation to save my skin, but to save both our kingdom and your empire." Alex let that hang in the air for a moment and studied his face. She wanted to make sure Victus understood that, too.

When he nodded his head in agreement, she continued. "I am happy with my decision, but I would be more at ease if I had their approval. Having you by my side will complicate matters. These men have been with me through the worst; they will do me no harm. Please, go back to the inn and I will find you there when I am done. I promise I will let you babysit me for the rest of the day after this."

He reluctantly left her side, but to her disappointment, he didn't go far. She watched as he slipped into the shadows to follow her covertly. His prince had commanded him to protect her, and it seemed he didn't intend to fail.

"Fine. Waste your time. They won't hurt me. You'll see..." Alex whispered, more so to herself than to him. There was a lump in her throat and her heart felt like it was being squeezed.

Alex continued her walk to the warehouse and then, after a moment's hesitation, she slipped inside. To her relief, there weren't as many unfriendly stares as she had feared there might be. There were a few, to be sure, but Artorians were easy to persuade. They merely needed a reasonable explanation.

Drawing a deep breath, Alex began with a warm smile. "Yesterday, as I'm sure Vallen has told you, I married Prince Marcus Evandrus of Luxor. You all must know that they did not trick me into doing this. They did not force me, either. Marcus and I married to help end the war and to save everyone we can. I can help none of you from the grave. I was misguided by Nicholas into believing that I could."

Andrian interrupted, a look of concern etched across his scarred face. "That morning was the bastard Nicholas' fault, not yours. We know that, but Marcus is the heir of the Evandrus family we've sworn an eternal hatred for. He is our enemy, Alex." A long, ugly scar stretched from his brow down to his chin. He was still so young when it happened, and Alex could remember believing they'd lost him, but he survived.

"Then you must see me as your enemy too, for my name is now Evandrus." Alex spoke solemnly. Her voice sounded haunted, but resolute. She could not back down from this decision.

"No, Your Highness." "No, we don't." "Don't think that." "No." Assurances fluttered through the room while she stood before them, crestfallen.

From there, they continued their discussions. For nearly five hours, she stood amongst them and gave each man time to air his concerns while also offering them assurance that they could return home now with their heads held high and knowing that the war would soon be over. It took some convincing, but the result was worth it.

"Will you continue to accept me as your princess and trust my judgment?" She asked, her voice booming with pride.

A resounding "AYE!" filled the warehouse, making her smile. She looked out over her men and couldn't be any prouder. They might not trust Marcus, but they still loved her.

Tears formed at the corners of her eyes when Kaden sat up to bring his arms around her. "You already look so strong, old man. Be safe, Kaden. I'll need you with me in the capital if I am to survive this," she whispered, and sat down beside him as the men dispersed back to their cots. Gently, she ran a finger over his pristine white bandages. So much color and life had returned to his face, where just a few days ago she had seen none. It made her heart sing to see him doing so well now.

"You can count on it. I'll be here for you no matter what path you choose," Kaden swore and brought his fist to her chest to give it a light punch. "Now, get out of here. You have more important things to do today than to sit in here with us!" He laughed and patted her back to send her on her way. Her men were going to be just fine, especially with Kaden there, to reaffirm her message in her absence.

She stepped outside a few minutes later with a fully armored Vallen by her side. He peeled his one good eye wide, but there was nothing to fear. They would probably beat Victus back to the inn. She glanced over at the treeline she'd seen him disappear in, but she couldn't spot him. Oh well.

Everything was going to be all right. Her men didn't hate her, they were just worried about her. Now that they knew those worries to be unfounded, she could put their anger to rest as well. For the good of their people, she would make things whole again.

CHAPTER 11

Commander Prevak awoke as he was being bound. Only a couple of Marcus' praetorians had stayed behind to help shackle the unconscious man and assemble his escort home. Unfortunately for them, Prevak had more men waiting in the shadows for when Marcus and his commanders sealed themselves away to conduct their meeting. They had to hurry.

Thirty legionnaires swarmed out of the surrounding buildings when Prevak awoke. They cut down the praetorian that was guarding him without hesitation. They put an arrow through other's skull just as quickly, even though he tried to run. Marcus had humiliated him, but he had a plan. He would restore his lost dignity by robbing someone else of theirs–a whore who deserved it. He grabbed his ten best men, told them about the special music box in his tent, and gave them instructions on where to deliver her.

"But, sir, where will we find her?"

"She'll be sucking off her men just like she does every day. Now, go!" he roared as a few others helped him up. They would save the empire and bring about a new rule, but they were going to have a little fun along the way.

The ten soldiers he sent were rather unremarkable upon first glance. It would take a trained eye to notice the legion markers on the shoulders of their armor designating them as members of Prevak's Punishers. The lead man had a sergeant's colors in the plume of his helm, denoting his rank.

The sergeant and his men sank to their knees in front of Alex and Vallen when they stepped out of the warehouse. "My princess, it is an honor to meet you. They asked me to present this humble gift from our commander, to commemorate your recent wedding. It plays a pleasant melody, which he hopes you will enjoy. He asks that I bring him back word of whether the tune was to your liking," the sergeant said in a calm, level voice, devoid of any emotion that might betray his mission.

His men were careful to keep their eyes fixed respectfully on the ground, while he kept his gaze trained upon the skirt of her dress. He held the music box patiently above his head. Should she refuse to open it, he had a rag soaked in a sleeping elixir at the ready, but the music box would be a far more efficient tool. Its song enchanted anyone who opened the box.

It made the victim pliable, and compelled to obey any instructions given by the one who held the winding key to the box. It was a sinister form of magic, one that could compel its victims to action. Worse still, the mind remained aware of what transpired, but was helpless to stop the body from obeying every command. It was like being a prisoner in your own body. The music box contained a magic long forbidden by law, even for a senator's son.

Alex was none the wiser. She smiled sweetly at the kind gesture, grateful to see it being extended from Marcus' men. Perhaps she wouldn't have to work so hard to win over the warriors of Luxor, after all. If only it could be so easy with the scholars and councilmen who were presently drafting her execution order.

She took the delicate wooden box into her hands and admired the craftsmanship of its design. She opened the lid to let a sweet tune loose into the surrounding air. It was a beautiful song that, for reasons unknown to her, made her body feel strange. She felt her tense muscles relax, and her mind became less and less sharp every moment that it played. It was such a soothing song that she hesitated to close the box even after the tune was done.

For a moment, she wore a blank stare until Vallen gently shook her shoulder, snapping her out of it.

"P-Please thank your commander for me. He was right; it was a sweet melody and I shall treasure this gift as one of the first I have received as Princess of Luxor. If you'll excuse me." She curtseyed slightly to the men, who were still kneeling in front of her, and moved to brush past them. She tried to refocus her mind on finding Victus, who she knew had to be eager to see her return to the inn safe and sound.

others moved to stand watch outside. Then they tore the tarp off.

After adjusting her gaze, Alex could see the five men who had brought her the music box and the other five who had murdered Vallen. Commander Prevak sat in a chair in the middle of the room with a smug look of victory plastered across his face. Victus was not among them. Had they murdered him, too?

She watched helplessly as the sergeant handed him small, golden key, and as soon as the handoff was complete, she felt a tingle shoot through her body. The key. Her eyes locked on it.

"You're mine now," Commander Prevak said with a sinister chuckle that gave her reason to take flight, though only her heart obeyed. He snapped his fingers, and without a word, they hauled her out of the cart and tossed her onto a pile of hay in the middle of the floor in a loud, painful thud.

For the first time, she could see what Prevak and his men had used this barn for. The stalls were brimming an arsenal of torture devices that would make an inquisitor pale. A few feet away was a table with straps obviously meant to hold a victim down. Blood stained floor beneath it and had mixed with the hay, giving the place an unhealthy odor of rotting, wet grass and As her gaze lifted to meet Prevak's again, he grinned, knowing she had realized what this place was— she was in a torture chamber.

Her heart thundered in her chest and she rapidly through every likely scenario, each more

"Princess, don't move. Don't make a sound or signal to anyone that anything is wrong," the sergeant said suddenly. Out of thin air, the melody played inside her mind, forcing her body to act exactly as he told it to.

Vallen didn't know what hit him. While they had listened to the cursed tune, five more men had circled in behind, using the crafty little box to hide their own footsteps until they were right on top of them. With their bodies shielding the scene, a burly soldier clapped his hand over Vallen's mouth, and with a swift jerk of his arm, cut Vallen's throat to the bone. An uttered groan passed the frail man's lips, but nothing more.

Alex watched the light leave her old friend's eyes. She tried to scream, but her lips only quivered. She tried to kneel to grab him, but her knees didn't even quiver. Her whole body froze in that moment, save for her own eyes, which were open wide with terror. Tears trickled down his face and blood coursed from his open mouth as they dragged him away.

She knew he was dead, her Vallen. They stole the very first man she'd ever won over, not by her charm or by her name, but by her skill on the battlefield. They had snatched him away from her side so abruptly that it felt like a horrid nightmare from which she could not wake, but that also could not be real. She watched until his feet disappeared behind the back of the building, and she saw him no more.

Alex tried to scream out again for her men, who were just inside of the warehouse, mere feet away. She drew the breath she needed. She stiffened her stance, as if to prepare for a fight. But her lips didn't even twitch this time. Not even a whisper tickled her throat. She couldn't scream. Her fingers couldn't curl to form even a loose fist. She couldn't fight. She'd heard legends of magic as insidious as this being a popular tool in the early days of the war, but after Marcus' antiquated interrogation tactics, she thought time had destroyed the cursed magic Luxor was infamous for.

How was this possible? How had a relic as powerful as this survived for so long?

The sergeant just smiled and sized her up freely now. "Magic is grand, isn't it? My commander has plans for you, whore. Now, hand me the box." After she complied perfectly with his command, he turned and walked away so his men could fall in around her.

"Do not make a sound and lower your head. Now, follow me." Quite against her will, Alex followed along meekly with her eyes pointed down. They moved silently through a few back alleys until they reached a small, covered cart on the edge of a forest trail. She felt her doom looming beyond the canopy of those trees, but she was powerless to resist the spell. The mystical tune twined around her skin, muscle, and bone.

Her only hope was Victus, but he was nowhere to be seen! Was he in on this? Was this his doing? Her mind reeled as she fruitlessly fought her invisible tethers.

"Lay down under the tarp and don't make a sound," the sergeant ordered, and again she found her body

acting without her permission. He quickly tied do
the tarp, and he and his men headed out.

Between the camp and the town was a s
abandoned farm with a barn that she could see
approaching through the slats in the cart. It was r
enough to be convenient, but far enough away t
screams his men would surely relish hearing w
attract unwanted attention. They were g
murder her.

They had trapped Alex with the echoing
the music box, forcing her to lie still as she a
her demise. She ran the situation repeate
mind as she tried desperately to think of a
this, but nothing came to her. It was as if th
had not only removed the control she had
body, but had clouded her mind as well.

Alex may have fallen for this trap,
truly damning was that she didn't know
about this artifact or how to break its
only pray that Marcus and his praetori
looking for her. That they would soo
pool of Vallen's blood left behi
warehouse. That they would follow
was undoubtedly leaving and that t

She wished with all her might t
her before this commander could p
the dream of peace they had craf
that she couldn't even whisper...

Once they wheeled the cart
of his men closed and guarded

harrowing than the last. Ten of his men. Even if he gave her permission to move, which seemed unlikely, it would be impossible to fight them all off without a weapon. She scanned the barn but saw no suitable weapons short of those that the soldiers held on their hips. For the first time in her entire life, there were no options left for her. She was completely out of control and powerless.

"Kneel, princess. You may also speak." Prevak granted her that much, but she didn't immediately use it. She was somewhere between begging for release and bargaining for a quick death. Best not to say anything.

"Oh Princess, don't be shy. Come now. Why don't you say something? Better, yet. Why won't you stand up? Too accustomed to kneeling with your mouth hanging wide open?" Prevak taunted her, a leering smile on his face.

"You know I can't," she hissed, fire lighting her eyes as she glared up at the eleven men who had her cornered.

"Oh, is my little toy holding you down? Am I not playing fair, Princess?" He sneered at her and sat on a wooden table in the middle of the room. The bloodied wood creaked beneath his weight and he twirled his finger in the air.

His men saw that and formed a semicircle between Alex and Prevak. "How about this? In the interest of fairness, I will give you a chance at freedom! If you can take this key from me, I will let you go. You may walk right out that door, and I promise nothing bad will happen to you ever again at my hand or my command. You may do as you wish."

His last sentence was all he had to say to free her. In an instant, she felt her limbs shake free of the bindings that had held her down until now. She paused and weighed her options. This was a trap, but if she didn't at least try...

"Men, our guest seems nervous. Throw down your swords." Prevak chuckled. The sound of swords being unceremoniously tossed into the dirt echoed through the barn. These men weren't actual warriors. They were thugs hiding behind a powerful name.

"So, not a quick death." Alex remarked, realizing what this meant.

"Of course not. Now, if you don't even want to take back your freedom, we can get start-"

Alex sprang to her feet, prepared to claw, punch, kick, and bite any man who stood in her way, while also desperately searching for a sword, but they were smarter than that. This was to be a contest of strength, and they painfully outnumbered Alex, but that didn't matter. She had at least try to survive.

She lunged for the center of their line, hoping to break through on speed alone. If she could grab a sword, she might have a chance. Unfortunately, the soldier there saw the move coming, and lashed out with a powerful punch that forced her to roll to the left to avoid losing a handful of teeth.

She tumbled right into the arms of another soldier who laughed and squeezed her breast painfully tight.

Digging his fingers into the dress and yanking on it, he loosened the strings before she could deliver a knee to his groin that sent him reeling.

She spun, thinking to use this as an opening, only to find two arms wrapping around her torso, binding her arms to her side so they could lift her off the ground. She shrieked in anger as another soldier tugged her boots free, but she delivered a kick to the man's face that made him withdraw.

Kicking with the might of a mule, she struck the kneecap of the man who was holding her and backed away from the hungry hands of the other men who'd yet to claim a piece of her. She tumbled on the ground in a roll that brought her back to the center of their circle. The sound of one of her tormentors howling in pain was music to her ears.

"Stop! I am your prince's wife. Harm me, and he will find you. If you stand aside, I will protect your lives," Alex promised as she fought to catch her breath. Before the words were even out, she knew they had fallen on deaf ears.

Another man, one of the burliest, lunged and forced her to dodge to the left to avoid being trampled, but another man was waiting to wrap his arms around her shoulders. While they held her fast, another man came to rip open her dress, baring her breasts to the lusty men who cheered in victory. Without sympathy or mercy, the man tore off her skirt, leaving her in nothing.

The sound of her clothes ripping and tearing, the sensation of goosebumps rising along her flesh as the cold air met her exposed skin, the cacophony of men cheering, the feel of their hands pawing at her most intimate places, their eyes leering at her bare body–it was all too much. The flames of rage sparked within her and exploded in sheer, primal fury. Frenzied wrath was the only way her mind could process the feeling of hopeless fear these men had implanted inside her.

With a battle cry full of hate, she brought her legs together and snapped them up into the chest of the man who was reaching for her. Still held from behind, the force of her kick threw them both backward and slammed her head into her captor's face, her vision blurring with the sickening, wet crunch of the impact. A loud groan rolled through her ears and the surrounding arms went slack.

Spinning, she swept her leg and knocked the last legionnaire off his feet. She had fought her way through all ten men, leaving the path to Prevak finally open. With a snarl, she broke into a dead sprint, her hands curled into tight fists. She geared up to throw herself at him to claim that key, but Prevak just smiled, tilted his head to one side, and dangled the key she was so desperately fighting to reach.

"Stop," he commanded softly. With a shriek of outrage, she skidded to an immediate stop just three feet from him. Her bare chest was heaving, and she stared at him with murder in her eyes.

"Now my dear, sweet little warrior, I will show you what actual power is," Prevak sneered with promise in his voice. He would turn her dreams of peace into nightmares that would haunt her for as long as he kept her alive.

CHAPTER 12

Marcus sat alone in his command tent, plotting his next move, when Victus burst in. "Prince Marcus, your bride is gone!"

"What?" Marcus asked incredulously, staring at the man in shock. "Speak up, man. What the hell happened?"

"Sir, she said it would make it harder for her men to believe that she had married you of her own free will if I were standing at her elbow. She asked that I wait for her at the inn and swore she would return the moment she finished speaking with her men. I waited across the street for hours, watching over her from afar. When she emerged, a group of our men approached her. I didn't notice until it was too late that they wore the Rustionage sigil. Before I could intervene, they murdered her older guardian, and the princess was walking with them as if in a trance. I knew I couldn't rescue her alone, so I came to find you." A cold sweat trickled down Victus' brow, all color drained from his wan face.

"You let those Rustionage dogs take her? Damn it, Victus, I trusted you!" Marcus shoved the shamed praetorian out of his way and raced out of the command tent toward the warehouse housing Alex's soldiers. A party of men fell in behind him, unsure of what was happening.

"Men! Search the area! Commander Rustionage's men have abducted the princess. Report back to me in five minutes!" He barked, sending his men scurrying through the area. None of this made any sense. Victus had missed something. She wouldn't just walk off with the men who had slaughtered one of her guardians. He needed to sort this out now.

With that in mind, he burst through the warehouse doors and charged at her, men. "Your princess has disappeared! Tell me now if you know anything about this! If any of you helped the maggots who took her out of spite, I swear I will burn down this warehouse with you locked inside it!" Marcus roared, his face flushed with anger, his eyes darting about in worry as he struggled to find some clue what was happening.

His praetorians searched the courtyard outside, looking for signs of foul play and questioning soldiers and citizens about what they'd seen. They came up empty-handed until they found the blood trail that led to Vallen's body, dumped just beyond the treeline. What the hell had happened?

"Do you really think we're so dishonorable that we'd harm the one we have dedicated our lives to protecting just because she married you? Your bumbling men are the ones who lost her. We have nothing to do with this," Kaden snarled from his seat on his cot. Marcus examined the crowd of soldiers, and not one of them looked guilty or ashamed. They looked worried.

"She left after assuring us that her marriage to you was legitimate and was best for our people. You are doing little to affirm it right now." The tension in the room was so thick that even the strongest steel would have had trouble slicing through it. Then, a man hidden away in the corner spoke up.

"I heard somethin'!" said a man with an eye patch over his deeply scarred right eye. Kaden rolled his eyes in frustration and grunted. "'Twas like a music box."

"You heard nothin', Leon. It was just some kids fucking around out there. We have to think about where she might have gone. We know her best." They started a lively conversation about who was right, who was wrong, and who knew nothing about nothing, each idea more useless than the next.

Marcus couldn't remember ever feeling so frustrated, but Leon only kept shaking his head and running his fingers through his dirty blond hair. "I knowed I heard a music box right after Princess Alexandra left us. I just knowed it." He sighed in frustration and slunk back into the corner while the rest of the men bickered about where she might be at that very moment.

"Wait just a minute. A music box? A music box, you're sure? Damn it, how could this happen to me again?" Marcus whispered as a bone-chilling revelation came over him. His eyes took on a haunted cast as he staggered back against the door, breathless.

"Your highness! We found a fresh trail just beyond where they dumped the Artorian's body. Should we follow?" One of his men asked.

"You three secure horses! Now!" Marcus bellowed.

He knew now how they had taken Alex. Prevak had always been close with Antonius and was a firm believer in the purity of the Luxorian bloodline. He knew all about the music box and how it worked. His stomach dropped as he thought about what was likely happening to her, and he almost retched.

Just then, his left ring finger throbbed, and he lifted his hand to see what was wrong. The iron of his wedding band seemed to shine, and he had felt it tugging him. She was calling out to him. He spun in a circle, and when he faced the east, the pull increased tremendously. The trail. Alex was crying out to him at the end of that bloody trail. He needed to save her.

Marcus and twenty praetorians rode like madmen through the forest. The closer they came, the more his heart throbbed in anguish and fear seized his mind. He knew what a man like Prevak would do to her, and he just hoped he could get there soon enough to save her. He couldn't fail. Not again.

Marcus slowed his horse from its maddening pace when the trees thinned and he spotted a large barn on the horizon. Dismounting, they tethered the horses and crept silently on foot. His ring pulled him toward the barn with ever-growing force as they crept through the brush as quietly as they could. A handful of Prevak's legionnaires patrolled the exterior, but there was no telling how many men were inside. Once they were within a hundred yards, Marcus quietly drew his sword.

"Kill them all, but leave Prevak and any men inside that barn alive for me. If they're doing what I think they are, I intend to castrate them," Marcus hissed. He turned his horse toward the barn and charged, bursting through the trees with his blade held high. He would not pause, and he would not wait to deal with the men outside the barn. They were for his praetorians. He locked his gaze on the barn door and a sniveling coward's sword wouldn't stop him.

He gave the signal, and they rushed the barn together as a small, lethal unit that the inexperienced boys Prevak had stationed outside couldn't hope to contend with.

Two fools stepped in his path with weapons raised. With a scream of rage, he used his sword to open their throats, spattering his face with their blood. Not wasting a moment, he raced to the barn door, vaguely aware of his men engaging the other soldiers all around him. Marcus ran full pelt and threw himself into the air, slamming full force into the doors. They flew open with a resounding crash. He just stood there for a moment, staring at the scene before him in shock.

Alex was on a table, being rammed by Prevak with the desperation of a crazed maniac drunk on power and lust. She wasn't moving, and her head had lulled listlessly to one side. She looked like she was dead. Her gaze was empty. Her nose and lips were oozing fresh blood. A whole gang of Prevak's men stood around the table, waiting for their turns with her.

"PREVAK! I'LL HAVE YOUR HEAD!" Marcus thundered. Prevak threw Alex to the ground, unknowingly dropping the key. Three of his men rushed forward, ready to kill their prince. With his path obstructed, Marcus whirled his blade like the gavel of a god, slamming it into the men who'd foolishly tried to tackle him. They fell before they could even retrieve their blades.

Marcus saw Victus rush forward out of the corner of his eye and grab the golden key that had fallen into the dirt. That accursed key was the source of his power over Alex. "Victus! Tell Alex she's free!"

"Not yet!" Prevak bellowed as he snatched Alex up by her hair and pulled her limp body off of the table. He held her like a rag doll in front of his half-naked body as a shield. Marcus froze. His men continued fighting Prevak's men to push them back, but none of them dared to get close to Prevak now that he had the princes' bride in his hand.

Prevak put a fraction of what Alex had endured on full display by hanging her up by her hair. She was just out of his reach. They had branded her lower abdomen and all along her legs with searing hot iron. Ripped off three fingernails. Blackened one eye so badly that it had swollen shut. Worst of all, they had raped her. A torrent of blood was also cascading from her scalp from a gash on the side of her head. Was she already dead?

"Don't look so distressed, your highness. She is alive, for now. If you want her to stay that way, you will call off your men and let me and mine leave unharmed." Prevak said. He shimmied his trousers back up his legs and drew a dagger up to Alex's exposed throat. That did it.

"Men, stand down. Let them pass." Marcus commanded as he stretched out his hand, silently pleading with Prevak not to do this.

His men backed up enough for Prevak's men to gather their belongings and to walk towards the door. They hung back just enough to wait for their commander.

"Make your escape, but please let her go." Marcus pleaded.

"Drop your sword. Tell your men to do the same." Prevak pushed the blade harder against Alex's neck, cutting off her air.

Without a word, he dropped his sword, and his men followed his lead. "You'll find her up the road. After I drag her through town behind my horse for a while, I'll cut her loose." Prevak sneered as he tried to take a step forward. Alex was limp and her dangling foot was in the way. "Move!" He barked, clearly growing anxious that this plan might fall apart if too much time passed. He was also too afraid to relinquish his human shield.

"You heard him, Alex. You can move now." Victus said as he gripped the key in the center of his palm, but

Alex still dangled in Prevak's grip. With a hiss of frustration, Prevak sheathed his dagger and reached around to grab her chin.

"We didn't smack your head that hard. I said move-"

Marcus watched in stunned silence as Prevak's look of frustration turned to confusion, then pain. He roared in agony as Alex bit the thumb Marcus had broken a few weeks ago back at camp so viciously that blood spurted everywhere. Prevak had no choice but to let her go, but the moment he did, he reached for his dagger.

He was too slow. Alex spun, dug her heel into the back of his knee and snatched the dagger out from Prevak's sheath. She slammed that blade deep into his belly before anyone could stop her and fell to the ground on top of him. Once he hit the dirt, she slammed the dagger into his chest and his gullet repeatedly and unrelentingly.

All of Prevak's men ran forward in near-perfect unison to stop her, but with a murderous cry, Marcus was among them before they could touch a hair on her head. He picked up his sword and sliced open the bellies of those who came closest to her. In the time it took for Alex to stab Prevak no less than forty times, Marcus' men regained their weapons and control of the situation. Only two of Prevak's men were still alive to watch their commander meet his fate.

Alex fell back, and Prevak struggled for breath beneath her. She'd finally stopped stabbing him once his entrails popped out of his swollen gut. He gargled and choked on his own blood, streams of it gushing past his lips. He was trying to say something, but no one could understand him now. Her good eye did not leave his, even at the risk of her own life. That glassy look in her eye. That's what would stay with him forever. It was the same look Meridian had given him right before his brother slaughtered her.

No, stop! She isn't dead! I must get her out of here!

He rushed to Alex's side, but she unleashed an attack with the dagger she'd used to gut Prevak. It was clear she intended to pierce his kneecap and tear him down, but she couldn't have known it was Marcus. Alex wasn't even looking at him. Alex was still staring directly at Prevak with a haunted look in her dim eyes. She must have heard him run at her. She must have thought he was going to attack.

"Alex! It's okay! It's me!" Marcus cried out.

He was nothing but a man with a sword to her at that moment, so he threw his weapon aside and caught her arms before she could take another swing. Marcus saw it then. He saw recognition creep across her face as she lifted her head. It was as if he had awoken her, only she hadn't been sleeping and this wasn't a dream. He had to get her out of here before anything else could happen to her. He had to make her safe again.

Ripping off his cloak, he threw it around her shoulders and the bloody dagger dropped to the barn floor with a clatter, making Alex flinch. She wasn't crying; she was crashing. The moment the cloak settled onto her shoulders, she buckled as if the weight of it were far too great. Marcus was there to catch her, but the invisible cuts Prevak had left her with ran too deep and he didn't know how to stop the bleeding. There, in his arms, she choked on her tears as the distress of what had just happened pushed her into a state of panic.

Feeling every tense muscle in her body shake violently, he sprang into action. "Move!" he shouted, and scooped her up into his arms. He sprinted with her out into the yard and away from that hellscape, as if it was on fire. The barn was more grotesque than any battlefield he'd ever witnessed, and he wouldn't subject her to it for another moment more.

He carried her quivering body to an old oak tree at the edge of the property where they could be out of earshot and sight of his men. He didn't know what else to do. The man who had orchestrated this monstrous crime was dead! What else could he do to help her? First, he needed to make sure Prevak hadn't stabbed her anywhere, but she had the cloak drawn around her so tightly that he didn't dare try to pry her arms apart to check.

"Alex, please. I need you to say something. I need to know that you're not dying. Can you tell me if he cut you? Did he stab you? Alexandra! Say something, please!" Marcus begged, and looked into her eyes. She wasn't there. It was as if the princess had detached herself from this world almost entirely, and all they left him with was an empty shell.

Then, a miracle. She came back to him. "Get me out of here. Please." Her voice was a shattered whisper, but he heard her plea as clearly as if she had screamed it at the top of her lungs.

He whisked her to his horse, sat her sidesaddle, and climbed up after her. He would not make her wait until they could bring the carriage. All along the ride back to the inn, he feared he might still lose her. She asked to be taken away from there, but could he really do it? Was it possible to save her?

Hours later, he felt like he had his answer as he watched her scour herself in her third scalding hot bath of the evening. Tears fell silently down his cheeks as he watched her scrub her right breast to the point of bleeding. The water was so hot, but she insisted she didn't feel it.

Marcus had kept his distance and given her what she asked for. He only stayed in the room because she asked him to, but he couldn't stomach anymore. He crossed the distance between them in three long strides and reached out to still her hand when it became clear she was just hurting herself.

"You cleaned that spot already, Alex. I can get some women to help you. I know the last thing you want right now is a man to touch you." The gentle smile he offered faded more with every moment of silence that passed between them. The silence was almost too painful, but he knew he needed to let her be the one to break it.

The depth of pain he felt shocked him. His tears fell into her hair when he breathed in her scent. He had married her because he respected her and she didn't deserve to die, but he was coming to see that perhaps his emotions went deeper. The thought of losing her was something he couldn't even imagine without feeling his own throat seal up.

"I don't need any help. Just leave me alone. I'm fine. I just have to get this shit off, that's all," she muttered, with blatant anger. She moved to her inner thigh and started the same aggressive scrubbing that would cause bleeding if she continued much longer.

Marcus let her push him away, but it hurt. He could see in her eyes that she wanted nothing to do with anyone right now. She didn't want his help, his comfort, or his touch, just his protection and more hot water. He could understand that, but he would not let her hurt herself, even if it gave her a small sense of relief. He stepped forward and clamped his hand down on her wrist.

"What?!" she shouted, her voice on the verge of cracking as she thrashed in the water.

"If you don't want me to get some women to help you, that's fine, but I will not let you hurt yourself anymore. You're scrubbing the flesh off your bones! I know you don't want his filth on you, but you will not rip yourself to shreds over it. Now, what's it to be?" Marcus asked in a low, controlled tone. He wished Prevak had lived; he would have tortured that bastard for weeks for what he had done.

"I don't need anyone's help! Why would you think I would want even more people to see me like this?!" She was screaming at him as silent tears trickled down her cheeks from an eye that was still wide with agony. Her voice didn't hitch, nor did she sniffle.

Before he could think of what to say, she defiantly snatched the cloth back. "I don't want you, your men, or any of the women you're thinking of recruiting to touch me. I can still feel it. He squeezed my breasts, his fingers, and laughed as he twisted them. While I let him." She broke down into a cracked whisper and rolled the cloth over her deeply bruised breasts.

"Alexandra, you cannot blame yourself for this. Look, I don't know what to do, but I know someone in this camp who does. First, let's just get you out of here, please. You're clean now, I promise." Marcus gently took her hands and lifted her out of the tub. She followed his lead, but he could tell it was with great reluctance.

When she finally dried, dressed, and tucked herself into bed, he let the innkeeper's wife into the room for the third time to drag the tub into the hall, where his men could take care of the rest. They knew something was horribly wrong, but Marcus was grateful that they didn't ask for confirmation of their worst fears. They just quietly went about their duties while Alex burrowed beneath the security of a thick wool shield.

Once they were gone, Marcus softly called out to her, but she didn't respond. Whether she had actually fallen asleep or was just pretending so that he'd leave her alone, he couldn't be sure, and he was too afraid of hurting her more to find out. He'd let her rest, for now, if only because it bought him time to reach out to the one who knew her best.

Victus appeared at his side the moment Marcus stepped out into the hallway with a tormented, mile-long stare. "I should have jumped in. I should have saved her. Marcus, I am sorry. This is my fault," he croaked. He reached out to grab Marcus' shoulder, tempting fate to provoke him into the violent retaliation he felt he deserved.

Marcus paused there in the hall. The gazes of his curious praetorians made his shoulders slump forward. He took three deep breaths and turned to face Victus. "This is not your fault. You followed protocol. They outnumbered you, and they would have killed you both if you had acted rashly. You did the right thing." Then, Marcus' face changed from that of a compassionate friend to a merciless warlord on a mission. "Now, let go of me or I will break your arm." He snatched himself away and marched down the hall, the look in his eye causing men to trip over themselves to get out of his path.

Victus crashed to his knees, but before Marcus could reach the stairs, he called, "Wait for me! I can help her!" Marcus barely heard him. He marched down on a path he could only hope was right, but Victus was soon close behind him with a wealth of knowledge that might save the princess yet.

The pair stormed out into the streets just as the soft sound of thunder rolled through the town. The enormous crowd that had gathered outside of that tiny inn was staggering and divided. On one side of the street stood a group of house representatives, legionnaires, and men loyal to the recently departed Prevak. On the other side stood the Estradian representative, the praetorians, and the commanders loyal to honor and common sense.

Clearly, the princess was not at fault for being raped, but the legionnaires and the noble houses perceived her reaction to be too severe. She had not simply killed a Luxorian; she had killed a senator's son for a crime they may have pardoned him of in trial. It was unthinkable and would shake the very foundations of the Luxorian nobility once they caught wind of what had happened.

Notably absent were the house representatives for the LaClair and Alvarado households, who were not sure where their masters would think of this turn of events. Some representatives on the street that day were ready to see her pay with her life. The Rustionage representative pushed his way through the crowd, his face curled in disgust.

"Do you understand what she has done, Your Highness? That savage has to be put down before she turns her blade on you, too!" he shouted in disbelief at the circumstances he faced. Informing Senator Rustionage that his son was dead would make for a very unlucky day for the messenger, and he was going to have trouble finding a man alive willing to undertake that mission.

"Do you understand what she has done? She defended her life and virtue after that vicious pig you called your master raped her! I suggest you be very careful about the next words you choose." Marcus attempted to walk past him, uninterested in having this fight while his wife lay suffering in bed, waiting for anyone to be of comfort to her. She needed Kaden by her side, and he wasn't willing to stall for anyone, least of all for the likes of this serpent.

"It is not what I would accuse her of that you should worry about, my prince."

"Was that a threat I just heard?" Marcus stopped and turned, his voice growing cold and quiet like frost.

"It is no threat, Your Highness. Rather, I am simply advising, as you will recall is my role. Frankly, I'm surprised you can hear anything at all that scheming, barbarian whore did not whisper directly into your ear."

Victus surged forward with a look that could have ignited the man in a fiery blaze had he been the flaky little leaf Victus suspected him to be, but Marcus stretched out his hand to stop him. "No, Victus. That's fine. I am certain we misheard the gentleman representing the Rustionage house. He would not insult the wife of the crown prince of his empire and threaten that same prince in a single breath, especially not today. Isn't that right?"

This was a very deliberate moment of restraint for Marcus, and it was crucial for his men to see it. He had to prove now, in the most difficult of times, what kind of ruler he was going to be. Would he be a distant ruler like his father, a tyrant like his brother, or would he continue to be a man among his men now that the promise of power rested on his shoulders? He showed that his men, even those he despised most, would have a fair chance of being heard before receiving his judgment. This, however, was the extent of his tolerance. One more word out of this idiot's mouth would mark the end of his miserable presence in this camp.

"She may have a bruised cunt, but my master has lost their only son because of her. I'm sure we can agree on which is the more serious crime. So, what are you going to do about it?"

"You all heard me give this fool a chance to leave unharmed, didn't you?" Marcus called out before spinning to slam his fist into the representative's mouth, sending him flying. After a quick scuffle, Marcus had his throat pinned beneath his boot and looked ready to apply those extra few pounds of pressure he'd need to snap his windpipe.

"Victus, bring around his horse. I think a ride around the camp, dragged behind me, ought to smooth out the rough edges of his tongue. Then he can ride home to tell Senator Rustionage himself how his son died."

It was a death sentence that the Rustionage family would likely carry out in a moment of intense rage, but it highlighted Marcus' cunning and silenced both sides of the street for now. His praetorians rushed forward to bind the man while Victus brought his horse over, but then Commander Hardin came forward and gently placed his hand on the prince's shoulder.

"I'll see to it. We will strip him down and drag him through the town. A prince should not dirty his hands like this. Go tend to your wife and find me when she is well enough to be without your company for a while. There is something we should discuss," Commander Hardin remarked calmly, his gaze unwavering and certain as he looked into the rabid gaze of the man he'd mentored since childhood.

Marcus' fists were quivering by his side, itching to throw another punch and then another, but he knew Commander Hardin was right. His brother had reveled in carrying out torture, and no matter how much he wanted to, he knew he shouldn't be the one his men saw administering this sort of punishment. He had men who would gladly take up the cause for him, no matter how brutal the command. Those who doubted him needed to see that.

"Very well. When you send him on his way, please send two of your own men with him to ensure he carries out my orders. I'm sure the coward would sooner slither into poverty than face his master right now."

"Yes, Your Highness." Commander Hardin bowed and signaled for the rest of his men to follow suit. For now, they set aside Prevak's death completely. The cost to anyone foolish enough to attack Alexandra for it was going to be put on full display shortly.

Marcus stormed into the warehouse with a crestfallen look on his face. One look at him told her men more than any words Marcus could have said. His appearance was just as ragged as the frayed hope that he was barely clinging to.

Kaden stood to his full height of six feet, eight inches, and sighed, with his arms crossed over his chest. "Well, where is she?"

Marcus felt as though he were standing before his wife's father as an immature boy, not the man she needed. "She's resting at the inn. She... she..." Marcus' voice caught in his throat and he bowed his head to hide his tears.

Taking a moment to compose himself, he lifted his head to match Kaden's gaze and just let the truth come tumbling out. "One of my commanders kidnapped and raped her. She's alive, but I don't know what to do to help her. Please, you must help her. She killed the monster who did this, but I'm afraid it's not enough."

Kaden stared at Marcus, and his face gradually grew a color red that was heretofore unmatched. He had the look of a man who was trying to restrain himself from ramming his boot down the prince's throat. Then, with a deep hiss of a breath, he said, "I don't have time for your tears. She needs me. Take me to her, now."

CHAPTER 13

There were three rivers of thought on how to proceed now that Alex was safe and under their constant guard. First, there was Marcus' plan: constant surveillance, coddling, and overprotectiveness to where Alex felt suffocated.

Next, there was Kaden's approach. She loved Kaden like a father, but he knew what to do, least of all. Once he saw she was alive and physically well enough, he just wanted to shake her out of it. Marcus had to hold him back from being too rough with her, which resulted in a grand gesture of Kaden sitting on his hands and muttering under his breath about Marcus' lack of overall good qualities. Marcus became even more protective to compensate for what he felt were his faults.

However, neither of these ideas helped Alex in the slightest.

Finally, there was Victus. He never left her side, except to relieve himself in the privy, and slept only during the brief moments she found rest, too. Victus was the only one who truly listened to what Alex wanted, but his efforts were constantly being pushed aside by the other two, who acted more and more like competitors with every passing hour. Still, he was patient and vigilant, waiting for her to choose which of them she needed at that moment. He was always ready to accept her decision without hesitation. All she needed was time to make it.

On the sixth morning since they'd begun their vigilant watch over her, Alex made her first decisive decision since that horrible day. "You two, go outside," she commanded Marcus and Kaden. They had devolved into another fight under their breaths about what was best for her, and she could take no more. Victus was the only one not pressuring her, which made him tolerable. At least he was trying to think of what she needed and not just overcompensate for his wounded pride.

"Until when, my dear? I'm worried. I really think you need to eat more than that." Marcus motioned at her untouched breakfast plate, clearly upset that she'd just moved her food around a bit rather than put any of it to her lips. The sausage was annoying her, but she didn't want to talk about it.

Marcus must have followed her gaze. Quickly, he reached to grab the offensive piece of meat off her plate, but Kaden's hand shot out and pinned his arm to the table. "Of course, she'll eat more! She's a Raybrandt. She'll finish the entire damn plate before you even look at yours! Go on, Alex. Show him what you can do,"

Kaden urged, and shoved her plate closer to her, almost tipping the whole thing over onto her lap.

Alex caught the lip of the plate just in time, and with fire in her eyes, she repeated herself, "I said get out, and don't either of you come back until you've worked out your differences. I'm sick of it. I'm sick of the bickering, the unhelpful 'helping,' and the pressure to hurry and get well. It's all making me feel worse. I don't need either of you as you are now, so get out!" she screamed, sending the two men into a tailspin as they tried to figure out how to make her change her mind.

When it seemed they might protest, Victus, who had been sitting off to the side, interjected. "May I stay, Princess, if I can make them leave?" When she gave a quiet nod and turned her head away from them, Victus sprang into action.

He led Marcus and Kaden out of the room and into the hall. They followed only because they didn't know what else to do. The woman they each cared for most had just dismissed them. How could that be so? They were her closest allies. Had she forgotten that? Why was she choosing Victus over them?

"Listen, you're only making this worse. Trust me. She doesn't need you, her husband, or you, her guardian, jumping at each other constantly, ready to put the other in his place. She feels the need to protect the both of you, when really all she needs to do is work on herself right now. So, go out there and find some middle ground before she falls out of love with both of you!" Victus shut the door behind him without letting either of them get in another word.

Once they were gone, Alex fell into herself again. She let her head slump forward and drew her knees up into her chest. Alex was also shivering, as though she had been crying, but her face was devoid of any actual tears. She couldn't cry anymore. Her eyes hurt too much.

"If you hate the plate that much, I could go find you something else," Victus casually offered, and dug into his own meal while he waited for her to answer.

"It's fine," she shot back, stabbing a few pieces of eggs and slamming them into her mouth just so she didn't have to talk about it anymore.

"Good. Just let me know if you need anything," Victus smiled and ate his meal in a normal, relaxed manner. That was what she needed right now: a sense of normalcy. Someone to show her that everything was going to be all right, and that she was free to talk about it if she was ready. It was her choice. At least Victus got it.

With Marcus and Kaden out of the room, it didn't take long for her to take part in conversation again. She needed to speak, now that she felt free enough to do so. "What am I going to do, Victus? I can't even see straight anymore, and everyone just expects me to forget what happened."

"I know it feels that way, but no one really expects you to forget and move on. They just want you to feel better and they don't know how to help you get there.

A few hours of sleep is an important first step, I think." She looked up at him and really took stock of him for the first time in days.

He was wearing a simple white shirt, a pair of brown pants, and a set of leather boots. He'd tied his long, light locks back in a loose ponytail, and his thin face was as stoic as ever. Though he wasn't wearing his uniform, it was only so that he could help her relax. No weapons. No Luxorian colors. Nothing to set off panic or unease.

"How did you know I hadn't been sleeping?" Alex asked, having been so confident that she'd been hiding her secret struggle.

"Because whether you realize it or not, you will literally inhale those eggs in a couple of seconds if you don't lift your head up." Victus chuckled when her head suddenly drooped forward and she barely caught herself in time to stop his prophecy from coming true.

Out of frustration, she shoved the plate away and laid her head down on her arms. "I just can't sleep. Every time I try, Marcus crawls into bed next to me and tells me how brave I am, how sorry he is, and how much he cares for me. Then, when Marcus isn't muttering in his sleep about how he'll avenge me, I see Prevak's bloated face laughing at me. It's as if he's mocking me from the abyss for falling for such a stupid trap," she admitted, her voice fading into nothing but a broken whisper.

"Alex, you know that what happened wasn't your fault, right?" Victus asked with all sincerity. He sat his fork down and looked into the eyes of the woman he had failed.

"Wasn't it? Luxorian generals use magic like that as a popular weapon. At least they used to. I even feared it when Marcus first captured me! I just really didn't think that it would lead to anything like this when they handed me that damned box." Tears pooled in her bloodshot eyes. "I thought they were accepting me."

"It wasn't your fault, Alex. Listen, I won't burden you with my guilt about all of this, but you should know that Kaden should have done more to prepare you. Marcus should have done more to inform you. I should have done more to protect you that day. That's all that could have changed. We let you down, but we'll redeem ourselves, you'll see." Victus fished around in his pocket for a vial that contained little blackish purple seeds that were no larger than spring peas. "Now, go get some rest while they're gone. You can take two of these. They'll help quell the nightmares."

"What are they?" Alex asked as she lifted the vial. She tilted it upside down, listening to the quiet clinking sound of the seeds dropping one by one against the glass stopper. It was such a soft sound.

"They are seeds from a well-known plant near my hometown. They will help you sleep. Your mind will be void of dreams, but you'll still be lucid enough to wake up and move around if you want to. I promise you that," Victus swore on his honor.

"How do you know?" Alex asked, not even attempting to mask the skepticism in her voice. He was asking for too much. Her unbroken attention to her surroundings was a lot to give up. Now more than ever, she needed to feel in control of her body and mind.

"Because most nights I use them myself. A few years ago, I went through the same thing with my younger sister. I was away on a campaign and bandits attacked her. I rushed to her side when I heard the news, but the damage had already been done. Helping her through it all took its toll. But it's also why I know how to help you now. You need rest, quiet, and stability. I'll make sure you get all three."

Victus produced a notebook from his other pocket and tossed it onto the table for her to take. The cover was leather and branded with Alex's initials. He had scorched AME into the trunk of the tree of life he'd had pressed into its surface. "This will also help. Just start writing whatever comes to mind. Day-to-day occurrences, poems, songs, memories, private thoughts, anything really. Push those feelings of guilt out like your body would a splinter. You'll feel much better. It starts with these first two steps: rest and reflection. Are you ready to take them?" Victus asked quietly.

"Yes," Alex said and nudged the vial back toward Victus, "but I don't need these. I'm stronger than the vestiges of his memory," she asserted with the voice of a monarch and the will of the warrior she'd always been.

Walking over to her bedside table, she took a quill out of the inkpot Victus had brought in for her and plopped down on the bed with her new journal. Meanwhile, Victus focused on watching the world outside her window. He didn't challenge her when she said she didn't require the seeds, and for that, she was grateful. He could be her eyes and ears while she slept, but she would not risk her senses being dulled ever again.

On the very first page of Alex's new journal, she wrote, "Entry Number 1: This journal will forevermore be a testament to how I triumphed over you. I'll start with a good, long nap that you can't touch. I won't let you, so don't even try."

With that letter written to his ghost, she fell over and forced her eyes shut. Finally, when she drifted off to sleep, she did not see Prevak's cruel face or hear his malicious laughter, but by the sounds of a quiet autumn night that existed only in her mind. In her dreams, crickets sang for her and the flames that had once warmed her cheeks danced in a fire pit before her. She watched the stars fall from the heavens above and lay there unmoving for hours.

Even after the serenity of that dream, she knew she had not done enough to rid herself of Prevak entirely, but she had at least begun the journey, and someday this road would lead her to the dawn.

·   ·   ·

Marcus and Kaden walked across the camp to Commander Hardin's tent now that Alex herself had officially dismissed them. "You know the only reason I haven't run you through is because it would hurt her, right?" Marcus said. There was no need for him to pine outside of Alex's room. She'd decided that he and Kaden would need to come to some sort of peace over what had happened before she'd let them anywhere near her again. The only problem was that he wasn't sure how he was going to accomplish what she asked. If he said left, Kaden barked right. How could he make this work when he only answered to Alex?

"I'd like to see you try, little man," Kaden growled and ran his bulging fingers through his red mane. Marcus truly couldn't believe that, along with this blundering fool, Alex had told him to leave!

"We've already seen what would happen, you forgetful oaf. So, rather than threaten me, why don't you make yourself useful and help her?" Marcus snapped and turned on Kaden, whose eyes had landed on a pair of caged, blistered and dehydrated men. A week of sun exposure had that effect. They still wore their torn legionnaire uniforms. The older, more powerful of the pair wore it proudly, while the younger, fairer boy looked ready to heave.

"Who are they?" Kaden asked in a dangerously quiet voice. His back stiffened and his chest swelled to almost twice the size. He stared at the caged men like a rabid wolf who'd found an easy meal for itself. He might not get at the son of a bitch who'd torn down his princess, but he'd settle for these two if they were involved.

"They're two of Prevak's legionnaires that we cap... HEY! STOP!" Marcus grabbed the behemoth's arm, to no avail. Kaden nearly threw him with the forceful swing of his arm and charged forth, slamming his beet-red face against the bars to stare into their souls with immeasurable hatred. He tried to grab the trapped men, but they were both able to avoid his vengeful hand by rushing to the other side of the cage.

"I'll be your fucking end!" he roared, and slammed his fist into the bars, denting the metal.

"Step aside, or by the Gods, I will be yours!" Marcus commanded in a thunderous voice. He drew his blade, making the unarmed Artorian take a few paces back, though his eyes never left his would-be victims.

"Thank you for not making me do that. Look, I'm as incensed as you are that they're still breathing, but I had a thought."

"Yes?" Kaden turned to look at Marcus, every vein in his head protruding from his face like striking purple rivers. The man was in agony, and although Marcus could sympathize, he could not allow him to be the spark that continued the war between their two peoples. Keeping Alex safe was going to be difficult enough without her right-hand man becoming a vigilante on her behalf.

"Yes. We'll let Alex decide what to do with them, as is her right as their princess. Maybe then she'll see that they're just men that she would have laid to waste in a fair fight, and not the monsters she's built up in her head."

"I like it. When do we tell her?" Kaden asked after some thought. He followed Marcus until they reached Commander Hardin's tent, where Marcus paused.

"Whenever I see her next, I think. She seems to have recovered some of her grit in these past few hours, and I'd like to see her put it to better use than on our backsides. Now, I need to speak with one of my commanders about where we stand. You may come in because I trust your single-mindedness, but if you give that man a reason to execute you, I won't stand in his way." Marcus turned on his heel without a second look.

"Ah! Right on time, Your Highness. Your ears must have been burning." Commander Hardin bowed when Marcus walked in, his heavy green eyes lingering on Kaden for a moment before motioning the courier forward. He was a small boy of only fifteen, and he looked terrified to stand in a tent among such giants. He wore the imperial colors of silver and blue, but had little more than an official scroll in his possession. With his eyes fixed on the ground, he handed the notice to his prince and stood back to await the end of his assignment.

"When did you arrive, courier?" Marcus asked in a neutral tone.

"Just an hour ago, Your Highness," the courier responded. "This is from the Council. They asked that I wait to bring back any reply you may wish to send."

Marcus took the letter and stepped away to read its contents.

"It has come to the attention of this esteemed council you hold Princess Alexandra Monica Raybrandt of Artoria prisoner in your camp. Negotiations have occurred with Nicholas Altan Raybrandt, and he has offered terms of peace. We require you that immediately execute the exiled princess, and send a courier with her head into Artorian territory to deliver it to the border town of Yenus. They will withdraw their troops once it is done. Should you fail in this task, they have promised us a protracted war. The Council has voted with a heavy majority to accept these terms."

Marcus said nothing. He simply walked out of the tent, and with a firm hand, threw the missive into a nearby campfire. The courier let out a startled croak and stared at Marcus in surprise.

"Courier, I will give you no paper to deliver to the Council. Instead, I give you a message to relay to them. Tell them my new bride, Princess Alexandra Monica Evandrus, and I will soon come home. Now, I've wasted enough time on this dishonorable nonsense. Eat your fill and be on your way to deliver my message." Marcus seethed, his gaze pinning the courier in place until he turned to resume his meeting with Hardin.

"I presume that notice didn't congratulate you on your nuptials or offer condolences for the princess." Commander Hardin sighed with an arched brow as he poured himself and his guests a glass of wine.

"It was a command to surrender Alexandra's head to the border town of Yenus, where they know her as a local hero. I won't have such a foul, cowardly idea spread throughout the camp when she can't even muster a defense for herself," Marcus raved, snatching the bottle to take a long swing before slamming it back onto the table. He was exhausted and no longer thinking clearly. His mission had become ensuring Alex's well-being, and because of that, he couldn't see the forest for the trees. Thankfully, he had advisors who could.

"Of course she has a defense. She has you, and by extension, many men in this army are ready to draw their blades for her. She also has this tree," Commander Hardin chuckled and gestured over to Kaden, who was crouching just below the canvas, his head still poking it up a bit.

"Sorry not to be a dwarf like the rest of ya. So, what are you saying then? That you're willing to defy the Council for our princess? Do you think I'm as stupid as I am tall?"

"No, I don't think the Gods would curse a man with a face like that and the mind of a jester. However, disrespect me like that in my tent again, and the worms may find a better use for your tongue than you ever did," Hardin warned. He ran his thumb over the hilt of his sword as a warning, deflating the unarmed giant for the moment.

"So, what are you suggesting, Hardin?" Marcus asked, drawing his attention back to the topic at hand: Alexandra. What were they going to do about their injured princess, and just how far was Hardin willing to go with them on this journey?

"You've never been in this position before, so allow me to give you some advice. Don't be so eager to prove your allegiance to her, not yet. You think some men hate her now? Just wait until the Council pins every breath she takes as the sole reason for their homes being burned to the ground and their kin murdered in cold blood. You won't find a kind thought to spare for her, not in this camp. Nicholas means to break us, and we're not prepared to stop him. So, rather than antagonize him by spitting in his face, let us buy some time."

"Buy time? But how? He wants her head in a bag! That isn't something so easy to fake," Marcus shot back, unappreciative of the bush that Hardin was beating around.

"If you want to protect one person above all others, you have to be prepared to kill everyone else. So, my suggestion is this: find a substitute among the camp followers or in town and cut off her head," Hardin instructed flatly, his tone eerie and neutral as though he'd simply told Marcus to go out for a walk to clear his head, not rid an innocent woman of hers.

Marcus' face dropped. Would he have to resort to such savagery to keep his bride alive? He felt the color draining from his face to the tips of his toes, but for the color he lost, Kaden regained it in spades.

"No. No, Alex would never allow that. She lives for the people. If she found out about this, it would crush her!" Kaden roared in disbelief.

"Then she will die for them, as well. I did not expect this to be easy for you and certainly not for her, but this is what we must do in order to keep her safe."

"What then? The men will know the truth, and those who want to hurt her will use the knowledge that she is alive against her. The Council and Nicholas will find out the truth from their whisperers before we can expand our forces out to the furthest borders, which, by my approximation, should take at least two months."

"You can't seriously think this is something Alex could live with? We must think of something else. A pig's head, a straw head, anything but this!" Kaden insisted, pushing for a less gruesome solution that his princess could stomach. Marcus knew that she'd never want to think such a conversation was being held in her name. She'd never even consider it, but what choice did they have?

Hardin ignored the bellowing oaf and focused on Marcus. "The decoy is all the proof you will need for a while. Whispers of conspiracy will spread no matter what you do, but it's hard to argue with flesh and blood. While you have that advantage on your side, you and a small party could slip away to the Izmari swamps. Ferrymen there regularly bring clams, crayfish, and swamp mud into the capital for trade; you could easily purchase your way onto one of their ships. It will be a rough journey, but in the end, I believe Princess Alexandra will be safe. By that time, it won't matter if the truth comes out because we'll be ready."

"I don't know how to feel about any of this. I need time to think." A decoy? How could he look at any woman alive and think of her as just a decoy for his wife, who'd sooner throw her own self on the sword? There had to be a way around this, a way he couldn't see. He didn't know her cousin, not like she did, so maybe excluding her from this conversation was the fatal flaw in all of this. Maybe she could point them down an alternative path and save them from becoming the monsters they all fought so hard against.

"I'll hold back the courier, but I don't know that my answer will change. My wife and I need some time together. I need her to understand what's going on, and I need her to make a choice. She doesn't deserve to go into this blindly without knowing what is going on around her. What I regret most is protecting her from the knowledge of men like Prevak, who she could have been on the lookout for if I had only trusted her like she trusted me. Don't follow me," Marcus warned, and turned away from them without another word.

That very hour, he relieved Victus of his guard and watched her sleep, free of the man who had torn so much away from them. It was a relief, and when she woke, he told her everything, knowing deep down that he needed her uncanny knack for survival to help carry them through another day.

CHAPTER 14

Alex chose a powerful, scarlet-red gown with gold trim on the square neckline, the edges of the long, billowy sleeves, and the hemline. Her hair hung loose free of the mangled braid she had kept it in these past several days and was all the wavier and more lustrous for it. She noted how his men were careful not to cross her path and stayed a considerable distance away. She supposed they were doing it for her comfort, but she felt like she had the plague.

'I wonder if that's how I made them feel that night.' Alex thought. 'That I blamed them. That they repulsed me. It's not true. I don't...'

Alex remembered how she had shied away from everyone, including Marcus, when they found her. Now, she looked regal as she enjoyed her breakfast of cured ham, runny eggs, whole wheat bread, and sweet, sugary tea. She ate two whole servings before her stomach reluctantly insisted that she leave the table to go about her day. She marched out of the inn with her head held high, acting as if nothing had happened and she had been suffering from only a slight head cold these past few days.

In reality, she was trying to hide the fact that she trembled every time she had to stand still, and that she was overly vigilant for anyone who might offer her more pain. Paranoia had rooted itself deep inside her heart, but with every forceful stride she took, she coaxed herself into believing that she'd be fine.

Today she was on a mission. She couldn't just let him execute the two men they had captured that day, not until she'd stripped away the power they held over her layer by layer. She needed to see them for the weak worms that they were and not the titans she feared them to be. At least, that's what Marcus had convinced her was true.

He stood upstairs inside the inn, watching this unfold from the window of their room, his face somber. They talked about it. He said he wanted to be at her side, but he also didn't want her to feel or look weak. Still, he certainly would not let her out of his sight when she was near these men. A bow sat propped against the windowsill, with a full quiver nearby. No chances.

It didn't take her long to find their well-guarded cage, where they had sat for almost an entire two weeks now. Alex had been told that they'd watched day and night as his men heated instruments of torture to a searing, hot white, and they tried to dodge their fiery touch. His men denied them everything from dignity to food; the guards intentionally prepared their meals

blessing to rip his throat out. I'd like to hear what this young man has to say."

When the men hesitated for a moment too long, she turned back to them and spoke in a calm but firm voice. "That was a command." Her frigid gaze lit the fire beneath their feet better than any threat would have. They hastily removed the prisoner so they could deliver him to Marcus without delay.

Turning back to the other prisoner, who sat groveling in the cage, she gave a moment of pause. He pressed his light blond head to the ground and sobbed like a baby. The sight of his hair gave her an idea, a hideous one. Just what sort of man was he? Was he a repentant rapist who'd had no choice but to follow the commands of one more powerful than he, or something much worse than the filth she had just dismissed?

"Stop crying and stand on your feet. Have you already forgotten that I was the one who first begged you for freedom?" she hissed, her heart thundering in her chest when he lifted his blue eyes to meet hers. Once he picked himself up and lean his head against the bars, she resumed her interrogation. "I have asked you quite a few questions, all of which, I noted, you refused to answer. I'll have you stand on hot coals until your heel bones turn black if you can't muster the truth. Now, why didn't you stop Prevak? Why did you not take the escape I offered you? Why did you do nothing while he raped me?"

The prisoner was crying so hard that snot was freely flowing out of his nose with every ragged gasp of air, spreading his mucus all over his lips. He was a pitiful, dejected sight. Finally, he blathered a reply. "He was muh commander! We fucked lots of barbarians, lots of heathen whores! Said we were doing them a favor! Was our right! I swear, I'm so sorry. I won't do it again!"

He broke down sobbing for a minute before he brought himself back to answering her. "How would I stop him? He's the son of a senator. I'm the son of a blacksmith. He gave us lots of barbarians to use and good food too! What more could we want? What would you have given me? Prevak gave us your body. There wouldn't be nothin left. Didn't think you would survive; why worry about getting caught if you were already dead?"

His answers flabbergasted Alex. She knew what to do with the prisoner she'd sent Marcus, but this boy hardly seemed old enough to wield a sword, let alone turn a blind eye to a woman being raped. His face was angelic, more like a girl's, really. He didn't look like someone capable of such a horrible, insidious act, yet she remembered him as one of the first to press that white-hot piece of iron into her flesh to mark her like a cow.

"What would I have given you?" she asked, her voice taking on a very dangerous tone that even Kaden had only heard her use perhaps twice in her life. He was in the crowd too, of course. Silent, observant, and patiently awaiting her judgment to fall on this boy's head. He knew she did not take kindly to the lad hiding behind his fear. Betraying his commander had never even crossed his mind, by his own confession, but now he was a sniveling coward, practically pissing himself in fear and false regret.

A sudden scream made Alex turn. Marcus had probably just sent the legionnaire she'd sent away to meet his commander in the pits of the abyss. When her thoughts returned to the sniveling worm in front of her, she realized how many men had gathered to watch the interrogation. Men intent on listening clogged the street now, but most had already passed their own judgment.

All her men were there, and they were at least now well-armed, dressed, and accounted for. She also spotted quite a few of Marcus' men, with their fierce gazes locked onto the shivering coward in the cage. Their glares could have taken even the fiercest beast back, and she knew then that this boy didn't have a hope, even if she forgave him.

Turning around to face her gutless prisoner once more, she answered her own question since he wouldn't. "Well, I recall freedom from this hell you've found yourself in was what I offered to any man who helped me to escape. Now, tell me something else. When you say 'lots of barbarians, lots of heathen whores,' what is 'lots' by your standard?" She stood deathly still, not taking her eyes off his. "Come now, don't be shy. Honorable men who I am sure are all dying to hear your esteemed definition of 'lots.' surround you now."

Just then, another scream that carried far louder than the last made Alex's blood run cold. What was Marcus doing? Why wasn't the prisoner dead yet? She'd given him this opportunity to execute a man who had hurt her, not so he could torture him, but so that he could feel some sense of closure. Who did he think he was? Antonius?

Rather than seeing the formidable, intelligent, compassionate royal standing before him, all the prisoner saw was a barbarian slut who was obviously far less refined and worthy of respect than any Luxorian woman. He found himself forced to endure this interrogation from someone he thought was weak, someone he didn't think could hurt him in a hundred thousand years, and who never would have if Marcus hadn't found her. He was clearly annoyed, and his mask was cracking.

"Lots means lots." He shrugged defensively. "I dunno, before we came back to the main camp, we took lots of barbarians that way. Had a couple a night for a few weeks straight."

It seemed to occur to him that perhaps he was saying the wrong things. Perhaps he saw that glint in her eye, because his sobs became more forceful, and the almost insincere terror washed over his face once more. "But I swear, I promise I won't do it no more. I promise! Barbarian women are good, and I won't hurt anymore! I swear!!!" He collapsed to his knees, banging his forehead against the bars as he clutched the cool metal for dear life.

Two women every night for a few weeks. So, at the very least, they had forced at least fifty women to endure this nightmare, and this boy had been there for it all. It made Alex feel sick, but she needed to be clear on just one more thing before she decided on his fate.

"Tell me, what did you do with these women when you were done with them? You've already admitted that the plan was to kill me, so what of the other women?" His counterpart's screech came surging forth at precisely the right moment, emphasizing the end of her question.

"Come now, I only wish to know if there are any women out there whom I might still help to recover from what you have done to them. If they are all as dead as you planned for me to be, I'd like to know that, too, so we waste no resources chasing ghosts. If you offer me honesty now, I will have your cage unlocked." The bait was tempting, and her tone did not betray her as a liar. In a moment, compounded by exhaustion, terror, and tremendous pressure, he snapped.

"We had to kill 'em. No choice. Couldn't soil the bloodline," he mumbled through his sniffles. He held his hands up in a pleading gesture, as though any other person in the world would have come to the same obvious conclusion. "Ya see? It was for the empire! We had no choice! Was fun, we were doin' them a favor! Did you a favor, too. We showed 'em what it was like to be with the civilized and proud men of Luxor!"

Alex felt her facade fall a little and her chest grow heavy when he confirmed that they had murdered all the women they had raped. Couldn't soil the bloodline, after all. Nothing but fun between heathen whores and civilized men.

It didn't matter which side of the border they had found their victims on, because they were all the same to him and he was doing them a favor. That word was like a blow to the gut that both enraged her and strengthened her resolve to see this sentencing through. No amount of baby-faced charm could help him now. Swallowing hard, she maintained her composure for the last few sentences that she could muster.

"Ah, well, you are right, of course. You did me a favor. You taught me a valuable lesson that I won't soon forget. Now, I promised to unlock your cage if you were honest with me, and I believe you were. Guard, remove the lock," she instructed calmly, waiting for him to comply. She saw a ray of hope illuminate the young man's face as it seemed she was about ready to discharge him for his honesty.

Alex glided through the wave of fast-approaching men who would pry him from the bars he had foolishly thought were his enemies. Stilling Kaden before she passed him, she murmured, "Don't let them burn the body."

A fresh scream rang out from behind her, sending a chill right down to her bone. She needed to see Marcus.

She needed to stop him. Killing the man was one thing. Torture was another.

"I'll see to it, Alex," Kaden rumbled softly, patting her shoulder before making his way forward to show the lad what a real man thought of his excuses.

Alex didn't turn back. She stopped in the back doorway of the inn that, for now, they had commandeered for these vengeful acts. The innkeeper, his wife, and his sweet daughter were nowhere to be seen, and for good reason. In a little brown stable out back, she heard a hoarse howl and then silence. She didn't know what she would find within those walls, but she prayed that among the horrors that were surely in there, her husband's soul would be there, too.

CHAPTER 15

Only when Marcus saw the first prisoner being brought toward the inn did he turn away from the window. His praetorians were watching over her now, and he knew her men must be in that crowd as well. He'd had Victus release them just this morning for this very purpose. He wanted Alex to feel safe when she stepped outside, and not like she was being eyed by a bunch of strangers.

He stomped down the stairs and rounded the corner to meet the prisoner, his face lit with a cold, feral smile. "The smithy, attached to the stable out back. Let's not mess up the inn. Heat some coals in the hearth," he instructed.

The guards dragged the man out back and tied him spread-eagle inside a stall. They viciously ripped off his cloth shield, leaving him as exposed as Alex had been that horrible day. When Marcus arrived, he took off his shirt, slid on a leather apron, and picked up a rather crude hammer. He caressed the head of the hammer as he looked down at one man who had attacked his wife.

"So, rape is a privilege, and you were doing it all for me? I suppose I can understand. I mean, hey, what man doesn't want his new bride broken in by a dozen swine?" His eyes were like chips of ice as he took in the vile creature. "I can tell you haven't been in my army long. My soldiers know that although I am a man of honor, I am also a man of little patience. Once you cross me or someone that I swore before the Gods to protect, my temper makes me more of a terror than my brother could have ever dreamed of being. This is an unfortunate situation you've created for yourself."

Without another word, he turned, and with a mighty stroke of his arm, he slammed the hammer into the prisoner's testes. The man's scream was loud enough to be heard clearly from the other side of town, but somehow, it just wasn't loud enough for Marcus. He grinned maniacally and lifted the bloodied hammer into the man's range of vision. Marcus delivered a swift, violent kick to his ribs to keep him from passing out.

"We're just getting started. That one was just for my peace of mind, reassurance that you will never touch another woman as you touched my wife." Marcus slammed the hammer into the man's kneecap, shattering it on impact and inverting the bend of his leg. This time, he couldn't stop him from blacking out, but he'd be sure to rouse him as soon as he could.

Once the coals were cherry red, their glow gave a devilish cast to Marcus' face as he held one in a pair of tongs. They woke the legionnaire once more with smelling salts. He groaned, sobbing in pain as his leg jerked involuntarily and his groin bled profusely. Marcus had lost himself in bloodlust and would not stop until he hollowed his victim out from navel to nose.

"My, my, my. It seems you're bleeding. We should really cauterize those wounds." He leaned down and pressed the hot coal to the bloody mess of the prisoner's scrotum. This scream outshined the last and filled Marcus' heart with twisted glee. Prevak might have been gone, but this man was as good a substitute as he could have ever hoped for.

"Now that we've gone through all the trouble to stop the bleeding, I've realized something. The part of you that touched my wife, that pathetic little piece, I worry it could still possibly function. I can't have that," Marcus said coldly as he lifted a hooked sickle from the coals of the forge. The blade was rusty and dull, but it was also glowing white hot.

"Now, this is going to hurt, I promise. The only question is, do I slice off your balls now and save your cock for later, or do it all in one tidy package?"

Marcus watched with pleasure as his prisoner hyperventilated. He knew he was going to die a horrendous death that paled to anything he could have imagined. Marcus kneeled at the prisoner's side and gripped the index and middle finger on his right hand.

"I've changed my mind. I'm having so much fun and don't want to rush it, so I'll just start by taking the hands that touched my wife's flesh," he growled as he hacked off the first two fingers, creating a spurt of blood and a fresh scream. The prisoner faded once more, but Marcus was just getting started.

"WAKE HIM UP!" he roared before he slammed the blade back into the coals. He walked out to let his praetorians get to work on reviving his prisoner before he could bleed out.

Marcus stood just outside the stable in silent reflection while they attempted to rouse him, internalizing every wound he had caused. Bile threatened to rise in his throat at the thought of torture, but the disgust was quickly drowned out by roaring flames of rage. This man had raped and assaulted his wife. Everything Marcus did, this bastard deserved.

Swallowing his heart, he grabbed a towel off a nearby stool and began cleaning his hands of the pungent blood. As he wiped the last smear from his palm, he heard light footsteps behind him and turned to see his wife approaching. It seemed that her own interrogation had concluded, and she did not look any worse for wear. Good. He wanted her to hold her head high once more. He wanted her to stand strong, but he hadn't expected her to use her strength against him.

Throwing the disgusting cloth into the stall, he stepped out into the light to greet her. He didn't reach out for her, but just watched her with a mix of emotions rushing across his face.

"I don't think you'll want to look in there. I've started making him regret the day his mother smiled at his father," he hissed, hoping she wouldn't make it difficult for him to turn her away.

Alex only offered a weak smile in return, but her steadfast stance made it clear she wasn't going anywhere, not without him. "I just came to say that it turns out our men cared little for what these beasts had to say. The younger of the two confessed to how his legion raped and murdered two women every night for weeks on end for the 'good of the empire.'" Her weak smile crumbled, and she took a step away from the stench of burnt flesh to recollect her thoughts. She had to squeeze the bridge of her nose just to stop herself from retching by the looks of it. He wished she would leave.

"I gave that boy to your men because I wanted to show them I don't believe that they are what he and his friend proved to be. I want them to know that I trust them to not take his side. Many of your men were in that crowd, Marcus. It made me content to know that so many would step forward for what was right, and now it's my turn. You need to end that man's suffering right now and come with me," Alex commanded, her stance stiffening a bit as she pushed him to make a hard choice.

"What about my peace of mind? This man tortured you while his commander raped you–MY WIFE! He knew what he was doing! He knew the cost! And now you want me to walk away and let this worthless piece of shit get away with a quick death?" Marcus roared, finding it more difficult by the second not to get right in her face. How could he make her understand? She was just standing there with a sullen, distant look on her face. Didn't she know he was doing this for her?

He was fighting just as hard as she was, but deep down, he knew she couldn't let him do this. The repercussions would last a lifetime and would only cause him more pain. She didn't want that for him. She wanted him to be the man she agreed to marry, not the man he was becoming.

"Yes, I do. I want you to walk away for yourself and for me. Do you think that by becoming my father, you're helping anyone? Well, you're not!"

"If your father visited the torments of hell upon men who raped women, then I would be proud to be like him. I can make certain he suffers for every woman he ever touched. I can make certain he feels the pain and terror he inflicted on you. He should know what you and others suffered before I give him the mercy that the abyss has in store for him." He was raving mad, but he was also crying out of sheer frustration. Why? Why was she trying to stop him? He couldn't understand.

"Marcus, please walk away. Do it as a favor to me. Please. I don't want to lose you to this. I need your help if I am going to make this idea of mine work," Alex begged, tears trickling down her cheeks like lonely, forgotten streams.

Seeing her in so much pain, Marcus paused. What was she saying? What idea was she talking about, and why did it matter now? Soon he'd have to take the life of not only this pestilent worm, but of an innocent woman who favored his wife just to keep her safe. His conscience felt like it was rotting him away from the inside and slowly putrefying his soul. Soon all that would remain would be a hollow, wretched pit. If that feeling was what she was trying to save him from, she was too late.

Swallowing a throat full of bile, he asked, "How will granting him the mercy he would have denied you help anything? What idea is worth that?"

"I won't tell you unless you agree to end his life now. I'll leave this decision up to you, Marcus. Meet me in our room at the inn once you decide to trust me." Without another word, she spun around and returned to the inn.

He watched her leave, quivering with barely restrained rage. A firestorm of lethal intent danced in his eyes. The fury, pain, and despair that had haunted him since the moment he found her in the barn were warring with each other in his gaze, yet he measured her resolve. Finally, with a monstrous sigh, he returned to the revived man, who was whimpering in his grief. Snatching a blade off the wall, he staved off any desire to prolong his suffering and resolved to trust his wife as she had trusted him.

"You are luckier than you will ever know," he growled, and slowly pushing the blade into his windpipe and leaving it there. Marcus doomed him to the slowest death he could in that moment. That blade would keep him from bleeding out too quickly, and would also have him gagging on his own blood until he drowned in it.

Not two minutes after Alex had propped herself up in front of a mirror to run her fingers through her shimmering gold tresses, Marcus walked in, looking just as dazed as she was. He shook his head and sighed. "What is this plan of yours? Please tell me," he panted, his hands corded so tight that his muscles were cramping.

Alex jumped out of her seat, knocking it over. She rushed forward to hold him tight, squeezing him with all her might until her arms ached. "Thank you for trusting me," she whispered softly into his chest. He doubled over her, inhaling her scent for comfort. She was still here, and she was alive, and slowly, she was coming back to him. He reassured himself of that repeatedly as his heavy tears washed over her scalp like salty drops of rain. In his backbreaking grip, she sobbed right along with him until her eyes were red and her chest hurt, but for now, her demons were silenced.

It took well over an hour for them to dry their eyes, but once they could see each other again, they discovered things they never really knew about the person they'd agreed to marry. Marcus, for instance, could see that Alex had a very thin scar just above her eyebrow that surely had a fascinating story, given its swirl shape. She had perpetually chewed up fingernails that she usually kept hidden within her clenched fists.

A few minutes later, she picked up her fallen seat from the floor and sat in front of the mirror once more.

He watched her pinch locks of hair between her fingers, inching up from her waist to her shoulders, pinch by pinch, as if she were measuring a piece of cloth.

"My plan is really very simple." A soft knock at the door interrupted her. It was Victus and Kaden.

"Princess, Kaden tells me we will not burn the boy's body. May I ask what you'd have us do instead? Filling the town with the stench of his rotting corpse hardly seems fair to those left to deal with it," Victus said.

"There is a woman in town that I met at the festival who is skilled at making wigs out of human hair. Her name was Giny, I think. She has a shop near here. Bring her to me, Kaden, and tell her to bring her supplies along," Alex instructed. Her tone told Marcus she would not explain herself. Kaden must have picked up on it too, because he left straight away to track the woman down.

"Marcus, hand me a small blade, please," she murmured as she outstretched her hand, clearly expecting he would do as Kaden had done and fall in line. He would not, not without knowing exactly what was going on.

"Enough. Tell us what your plan is so we can help," Marcus said. He drew a small blade from his boot and flipped it around so she could grab the handle.

"I'm going to have that woman make a wig out of my hair and then I will sew it onto that boy's decapitated head. He had a soft face. In death, I'm sure he could pass for a girl if he had long enough hair. I just need to give him mine. Then you can announce to your council that I am dead, send the courier off with the decoy head, and we can travel together as a smaller party, just as Commander Hardin suggested. It could be you, Victus, Kaden, and me. Any more and we'd risk a mole sneaking into our midst." She continuously pinched one lock of hair until she was just above her ear.

Marcus knew she would have to give herself the hairstyle of a young squire if she wanted this to work, and she was ready to do it. She was ready to throw away her treasured locks; she'd actually put effort and care into them all these years, despite her dirty skin, nails, and utter lack of feminine attire. Even Marcus could see her hair was something she'd taken pride in for quite some time.

If Marcus had learned anything about women from his time with Meridian, it was this. Every woman wore a crown on her head. It sat atop their scalp better than any piece of iron-cast jewels, and it framed their faces. Marcus would be damned if he would watch her do this to herself.

"Alex, wait. Let's talk about this." Before the words could finish coming out of his mouth, he heard a blade cutting through a clump of hair. Alex's hand hadn't moved. She was still pinching a doomed clump of hair and holding the blade up.

Beside him, he saw Victus slicing through thick chunks of his own hair, but he was cutting much closer to his scalp than Alex had planned to. Even she was stunned into silence as he stripped away his hair until he carefully piled it on the table beside her.

"You should keep your hair the way it is. It suits you." That was all that Victus would offer in the way of an explanation when he was done and left to stand guard outside. Those simple words had Alex swallowing back tears and made Marcus swell with pride.

In his company were good men, men he'd grown up with that knew how to care for hearts that were not their own. Years of battle, strategizing, and leading this campaign, and it was only now that he actually believed that he might have what it takes to rule because he knew how to surround himself with the right people.

The shade and length were almost a perfect match, and while he certainly had a nest full of frayed ends, no man was going to pay them any mind when they thought they had the Princess of Artoria's rotting head in a bag. They'd be eager to deliver it to Nicholas to earn his blessing, not knowing it would mean their doom when the boy's rotting flesh revealed his scalp's stitch work.

By the time Alex and Marcus talked through the remaining details, Kaden returned with Giny. They explained the covert nature of their mission and bought her silence. She worked diligently through the night and into the early morning hours to complete the wig. During that time, Kaden decapitated the boy and set up a pyre behind the inn.

In the time it took Alex to finish sewing the wig onto the boy and stuffing his head into a bag, Victus had recruited two praetorians who would explain to anyone who came calling that Marcus was inconsolable after executing his second wife to comply with The Council's edict. He'd done so in the most humane way he could, and no could blame him for granting the princess a private execution.

The only evidence that he had carried out the execution was an inferno that reduced down to nothing but smoldering ash come morning. Curious men seeking to verify this claim could find the charred bones they thought belonged to the princess if they wanted, and no one would dare question their grieving prince after the carnage he had unleashed on the last of Prevak's men.

Meanwhile, Marcus had notified Commander Hardin of their plans so that he could take charge come first morning light.

His men had broken the boy's jaw and mangled his face, which would help to sell their story. If there had been a revolt that resulted in the princess's death, she would have been unrecognizable. That was the story Marcus instructed the courier to tell on pain of death. What difference would the Artorian commanders or the elite know? They wouldn't care until the wig that Alex sewed into his head fell from his rotting scalp. By then, the courier would have his reward and they would have more than enough time to make it back to Valencius.

For now, at least, they were safe.

That night, she wrote, "Entry Number 2: Today I killed two of your men and dressed one of their heads up to look like mine. Perhaps he can do some good in death that he failed to do in life."

CHAPTER 16

They slipped away into the night once the courier rode away with the boy's head in a bag. Alex had obsessed over every detail until looking at his pale face made her feel uneasy. It was as if she just might hold her own head in her hands. Father Brenar caught them on their way, and in silence, he offered them a soft nod and a quiet prayer. An enchanted wind was at their backs and fate finally felt as if it was on their side once more.

They stayed clear of the main roads and towns where people might see her; though it slowed them down considerably, they kept to the shade of the canopy. The group used the cool streams for their baths and rested their heads on mounds of moss on the forest floor. By their tenth consecutive day of travel, everyone was weary as they approached the swamps of Izmari.

The air was heavy with moisture kept close by the mangrove trees that littered this dense, quiet swamp. Their boots sank deeper and deeper into the ground with every step they took. The animals that had entertained them throughout their journey had abandoned them. There wasn't a sign of life anywhere, from the purplish gray moss that hung from the canopies to the sludge they trekked through. An ominous stillness accompanied them the farther they walked, shading this place in a dark, oppressive energy. It made Alex uneasy, but the rest of her party seemed either blatantly unaware or uncaring. They were just ready for some decent food and a warm bed.

"Are we sure about this, Marcus?" Alex whispered as they passed through the gates of the town that seemed to be made of rotting wood. To stifle her uncertainty, she pulled the hood of the blue cloak Victus had lent her lower over her face. She was shivering and miserable, as were they all.

"This is the quickest and safest route we have, Alex. We need to keep you hidden, but we also need to make it back to the capital before Nicholas can poison my council against me. Just stay close to me. I'll keep you safe." He wrapped his arm around her shoulders, squeezing her tightly for comfort. Although they tried to be quiet, their voices seemed to carry like a low echo through the streets. They didn't belong here, and it was as if the driftwood homes that were slanted into the mud had taken notice.

They tried to keep their heads down as they walked past the townspeople, but Alex couldn't help but note the differences between them and those she had befriended in Tripsburgh. The faces of these people were hollow and frightening. For those living in towns where food was abundant and war was simply a three-letter word to be spoken in terms of profit. The farmers of those border towns fed the soldiers of both sides, and both crowns paid handsomely for the risk of living so close to the borders.

These forgotten swamps were amongst hit hardest by the embargoes. They didn't have the protection of their soldiers, and war was an unspeakable injustice on their livelihoods. They would find no love in these shacks, where skeletons lived and died. Best to move unseen.

Every morning, these men and women dove to the depths of this swamp to satisfy the exotic tastes of the elite for pocket change. There was always a chance a creature from below might unhinge its jaw wide enough to swallow them whole, and they might not find the surface of those murky depths ever again.

They didn't even have time to recognize one day from the next when the consequence was starvation and ruin. So, thankfully, no one had time to care about four interlopers. At least, not until they made it to the docks, where ships were so close to each other that one could walk from one ship to the next without breaking stride.

"Are you four looking for safe passage to somewhere?" a honeyed voice called from the mists that were billowing in from the sea just beyond the dismal swamp lands.

Alex turned to see a tall, luminous woman dressed in a violet top and torn brown leggings. She didn't look like the others. She looked well kept, with hoops of gold dangling from her ears, capturing what little light there was in this forsaken swamp. Stunning emerald green eyes locked onto her wary blue gaze, she draped her wavy black hair over her shoulder, and her skin was sun-kissed.

"We sure are," Kaden hummed as he reached out for her hand to deliver a soft kiss, which Alex swiftly slapped down.

"We are. Do you have a ship?" Victus asked with a skeptical stare that spoke volumes.

"I don't, but my brother does. We're just a poor family, sir, but we'll be leaving tonight for Valencius to unload our wares for the market. For three gold coins, we could ferry you away from this wasteland, if you're interested," the woman purred softly. She met Victus' fiery gray irises with pleading crystal pools of evergreen.

"Please excuse my master's guards. My name is Marjorie and I am my master's maid. We're interested. Could you please show us to your ship?" Alex interceded, not liking the way Victus was treating this poor woman. She'd seen enough misery throughout the town to know that this woman was just trying to make a living.

Besides, she had a good feeling about this. If this captain had his sister on board, that probably meant that she'd be safe from harassment from the rest of his men. Surely, the captain of such a ship wouldn't tolerate a crew of heartless men.

Looking up at Marcus, her large blue eyes met his, and he knew. She desperately wanted to go with this woman to see more about this ship. She was afraid. So, without further inquiry, he relented.

"Show us the way." He took the lead that Alex had given him.

He was to be Duke Darius from Fledger Castle. Victus and Kaden were his guards. She was his maid. They'd encountered a group of bandits along their pilgrimage to the capital to answer the emperor's summons, and only had a few gold coins they'd kept hidden left to sustain them.

That, at least, was the story that Alex had crafted days ago when they first broke away from the main camp. It was a sturdy vessel capable of holding a lot of cargo, with a crew of about ten men. It wasn't the height of luxury, but it was safe and dry, which was more than he could say for the rest of their journey leading up to this moment.

"You are faring well, given your environment," Marcus gently pressed, eyeing this mysterious woman carefully. "What is your name?"

"My name is Ezmeralda and I am not from this village. A family in town is skilled at fishing out the rare clams that my clients prefer. This was merely a pit-stop for us," Ezmeralda answered without so much as a pause as they walked up the plank.

Her story checked out. The ship was well-kept, and the route they were taking made sense. All they had to do was wait for the tide to come in so mangrove roots wouldn't puncture the bottom of their ship when they set sail. Even Alex could tell if they tried to do so now, their ship would quickly sink to the bottom of this forsaken swamp.

After being introduced to the captain and given a tour of the fine vessel, Marcus paid their fees, plus a little extra for dinner in the captain's chambers. Alex didn't press her luck or try to punch holes in Ezmeralda's story. She accepted it at face value, maybe because she was so tired and desperate to believe that they could have a brief reprieve. Just this once.

"A toast!" Ezmeralda raised her glass of red wine high into the air a little later that evening, when dinner was served. They stacked the grand oak table below deck high with cured meats, cheeses, breads, and rare clams that weren't for sale. It was a feast for the group of four who'd been living off of what they could forage for over a week now and politely waiting for their hostess to finish her toast to dig in was pushing Alex to her limit.

"To a safe journey! May the tides, winds, and profits favor us this week!" She smiled before taking a sip, obligating those at the table to drink after her. Alex drank long and hard, as did everyone else, before grabbing fistfuls of food. The refreshing wine dancing over her tongue made her smile. It was tart and dry, making her lips pucker, and less than halfway through the meal, she was on to her second glass.

The food reinvigorated her body. The laughs and smiles on everyone's lips fed her soul. Finally, they were warm, fed and happy.

Fifteen minutes in, she was trailing Victus and Kaden, who had committed themselves to a drinking contest, it seemed. Alex just laughed at them. "Stop drinking all of our host's excellent wine! Leave some for the rest of his crew!"

That's when it hit her. A ghastly look of fear had overtaken their jovial expressions. Why? Did they feel what she was feeling? A strange tingling sensation expanded through her chest and down the lengths of her arms and legs. She shook. She jumped up out of her seat and fought to remain standing as a paralyzing numb took its grip on her and her men.

"What's happening?" The sheer effort of trying to fight the terrifying sensation of losing control of her entire body all at once. Again. If she tried, she knew she could still draw her hand to the hilt of her sword, but she froze. Her hand twitched. Her instincts were screaming for her to take action, but she couldn't move. As her body slipped into senselessness, her eyes were wide and glazed. Tears spilled over her cheeks as intimidating crewmen she hadn't seen before came at them from behind the closed doors.

Ezmeralda let out a rueful laugh. "You're my prisoner now, Darius." She grinned, her beautiful green eyes sparkling with delight as she set her glass down and stood up to face Marcus. He had forced himself to his feet and was groping for his sword with one hand

and holding a dagger in another. It was pure adrenaline keeping him up on his feet now, and Alex knew that wouldn't work for much longer.

"Why don't you sit down, my pet," she purred, pushing back on his shoulder with the lightest of nudges, completely confident he couldn't muster a swing now even if he tried.

His body stumbled, while his mind rallied against the weakness that was overcoming it. His hands were twitching helplessly as he just barely drew his sword from its sheath before it clattered to the deck. He growled in frustration. All he had was this measly dagger, and he stood to lose that too in very short order. He swung out his arm like it was a wet noodle before it fell by his side. The blade sliced her left cheek, but missed actually killing her.

"Fuck. Aimed for the throat," Marcus muttered before his body couldn't fight anymore and he collapsed like a puppet with its strings cut.

Some of Ezmeralda's men were inching closer to Alex's limp body, as if their proximity to her would determine who got to have her first. They stopped dead in their tracks when Ezmeralda snarled and pressed her fingers against the fresh cut on her cheek. "Damn it. That hurt. Now, what should I do to discipline you?"

"You could throw his men overboard and give their maid to me," one of her men joked, flashing a charming smile at Alex as if to woo her. Ezmeralda simply rolled her big green eyes and pushed him away before bending to haul Alex into a sitting position. She propped the vulnerable princess against a leg of the table and backed away.

"No, there is no need to harm the weak. Just let me think for a minute, because something here isn't what it seems."

"You wretched sea witch! I will destroy you!" Kaden roared in frustration, desperate to move and charge after her.

"Gag the men and check 'em for loot," Ezmeralda commanded, springing her men into action. Why were they obeying her? Why was the supposed captain at the head of the table saying nothing at all? Something didn't add up.

"Wait! Are you the captain?" Alex exclaimed, trying to piece together what was happening. Her life and the lives of her men depended on it.

"You haven't figured that out yet? That man over there is my first mate, not my brother, and certainly not the captain. Would your master have stepped foot onto a ship captained by a woman? I doubt it. The richest of men are picky that way, you see. As if the dangly bits between their legs entitle them to unearned respect, but such is life. If I don't play the part, I don't get paid. What I'm trying to decipher right now is if you are who you say you are. What did you say your name was again?"

"... Margaret." Alex gasped when Ezmeralda suddenly drew a blade and pressed it to her throat. She cracked under pressure, which Ezmeralda was counting on.

Dropping her blade from Alex's throat, she smiled like a cat in the cream. "That's strange, because a couple of hours ago you introduced yourself as Marjorie. What's going on here? Are you perhaps the noble I should hold hostage?" she asked as she lifted Alex's hands, finding nothing on her fingers or her wrists.

Alex was smart about her jewelry and had slid her wedding ring into her boot during their travels. She also looked a disgusting mess from traveling for the past ten days. Noble, she did not appear. Ezmeralda seemed to have a sneaking suspicion she was hiding more than her name. This was bad.

"I am not a noblewoman. I have nothing for you," Alex asserted, for once relieved that cracks and callouses covered her hands. She wore a ragged green dress she'd stolen from the innkeeper's wife. A sheathed blade rested against her thigh that she could grab through a hole she'd cut into the hip of the dress, but Ezmeralda would have to know where to look to find it. Nothing to look at and no one to steal from.

"We'll see about that. Your hands and your dress may tell a story, but could it all be a mask? Those two men were flanking you, not him. Before I appeared, you were even standing beside your master, not behind him. Something's not right." Ezmeralda looked into her eyes and then back up at Marcus. Alex said nothing, and Marcus was silent too. They couldn't let her know the truth.

She pulled away with an annoyed sigh. "What did you find on them?" she asked her man.

The man who had been searching a very red and agitated Kaden said, "Nothing on this one but a large broadsword, a dagger, and a small map."

"Let me see the map." A grin of satisfaction spread across her lips. "Very good. What about that one?" she asked, nodding to Victus.

"A few daggers, a rapier, and a silver ring with a blue stone in it! Think it's valuable?" the ship hand asked, eager for his find. Victus was irate and shouting wildly into his gag as the boy held up the ring in his greedy little fingers. Alex's heart went out to Victus. To see something so important to be passed around as if it were nothing while powerless to reclaim it must have been his own version of torture.

"Possibly. Keep it and if it's worth something, buy me a drink when we make it back to port. Good find," she winked, ignoring Victus' agonized screams and turning to Marcus. "And what's on him?"

"Oh, nothing. Just the imperial crest," her second-in-command announced with a proud smirk as he produced the crest for her to inspect. Ezmeralda spun around with an excited squeal. She just knew something was off about this entire arrangement and she was right! She could only imagine what the ransom for a royal would be, and she could not wait to find out.

"Well, well, well. This changes things! Men, we are in the company of royalty." She raked her fingers through his hair to tilt his head back and look into the burning pits of his eyes. "Hmph. Whichever of the princes this is, he is going to turn our luck around, boys.

See that we take him below to the very finest cell in the brig. We have no more time to waste, but before that, I have a mission for his loyal servants."

"There is a bit of magic I wish to share with you, big man. You're going to make sure they do what I tell them to do, or you'll die." Ezmeralda pulled her twisted black dagger from her side, making Marcus scream in outrage against his rag. Alex was speechless. She couldn't speak out for him, even though she was the only one without a gag crammed halfway down her throat. She had to do something. At least scream, but in that instant, a part of her was glad that their attention wasn't on her. She couldn't speak.

Ezmeralda instructed two of her men to hold Kaden; she kneeled before him and slowly shoved the blade deep into his chest despite Marcus' protests. Alex looked on in horror, frozen. She could only bite the inside of her lip to keep from sobbing. Kaden gasped for air as the blade slid smoothly into his heart. Then, without drawing so much as a single drop of his blood, she withdrew the dagger from his chest and sheathed it.

"Hear this. You are to deliver a message to the Luxorian palace. Tell them I require four thousand pieces of gold. You will return to this port with the ransom for your prince. You will bring with you no armies and you will meet with this man, Andrie. He will stay at a local inn called The Crow's Nest." With that, the curse was complete and Ezmeralda turned her attention to her stunned audience.

"Just ask the innkeeper for Andrie when you get here with my gold. He will bring it to our hideout and we'll release the prince to you. Any act of betrayal will cause this big man's life being sacrificed to my blade on the spot. You will only have yourselves to use for this mission. No more, no less."

Ezmeralda licked her lips and looked over her shoulder with an exasperated sigh. "Andrie, dump them on the deck and give them provisions. They'll need enough money to buy three nags. The rest of you, move our prisoner to the brig. I expect he'll feel spry again soon, so tie him wrist to ankle." With that, they set work.

Just like that, they kidnapped Marcus. All it took was a couple of glasses of wine and less than half an hour. Alex, Victus, and Kaden had to save Marcus without costing Kaden his life. That became their new mission, as Ezmeralda's men threw them onto the docks unceremoniously. Alex risked shooting only one sympathetic look at Marcus as the men dragged them away. He looked... resigned.

Alex's mind was spinning as they lay lifeless on the dock while the ship sailed deeper into the treacherous mangrove swamp. The tide had risen. Their path to the open sea was now clear. Alex could still make out Marcus from where he sat until two of her men dragged him away. Tears of rage pooled in her eyes. Being so severely outnumbered, they could force him to endure any torture she desired. It made her feel sick. He was just as bound as she had been when she was under the spell of the music box.

Once Andrie gave them the money they'd need to survive by shoving it down the front of Alex's dress, he wandered off to find himself some shore leave. It wasn't often that Ezmeralda granted the second-in-command a few days to himself, and he clearly planned to make the most of it.

"Kaden, Victus, pick me up and carry me out of sight of the ship, if you can," she commanded, forcing them groggily to their feet after another ten minutes when they'd all sat up. They lifted her off the dock and dragged her by her arms deeper into the village.

They were on edge. Fearful. Agitated. Where could they go? What should they do? It was then that they passed by a dark alleyway where they heard a "Psst! Psst!" sound.

"Take me over there," Alex instructed, squinting her eyes at an old, haggard woman who came into view. She was using a crooked cane to steady herself, something Alex could relate to at that moment. She also had a jar of eyeballs swinging from a chain in her right hand, and a ripped cloak caked in swamp mud. Her bare feet squished in the green gunk below her hunched figure, making her look more like a toad than a woman. Still, there was something soft about her one good smoky blue eye.

"You have a powerful curse laid upon you! I can help you. For a fee." She chuckled darkly. Old, dark green rags covered her head, leaving only her crooked nose and mangled tufts of gray hair to poke out from the shroud. Most alarming about her appearance was the jagged, black scar over her left eye that had clearly been gouged out long ago. Alex tried not to notice it when she spoke.

"Are you a witch?" Alex asked, trying to contain the hope in her voice.

"If that is what you choose to call me. So, how about it, sweetheart? That curse is quite a doozy!"

"You mean the one on this man, right?" she asked, pointing at Kaden. It wasn't immediately clear who the hag was speaking about because she was pointing directly at Alex.

She cackled and stamped her cane into the muck. "No, no. That's easy to fix. I have just the trinket. I mean the one that was laid upon you, Serena."

CHAPTER 17

Alex, Victus, and Kaden followed the wretched old woman through the alley all the way to a crooked little shack half-a-mile south of town. Their sluggish pace matched her elderly stumbles perfectly. She refused to explain what she meant by referring to Alex as a cursed girl named Serena. It was just the old woman showing her age and was nothing to get worked up over, or so Alex told herself. If anyone could help them lift the curse off of Kaden 'easily', then Alex wanted to talk to her.

"We shouldn't be trusting a witch, Alex. No tellin' what she'll do," Kaden whispered in distress. They followed closely behind her to a shack that was wedged against a massive oak tree.

"Alex, I'm with Kaden on this one. This doesn't feel right. Let's get out of here. Marcus wouldn't like this," Victus grumbled, feeling vulnerable without his sword. At least Kaden had his brute strength to call upon, but there wasn't much Victus could do if this took a turn for the worse.

"I know it's a long shot, but I need to lift this curse off of you, Kaden, so that we can save Marcus. I'm not leaving him there to go find the legion. It'll take too long. He'd do the same for me, and you know it." She thought about the last words she had seen him mouth to her before she descended out of sight. Those unspoken words broke her heart. It was as if he was saying goodbye to her for the last time. No. She wouldn't let him do that. She'd be the one to save him this time.

"What if we just went to the capital on our own to get the emperor's help?" Kaden suggested with a rub of his broad brow. "You're the Princess of Luxor now. Surely they'd honor their heir's wishes and leave you unharmed until we can save him."

Victus just scoffed at the naivety of such a statement. "No. No way. She's not a princess of Luxor. Until the Council that is doing everything they can to kill her recognizes their marriage as legitimate, she will never be safe in the capital without Marcus by her side."

"Now, now. Settle down, you three. I'm just an old woman with a few tricks left before she dies, but I can help. Come on in, sit down, and I will make you a cup of tea." The old lady smiled as they walked into her shack, where many skeletal remains hung from the ceiling. The furniture was old and rotting, much like their mistress's teeth, and the floor was mushy. She had adorned the shelves with many artifacts encased behind dirty glass. It was an odd, unsettling home that had Alex's hair standing on end.

"While I'm preparing it, I want you to think long and hard about sacrifice and what the word truly means." She set a pot of water on an unlit stove, and with a flick of her fingers, a roaring fire came to life in the hearth.

Sacrifice. What did the word truly mean? For a warrior, everything. You sacrificed for your home, your people, your friends, your mind, your heart, and eventually, your life. Alex would have given her very soul if it meant Marcus was free of that woman. This was all her fault. It was her fault that they had to break from the legion so that they might get into the capital undetected. Tears welled in her eyes at the thought.

"Look, we know better than anyone what the word means. Just tell us what we have to do. Please. I can't lose him now," Alex begged in a soft, polite voice. She'd sit in this cursed house and she'd drink this woman's tea, but she would not waste any more time. If this witch could help her, she needed to do it now.

"The curse is the reason you are here. I am not powerful enough to remove it, but I can reveal who placed it upon you." She brought each of them a cup of tea, all but ignoring what Alex had to say. That went over as well as dumping a cold bucket of water on a feral hen might.

"Just tell us what we need to do! Please! I'll do anything you ask!" Alex begged, angered that this old witch was just spouting her own agenda. Marcus was in serious trouble, and she wanted nothing more than to rush after him. Was she really supposed to sacrifice

Kaden for Marcus? Could she? Gently, Kaden put his hand on her shoulder to slow her down.

"Now, now. I'm not that hard of hearing, young lady. I know what you want. You, the ninety-seventh Princess of Artoria, would like to save your Prince of Luxor from the pirate. I have my agenda, of course. She has stolen my magic dagger that was used to curse your big man, along with a crystal known as the Pearl of Illusion, to hide her island from everyone but me." The old woman took a seat at the head of the table. The table itself looked like someone made it out of the mossy bark of the massive oak tree. Everything here was alive and breathing.

Taking a deep shuddering breath, Alex tried to collect herself, and Kaden threw her a warning glance. She knew he would not allow her to abuse this old woman, no matter how much he feared her. She'd brought them into her home, and now Alex would hold her tongue.

"Almost, but you're wrong about one thing. I'm the one hundred and fifth princess of my kingdom, not the ninety-seventh. That princess would have had to have lived over a hundred years ago," Alex mumbled, trying to remember her family tree before slamming her hand on the table. What the hell did this have to do with Marcus? "Look, if it's the knife and this crystal you want, we'll get them back! Just give us a way to do that. Please!"

"Mmmmm, very well, but there is something I want from you before you go off to fight the wicked little bitch for me. This has to be a fair deal, after all. Can't have you running off saying I didn't pay for your services."

"Fine. What is it you want from me before you will lift the curse off Kaden so we can go get your things?" Alex was rapidly losing patience with this entire drawn out conversation that seemed to lead nowhere.

"I am a collector of eyes, not for what they are, but for what they can reveal. I want your memories of the night someone spirited you away, for in them lies the key to solving a lifelong mystery. Who started this war? Now, drink your tea."

Alex growled with frustration, yet sipped her tea all the same. Her fingers were quivering around the cup, and she tried to remain calm. "You're crazier than a fox with two heads if you think I have anything to do with the origin of the war. Kaden here has known me since I was born. Isn't that right, Ka..."

She looked at Kaden for reassurance, but he cast his head down. He couldn't bring himself to meet her eyes. "Kaden, this woman is crazy, right? Please, you're scaring me! You've known me since I was born, haven't you?" She jumped to her feet and pushed back on Kaden's shoulder so she could look him in the eye. Victus just stared, first at Alex, then Kaden, then the old woman.

"Alex, I've known you since you were three years old. I was there with King Jiordan on guard that day. That day you just sort of... appeared walking the castle halls, the day after our little princess died of a vicious fever."

"Kaden, what are you saying?" Confusion knit Alex's brow. She took Kaden's hands in hers. She'd known his face since before she could remember. This wasn't true! Was she an impostor? A stand-in to protect the royal line?

He pulled his hands away, shaking his head. "You were not born of Jiordan and Victoria Raybrandt. Your first name was not Alexandra when I met you. You wore an ancient-fashioned dress and were looking for people who were long dead. When asked, you proudly said your name was Princess Serena Isabella Raybrandt." He'd sworn to Alex that he'd always tell her the truth, but this had never come up before. She'd always just assumed that Kaden had known her since she was born, and he'd never had the heart to remind her of what her adoptive parents had worked so hard to make her forget.

"The scrolls showed evidence of a princess named Serena who disappeared at three years old, exactly a hundred years ago to the day you arrived. It was the same year this entire war supposedly began." Kaden trailed off, not daring to say what everyone in the room was thinking.

"That's the very moment I want to see," the witch said. "I want to unmask the true culprit behind the war that stole my child from me and the children of so many others. So, to save your prince, will you allow me to peel back the veil, though it may strip away everything you thought you knew?"

Alex was reeling and sat silently for a long moment. "Okay. Fine. I'll do it." There was no time to think this through or second guess herself. They needed to save Marcus, and if this priestess wanted to look into her past, then she'd quietly oblige.

"You're going to feel a little pressure," she warned. The woman walked behind Alex and positioned her hands on either side of her head. "Lean back in your seat." When Alex did as the witch asked as she hummed a soft, mesmerizing song.

Suddenly, Alex interrupted her. "No, wait. Let's make sure we have an understanding. I'll let you rummage around inside my head for memories of my childhood, and you'll lift the curse off of Kaden and grant us the power we need to rescue Marcus. Is that right?" She was nervous. She felt like her heart was about to beat right out of her chest and that she might heave at any moment. Was this all happening too fast?

Gently, Kaden took Alex's hand to give it a reassuring squeeze. "No matter what, I am your humble servant always. Never forget that. I won't let her hurt you."

"Yes. Now, hold still," the old priestess curtly retorted before settling herself back down behind Alex. Drawing a deep breath, she sang a soft song in a voice that couldn't belong to her. Whose voice was that? It was so youthful, soft, and gentle. It made Alex lean her head forward as a warm blush spread across her cheeks.

She missed that voice. Louder and louder, the voice grew until it was all she could hear. She couldn't hear Kaden's strained breaths or the soft crackling of the fire in the hearth–just this voice that was easing her awake from the nightmare she'd found herself in.

"Mommy?" she whimpered as her eyes eased open to take in a warm, smiling face.

"Yes, baby. It's time to wake up." A beautiful blonde woman who looked as though she'd been born of the moon smiled down at her. She bent down to hug Alex close. Her soft, short strands of hair tickled her nose, and her warm blue eyes made Alex beam. She had a soft face that made Alex feel safe. She felt love from the tip of her mother's lips that were pressed to her sweaty forehead, to the curl of her knees that were bent to support her. Alex snuggled in closer to press her face into her warm bosom, breathing in her sweet, motherly scent. She was home now.

After a few moments, she blinked up at her mother and smiled. She was wearing a gown of radiant white silk with magnificent gold patterns embroidered on it. She looked angelic to a pair of eyes that had not seen her in over twenty years. For so long, some other woman named Victoria had claimed to be her mommy, but she'd known it was a lie all along. She knew it! Her actual mother's name was Ariane Luisa Raybrandt.

"Mommy, I had a nightmare," Alex whined and sat up in her lap with a tired yawn. To Alex's surprise, she had no control over what her body was doing anymore. This was a memory. She was reliving it in her much younger body, rather than standing off to the side as a third-party spectator.

Her mother shushed her softly and scooped her precious baby into her arms once more to plant her neck full of kisses. "I know, baby, but we have to go," she whispered in reply, just as she sharply lifted her head. She was listening for something, but whatever the source of the sound that had startled her was, it did not present itself. Alex squirmed out of her grip to giggle and poke at her face. "Shh," she soothed her, putting her finger to her soft pink lips.

"Where are we going, mommy?" Alex gripped her mother's forefinger, shaking it softly in her tiny fist. Where was she taking her?

"Far away, baby. Remember this, always. We're playing hide and seek." Alex tilted her head in confusion when her mother sprang to her feet, rushing Alex through the servant passageways. Faster and faster she ran until she reached an unattended hearth in the kitchen.

"Mommy, mommy, I'm scared! I don't like it here. I want to go back," Alex complained quietly, not liking that they had come to the Luxorian Palace. "Mommy?" she whispered, tugging at her arm as she strained to look up at her face.

"I am not your mother, Serena." A silky male voice suddenly emerged from out of the shadows surrounding them. The impostor's grip suddenly squeezed tightly around the small, frightened child as her mother's face burned away to reveal a man she had met only two days before. Her daddy had called him Father Nicholas when they first arrived. She shivered in his grip, too afraid to scream out for help.

"Remember, we're playing hide and seek. Don't let them find you, for they only want to control you," he warned her as the hearth roared to life behind her.

"Mommy! MOMMY!" she squealed when he lifted her up and held her in front of the roaring fire. She could feel the flames licking at the back of her legs, pushing her to kick frantically, but no one would hear her. No one could save her. This man was more than he seemed. He was a powerful sorcerer with a taste for power and a plan to achieve it. The first step of his plot was to break the long-held friendship between two kingdoms by casting suspicion on the hosts of the Artorian royal family. He'd make sure that the grieving family would have no one to blame for their lost child but the neglectful, power-hungry slobs who he would dethrone soon enough.

"I'll see you again soon, Serena," he said before casting her into the blaze. Screeching in pain, she flailed frantically. A blazing light filled her vision. She didn't understand it, but it had been a spell of such strength that only a complete shock to every sense would allow for its completion. Something like being cast into a fire was exactly the trick needed. She would escape death only to suffer much later in life.

Somehow, she had resurfaced from those flames on the day after the real Princess Alexandra died, nearly a hundred years in the future. Because of that day, a century of war would weaken one kingdom to the brink of collapse and rot an empire from the inside out. All because she needed to hide from them.

Who was... them?

Don't let them find you.

Control her how?

Alex jolted awake with an exasperated gasp, and she woke in the Artorian courtyard beneath the bright morning sun. Standing shakily, she looked around for her mother with a dread-filled tummy that threatened to explode. Was that a nightmare inside a nightmare? Quickly, she picked up her stride, barreling through the halls as fast as she could for her mother's chambers. There, she found a sad woman dressed all in black looking over a tiny, empty bed.

Alex stopped mid-stride, a puzzled look on her face. "Who are you? Where's my mommy?" she finally demanded, breaking Queen Victoria out of her haze long enough to realize she had an unwanted visitor.

"Guards! Sir Kaden! Remove this servant's brat and ensure they whip her for entering the royal chambers uninvited!" Queen Victoria shrieked.

Outrage filled Alex's chest. Outrage and confusion. "You're not my mommy! You're not the queen! I am Princess Serena Isabella Raybrandt and you can't touch me unless my mommy says," she'd declared with a stomp of her tiny feet.

It took a few days of constant questioning, and Alex wouldn't answer anything asked by Victoria or King Jiordan. After all, they had dragged her out of her mother's room that day, kicking and screaming. The person she finally warmed up to was Kaden. He'd comb her hair, play her little dress-up games, and entertain every wish she had in exchange for nuggets of knowledge. Once they broke those nuggets down and used to paint this young girl's history, they agreed this girl had somehow transcended time. She was a princess, and by their laws, deserving of every right they'd have afforded their own daughter.

With time, Alex slowly accepted the name of her adoptive parents' lost daughter, all so she could take on a new identity the public would accept. They made it a game for her and eventually it stuck. She forgot all about her former life, throwing herself into aggressive regimens to unleash the pent-up rage and loss she felt, the source of which became lost to her as she grew.

She saw the rest flash before her eyes. Her world spun faster and faster, and then a thunderous clap brought Alex back to the priestess's small shack. She gasped for air and bolted upright, her back arching as far as it could without snapping. Tears poured down her face, and before anyone could say a word to her, she was running for the privy pot so she could throw up. Her head felt like it was going to split open with all that she had just remembered and had to digest. She wasn't from this time. They had stolen her from her mother while at some sort of gathering in Luxor. A treacherous man named Nicholas had fueled their grief. In this era, she called this man her cousin. Two families fanned a single flame of grief into an inferno that consumed two kingdoms.

She jolted when she felt Kaden's cool hand pressed against the back of her sweaty neck. She wasn't ready to be touched, but she had something to say.

"We're in big trouble, Kaden. Nicholas. I don't know how, but my cousin Nicholas was there over a hundred years ago," Alex confessed shakily, her wide eyes staring at her discharge in the pot. It was a weird purple color, but she felt much better for having let it go.

"What did you see?" Victus asked softly, trying to grab onto an anchor in all this madness.

"I don't know what I saw. Too much and not enough..." She ran her hands over her eyes. It took almost an hour to pull every detail they could needle out of her, but when she finished speaking, the three warriors sat there as if the truth had gutted them.

Victus was perhaps the quietest throughout the retelling of her story, though the competition for such a title was fierce. He just sat there in stunned silence, staring on in utter disbelief. Alex could only guess at what he was thinking.

They were defying a time lord by keeping her alive. Was that wise? Was it what was best for Luxor? He didn't know what to think anymore. He was told to guard her until told otherwise, but surely a part of him couldn't help but to believe that perhaps everyone in the world would be better off with her head on the ground.

The priestess, however, simply smiled. "I am satisfied with this revelation. I believe you will not allow the reason I lost my daughter to be in vain. Now, let's talk about Marcus and how we will get him back." The old priestess brought Alex back to the present with the name of the man she wanted to save. "Have a seat, Serena."

CHAPTER 18

His arms were sore. That was the first thought that penetrated the haze of Marcus' mind when he slowly drifted free of the slumber that the pirate's drugs had forced upon him. His head was hanging limply, his jaw agape because of the rag wedged between his teeth. His legs were numb beneath him, yet he dragged them forward far enough to lift himself upright. He had to pull himself almost onto his toes to relieve the pressure on his wrists; the excruciating pain that had woken him came from there. He blearily looked upwards and took in the iron manacles clamped tight to his wrists and the chain wrapped around a support beam that ran along the ceiling of the hold. His blood flow was being cut off.

They chained him up in a pirate hold, not the best place to be, but at least he was still alive, which meant there was hope of escape. The creaking and groaning of the timbers around him and the rocking of the floor let him know they were in deep water, no doubt on their way to this bitch's lair. He saw bags and crates bearing the stamps of many nations and merchant consortiums stacked throughout his prison, a clear sign the pirates had enjoyed a profitable run. Raised voices and a column of light coming from above, through the lattice grill of a hatch. He grunted and shoved his arms forward, pushing the chain along the beam, inch by inch, until he felt the light upon his face. He peered with squinted eyes at the harsh sunlight to see what was going on.

"Cap'n! Me and some boys, we think you owe us an extra ration of this bounty! We're entitled to enjoy the pleasures of the ladies we capture, but you sent away that pretty little thing last night with naught a squeeze to be had! She was the cleanest, firmest wench I've seen in years. What right do you have to deny us our prize? Just cuz you got tits yerself don't mean we're gonna stop enjoying the company of ladies," a coarse voice growled. The sound of bare feet slapping wood sounded above. Marcus peered up through the hatch, shifting until he could see three crewmen facing off against the captain.

"Extra rations? I seem to recall you were off in the corner just hopin' that prince and his party wouldn't overcome their poison. You feared the big one, didn't you? Well, look what I did. I made him work for me, just like you," he heard her purr right before her boots collided with the panels above. She'd been sitting on top of her desk, hearing her boys out, but she'd heard enough.

"The only reason you wanted that woman was because the clean ones won't go near you. Now, you might make the argument that I don't pay you enough, but I'd wager this entire ship you couldn't get one into bed of her own volition with all the rations you've ever earned. I don't drag my ass out of bed every morning to give you women to rape, but if you suggest I should again, I will make your face so ugly that even the disease-riddled whores you frequent won't consider it worth all the coins in your pocket."

"You sure talk tough for nothing but a stuck-up cunt! I'm sick of taking orders from you! You may be Captain Redtooth's daughter, but if you won't let us have fun with the pretty ones, I say you ought to take care of us yourself!" the man shouted, murmurs of agreement and shifting feet sounding from above as the three pirates advanced on their captain. Marcus hoped that the woman could somehow maintain hold over her crew. He didn't think these brash, impulsive pirates would see the point in leaving him alive for ransom.

A silence fell for but a moment before Marcus heard the slow, steady stride of the pirate captain above him as she sashayed her way to her men. "Now, why be so aggressive? We're all fighting for the same things and are on the same crew. That doesn't mean we can't come to some kind of understanding," she purred seductively. She drew closer and closer, never faltering in her stride. Then she stopped right in front of the three mutineers. He could hear her almost pleading when she said, "Please? I'll show you what kind of captain I can be if you'll just give me a chance."

Then something shifted. In a flash, there was a full-on scuffle on deck, and he couldn't tell who was winning. More pirates charged in until finally the less fortunate in this mutiny were subdued. He had reason to worry that the captain who had seized him and let Alex go was going to meet a terrible fate when the familiar song of blades rang in his ears, but then he heard her voice again.

"Tits or not, you will follow me. I am the leader of the Pirates of Dauhn and the only child of the ruthless Captain Redtooth. He was a fan of ripping off the ears, noses, and lips of any man who crossed him, but I hope I won't need to resort to that to earn your respect. Suggest rape to me again and I'll show you I'm my father's daughter by ripping away something he wouldn't dare take away from another man."

"No rations for that one. Tie him and his friends to the mast. Five whips with the cat o' nine for each of them. Make sure the men see. I need to go check on our prisoner; the drugs should be out of his system by now."

Marcus turned himself around to face her as she descended the stairs, his hands crossing above his head when he spun. He glared at her defiantly when she entered the hold, his eyes burning into her. Her hips swayed exaggeratedly, and she had a grin plastered on her face. He wanted to kick her, to shame her and her ego.

"Well, well. Had a nap, did we? We're almost at port, and then it will be a few short weeks before your pampered ass is back in the capital and we're all just a little better off for it." Ezmeralda leaned against the central beam, her long, dark hair framing her beautiful face. "Hm? Oh, that's right. You can't speak unless I permit it. Here we go." She pulled the gag out of his mouth to loosen his tongue a bit. "Speak," she commanded with a glint in her eye.

"Is that how you've inspired such devotion in your loving crew? Talking to them like unruly hounds?" Marcus rasped, flexing his jaw as he tried to work some moisture back into his mouth.

"Love? There's no room for that word on this ship. Obey—now, that is a word they know to the marrow of their bones. Why do they obey? Because I tell them to. Come now, you can't really be cross with me for gagging you, can you? Or is it you feel tricked?" she asked, clearly fishing for a reaction while she still had him securely bound.

"No, no, I love the accommodations. Reminds me of home. I think this has actually helped some back pain I was suffering from," he replied, not able to contain his sarcasm. "Do I feel tricked? Why would I ever feel that way? It's not as though I offered to pay for a service and then found myself drugged and kidnapped. Oh, I guess I did, actually."

"Home? Tell me, how many pirate ships have you frequented? How many swells have you beaten? How many throats have you slit? You know nothing of this world because it is mine. You are nothing but a tool for me, so I can make this world shine just a little brighter for those who deserve it. Don't worry, though. No harm will come to you or your crew, not as long as they obey my command."

"You've murdered, plundered, and led men who clearly thrive on rape. Don't expect me to feel that your world should shine any brighter, unless it shines with the glow of torches burning this vessel as your funeral pyre," Marcus growled, stopping when he coughed, his dry, ragged throat making it hard to speak. "You had best pray that my ransom never comes, because if I am released and any harm came to my w... to my people, because of your duplicity, I will reduce your world to ash and rubble!"

"Ooooh, such tough words for a man who doesn't even have his sea legs yet." She grinned and shoved him backward, knocking his feet out from under him. This caused him to hang from his wrists once more, halting his advance. "I thought commanders of men were supposed to be realists. I'm dumbfounded to think that Your Majesty's prowess could suppress an entire army of men. Consider me impressed." She laughed dismissively, attempting to dig under his skin and display her clear disdain for any threats delivered by the man shackled in her hold.

"Consider it a promise, and the only one I'll be giving you. I prefer that when I kill someone, they face me on equal ground. I swear if she is in pain right now, I will repay you a hundredfold for every bruise on her flesh," Marcus said, not noticing his slip.

"Her? You know, I'm thinking I should have kept that pretty little girl with us. I wonder what mood I'd have found you in if you woke up to her screams. I'd have three more loyal men at the helm and some much-needed leverage. Your tongue is quite sharp, but my blade is sharper. Don't tempt me into proving it to you, boy." Ezmeralda sneered and moved in close to prove to him she was not afraid or intimidated by any Luxorian, least of all a royal.

"You'd never find me even if I harm her, you know. Not even the wake of my ship. You'd spend your days scouring the oceans, chasing nothing but the breeze. That, I promise you."

"If you ever made the mistake of hurting her, no ocean would be large enough to hide you from my wrath," Marcus swore with a simple, solemn heat and sincerity that made it chillingly threatening.

"Well, that is up to her. For now, I'd worry far more about yourself. Your stay with us is going to be a long one, and I have men aboard who like pretty boys even more than they like pretty girls." With a whip of her hair, she turned away and approached one of her crewmen who'd followed her down to the brig. "Three strikes with the cat o' nine. Tie him to the mast and let the men see that royal blood is just as red as theirs."

Marcus wanted to fight back, but a night spent with his arms hung over his head had left them nerveless and unable to respond to his orders. When her men carried him up the stairs into the sun with the promise of punishment, he closed his eyes and thought,

'Stay away, Alex. Stay safe.'

Before Alex, Kaden, and Victus sat the most mesmerisingly delicious meal they'd seen in days. It was all thanks to that old priestess who had agreed to feed them before they'd have to make their way over to the Island of Dauhn to rescue Marcus. According to her, the pirates were based on a seemingly uninhabitable rock close to shore. Only the elders in town knew of the island, for the pirate crew's founder had ensured that they erased the unmemorable island from the maps after they stole the Pearl of Illusion, along with the dagger known as The Betrayer. To get both artifacts back and save Marcus, they were going to need a lot more luck than they'd ever had, and chances were high that not everyone was going to walk off that island alive.

It was a lot to process over breakfast, but they had all swallowed worse. They each had their own large plates full of biscuits, ham, eggs, potatoes, and grits. Kaden and Victus had long ago tucked into their meal and had scarfed down nearly all they could stomach before they noticed Alex was absently looking at her untouched plate with a forlorn stare.

"Come on, Alex. Eat up. This old bird can't clean the plates until you do," Kaden reminded her with a firm pat on the back that made her jolt out of her dazed state.

"It's my fault that they captured Marcus, and I'm sure they haven't given him a single bite to eat. I'm not eating until he's safe." Alex's voice cracked, just barely above a whisper. She wore in a dark red top that came down to her hips, a pair of brown pants, and a snug pair of leather boots. She looked like a brave, seafaring woman, ready for adventure with her blonde ringlets tied back. Inside, she felt like the wooden figurehead- the carved woman at the bow of the ship who spent her days being slammed in the face by waves.

"What have I always told you? You can't fight a war on an empty stomach. Even if you tried, you'd just be in the way when the time comes for us to land on that island."

"That's just it, though. How are we even going to get to that island? I don't know where to start."

"Don't know, or don't want to try? Hmmm?" the old witch asked.

"What kind of question is that? Of course, I want to look for him! But we don't have a ship or anyone who could man one to an island dolled up to look like nothing more than an ominous pile of jagged rocks! The second we tell any captain our course, he'll either laugh at us or throw us all overboard."

"So that's why you starve yourself? I may be a frail, broken woman who has let herself fall apart, but I have given you a way to help your husband. No, you are more interested in feeling miserable and moping around than finding a solution! Bah! You can do better, girl, and you will do better! Until then, allow me to help you. Do you think that the lads on that island spend every night twiddling their thumbs? No, they come back to shore to terrorize the merchants and the local girls. That is your way in, child, on their own ship. You might have come up with an idea like that on your own if you weren't so busy moaning about how much you are to blame for someone else's evil deeds!" The witch turned away with a snort.

Alex's face went from mopey and defeated to glaringly pissed off somewhere around the word 'twiddling.' She was hungry, tired, stressed, and frustrated that she'd let Marcus down. This was not the time to test her, which is why Kaden caught her eye. It was a stern, fatherly look that he rarely used against her, but he was using it now. He would not abide her, snubbing this woman's food and acting like a brat on top of it. He'd raised her better.

Alex drew a deep, centering breath. "Why, thank you. I hadn't thought of that. You're right, I should eat something. However, while I'm enjoying your delicious meal, why don't you explain what your plan is for once we get there? That entire island is crawling with pirates, according to you." Alex was barely containing her ire while she gnawed on a biscuit.

"In her defense, it really is a delicious meal," Victus said quietly, a small smile playing about his lips as he watched the two strong-willed women square off.

"Whose side are you on, anyway? Your prince is missing and all you're worried about is..."

"ALEXANDRA!" Kaden barked. "That is quite enough."

"I'm on Prince Marcus' side, and yours, Alex. That doesn't mean I can't disagree with you or point out that you are being foolish," he answered in a calm voice as he grabbed another biscuit. "The past is the past. No amount of worrying will close broken lines or bring the dead back from their graves. We can either mourn our losses and accredit blame, or we can put it all aside and focus on making the losses suffered mean something, knowing that in the end, we will have earned our right to mourn. Marcus told me that after my first battle with him, so I know he'd rather I enjoy this biscuit and be nourished than eat myself raw over not restraining myself from the poisoned wine." Victus took a bite of his biscuit and leaned back in his chair.

"Such a smart boy. I hope you pay attention to the lad while you have him, Your Highness."

"Ok. All right. Fine. The past is the past. Marcus is gone. However, we have nothing to mourn just yet. They want a ransom. Can't get a ransom with a dead prince. So, we need to make our way over there and be quick about it. The issue facing us now is that even the best blacksmith in the world would need time to make us some proper, formidable weapons. Unless, do you have any blades?" Alex asked, looking up at the old woman as she admired her artifacts and the power forged within them. Both terrifying and awe-inspiring, these artifacts were.

"Oh, so now you will ask for help again? Youth. So impetuous." The witch shook her head with a smile and shuffled back around the corner. She returned a few moments later with a large bundle wrapped in oilcloth. "This is a very special blade, one that harbors a dark curse but is powerful enough to win you the victory you seek." She laid the cloth before Alex. When Alex reached out to touch it, the old woman cracked her on the back of the hand with a wooden spoon she snatched off the table.

"Patience! Let me tell you what trouble you will face before you go grabbing at a cursed blade!" the woman snapped. "This, my girl, is a blade forged in days long lost, even to legend. Magic was common before the war. Priestesses and priests were figures of prestige. They shaped the fate of the world by their word, deed, and allegiances with humanity and spirits alike. This is the blade of the last King of Nurinar: The Last Vow."

The witch peeled back the cloth, revealing a blade as pristine and gleaming as one newly forged. With a long blood catcher down the center of the blade, the artisan who crafted this sword fashioned the pommel and hilt to resemble bramble-filled vines. If one looked closely, skulls and bones were visible within the wrappings of the vines.

"With this blade, the Dire King forged an unstoppable army, at least so they say. Every life stolen by this blade rose as an eternal servant in death, obeying the will of the blade, or the blade's wielder, whichever proved to be the stronger. More than that, every soul claimed by the undead slaves of this blade also rose. It is a dark, cursed magic that cost more than you will ever know to forge, and cost even more for the wizard kings of old to defeat. I would normally never hand over such an item, but I think that you might have the strength of will, or at least the sheer ornery contrariness, to overcome the corruption of the Last Vow." The blade emanated a dim purple light that swirled within the gleaming steel of the blade, as though it knew it was about to be summoned once more.

"Alex, don't touch it," Kaden whispered, drawing her hand away from it a second time. The distrust of anything enchanted ran deep in Artorians. Their forefathers had outlawed artifacts like this for a reason that Alex herself was very familiar with. This kind of magic was malicious and violently binding. If she lost herself to it, there would be no coming out.

"No, I must do more than touch it. I must wield it. She's right. With this sword, I could command the pirate army, if only for a little while. We'll find the captain that took Marcus and force her to bring us back to town. With her own army's swords pointed against her, she'll have no choice but to do as we say." Alex shook her head, her eyes becoming lost for a moment in the sword's gleam until she tossed the cloth back over it.

"What is the cost of using such a formidable blade? Are the dagger and the crystal truly all you want?" Alex asked, not deluding herself into believing that this was going to come without a price.

"Yes, but if you can only save one, grab the Pearl of Illusion. It is used to disguise that island. With it gone, our tormentors will have nowhere to hide, but I will. It is hard to keep those who might abuse these artifacts at bay when you reach my age," the witch explained with a tired sigh.

"The captain ought to know where her father hid it. Find it and return it to me. Also, take this," The witch pulled off a silver ring with an engraved bear on it from her finger and slipped it onto Alex's right ring finger before she could protest.

"What is this for?" Alex asked, bewildered that it wouldn't come off, even though it had slipped on easily enough.

"A little luck." The old woman smiled and craned her neck to look out the window. "Now go, while the moon is still out. You'll have to wait another day if you let the sun rise too high in the sky."

Victus rose first and peered outside. He waited for Alex to gather the wrapped blade while Kaden stood over her like a protective grizzly bear, both fascinated and fearful of the weapon in her hands. She gave him a reassuring smile and joined Victus at the door.

He checked the alleyway again, one hand reaching up absentmindedly to rub his scalp. Alex reflected it must have been shocking for him to only feel stubbles on his head where full golden locks had once grown. He glanced back at her before she could think of what to say and nodded, and the crew slipped out into the predawn gloom.

They moved quietly, following Victus as he wove a trail through downside roads and alleys, moving them ever closer to the harbor. When he pulled up the hood of his cloak, Alex and Kaden did the same. Finally, as the first hints of dawn's ruddy glow crept over the distant horizon, they joined Victus in kneeling behind a stack of crates that smelled absolutely horrid. Fortunately, the odor would keep away any unwanted visitors.

"Recognize anyone?" Victus whispered to Alex, pointing to a vessel in one of the best positions on the wharf, with only a single, half-asleep guard on watch.

"That's one man we saw when we boarded her ship. The witch was right. She must have left some of them behind to stock up on supplies. The problem is that he's still aware of what's around him. If we walk up with a mountain of a man, he will notice," Alex whispered back and wrung her hands with stress.

"I got an idea," Kaden murmured, though he was looking in the exact opposite direction.

"Yeah? Well, the boats are over here."

"I know, but our distraction is right over there." Kaden reached up to turn Alex's head toward a group of seven boys dressed in rags, looking for those to either steal or beg from. It was early morning, so the drunkards who slept out on the streets were easy pickings but offered low reward. Kaden just needed to make it worth their while, and that would not be very hard at all.

Kaden approached, but before he could get too close and scare them off, he called out, "Oy, boys. How would you like to make a pocket full of gold this morning?" He smiled charmingly and jiggled a purse on his hip.

"There's a place up the street where you can find boys to lie down for you, big man. We make an honest living! You try to touch any of us and I'll cut you open!" the oldest lad, perhaps eleven years old, warned in a feral tone. He drew a small but well-honed dagger from somewhere in his rags to accent his warning. "Go get yer rocks off on the pretty boys at Madam Vastra's. You'll get nothin' from us!"

"Wait, wait!" Alex called, emerging from behind the wounded and now downright sheepish Kaden before the boys could run away. "That's what we want to offer you: a handsome reward for an honest task." Alex opened up the purse so that they could see she wasn't lying about the prize.

"Do you see that man over there, half asleep? We need you to distract him long enough for us to make it onto his ship. To make sure you do a good job and don't double cross us, we'll even pay one of you the money in advance if you'll leave him behind to collect," Alex offered wholeheartedly.

The boys eyed her suspiciously throughout her appeal, though the sight of all that gold had the younger kids hungry to agree. The older lad had the look of one who had survived by seeing more than a boy ever should, and immediately snapped his arm out to stop one of the little ones from running forward.

"You wanna get turned into a boy whore, Terin? All of us leave except one of us? It's a trap, and it's one I've heard before," he scoffed as he led the boys away. "You want us to distract him? Then you pay up front. All of it!"

"Then how would we know you wouldn't just run away with the money, as any smart boy would?" Victus asked softly from the shadows, stepping forward slowly. "Perhaps we could meet in the middle, eh, lad? No one stays behind, but the gentle lady there just gives you some of the money now and promises to hide the rest, over there under those crates maybe, once you lead that man away so we can do what we need to do?"

"Well, I guess that might work. It depends on how much yer paying, though! I ain't dumb - I know whose ship that is. That sleepy old fart catches us and we're in for worse than what I first thought you were after!" the boy retorted, clearly trying to sound streetwise and tough.

"Fifteen pieces of gold. Enough to feed you and your friends for a few months, wouldn't you say?" Alex shot back. "But I'll only give you five up front. The other ten will be in our hiding spot by the crates. If we can't make it onto the ship, you can't get the gold. It's that simple." She hadn't meant to scare the boys, but enough was enough. If they would not help her, she needed to find someone who would, before the sun rose and the crew returned from the whorehouses.

"Deal. But if you cheat us, we'll come back and tell them you snuck on board," the boy threatened, and slipped his knife away. Cautiously, he came forward, ready to dart away at a moment's notice. He extended his hand for the promised gold, his suspicious eyes darting between the three strange figures.

Fishing in her purse, she secured the five pieces of gold and placed them in his four-fingered hand. "All right, you have a third. Now go earn the rest. We'll be hiding among the crates right over there. I'll hide the pouch in a nook on the ground. You shouldn't have to look hard to find it."

"And for the record, boys, I love women! Women have written songs—no, fables—about my prowess. Why, once I..."

"Enough. They don't care." Alex cut him off and led him back to their hiding spot to wait and see if her initial investment would pay off while she hid an additional twenty coins in a nook by her feet.

A few minutes passed, and the boys had scattered into the gloom. A couple of them worked their way toward the pirate ship, while the rest disappeared into the predawn mist. The ringleader strolled boldly as brass up the dock until he stood directly in front of the watchman.

"Hey, old man! Anyone ever tell you that your ship smells worse than a whale's fart?" the kid hollered. The watchman turned to see who was yelling when an egg flew out from behind a crate, cracking on the man's face. The yolk that smeared across his nose had a greenish cast to it, and even from where she hid, it convinced Alex she could smell the rot.

"You little shits! We've warned you!" the pirate growled, wiping the egg out of his eyes just in time to get a rotten mound of something Alex didn't even want to identify, straight in the face. "I'll have your ass for this!"

"Gotta catch me first! Why aren't you with the whores with everyone else? Did they stick you on watch duty cuz your third leg is a peg leg?" The boy turned and ran at full speed down the dock, the enraged pirate close behind with a cutlass in hand and bloodlust in his eyes.

"All right, let's move," Alex said, rushing down the dock and blindly dashing up the gangplank, her eyes peeled for a place to hide. "They surely have storage down below. We'll hide there until we make it to the island." They walked as quietly as they could toward the stairs, climbing down into a cavern. Not all the men who had landed here had the money for whores, and those who didn't were snoozing down here until the morning bell.

Thinking fast, Alex led them to the quietest part of the ship, which was stacked almost to the roof with crates. "We can hide here. Then, when they come to unload the cargo, we'll have our first recruits." She ducked down near the back with Kaden and Victus by her side, terrified of what should happen if she failed, and anxious about what should happen if she did not.

"Fenz, how many goddamn times have we told you not to leave the boat when yer on watch?" a grizzled voice rasped through the air, startling all of them until they glanced up and saw that the sound was coming from above deck, through a nearby hatch.

"Those fucking brats were causing trouble again! I just wanted to teach 'em a lesson! Besides, the others were still here!"

"Yeah, their snoring sure was a good deterrent if someone had wanted to slip aboard and steal from us! Yer lucky we don't have anythin' more valuable than eggs and pickled herring down there, or else I'd skin ya and use you as a new sail! Now, go wake up the boys so we can cast off!"

"But I thought ya said I'd have time to go ashore!" Fenz whined.

"Why, you already did, Fenz, my boy. Not my fault you used it to go chasing after smooth-cheeked li'l boys who want nothin' to do with you! Now get to work!"

All three of the hidden passengers looked at one another, and Victus finally motioned toward the corner, where a small clump of hay had leaked from some crates.

"Rest if you can, Alex. I'll keep my eyes on them." Victus laid himself against the barrels, sacks, and crates, tugging a bit of canvas over his head to help conceal himself as he set up to keep watch.

"All right, but just for a little while. Try to settle in, men. I've never been to sea, but I've heard she is quite unforgiving of those new to her ways. We're in for a long day," she sighed, not finding much to smile about other than what she knew those boys were sure to find right about now. They made twenty-five gold coins from a single act they seemed to take more pleasure in.

She wished she could see their faces, but realized that wasn't what charity was about.

"I've been on the open sea before. She's a wondrous, fickle mistress. I could have lived my whole life at sea if the service hadn't called to me," Victus mused quietly as Alex closed her eyes and listened to the creaking and groaning of a ship alive in the water.

CHAPTER 19

The difference between a wound from a cat-o'-nine-tails and a sword wound is simple but profound. A sword should maim or kill its target with maximum efficiency. It has a sharp edge to cut or pierce the flesh, and it's best to slide it into vital organs. A cat-o'-nine-tails is a vicious thing, a many-headed whip filled with barbed hooks. You can't kill anyone with it, but after three lashes upon a bared back, even the strongest warriors will crumple. The whip cracks open flesh, the barbed hooks grip and tear it open further, splitting your flesh apart like thin paper. It is no surprise that pirates use them to keep their minions alive, but in line.

Marcus kept his shoulders squared as he walked the sandy path up the hillside of the pirate's island hideaway. Her men had torn his shirt open when they strapped him to the mast, eager to see his blood spill. He hadn't been able to stop himself from grunting in pain from the impact, but he'd glared at Ezmeralda the entire time, never flinching. Egged on by his fortitude, her men gave full-armed swings at his back. His skin was beading sweat now, running into the wounds on his back and stinging like a demon with every step he took, but the blood loss had not been severe enough to impede him to any great degree. If he didn't get the wounds bound soon, though, he knew he was going to feel dizzy, disoriented, and weak.

He tried to keep his focus on the surrounding area. The pirate shacks down by the shore were obviously where most of them lived, but there were a few larger structures on a central mountain peak as well. These appeared to be storehouses and the homes of senior members of the crew. There was a large, U-shaped home built at the crown of the hill, a virtual villa compared to the other shacks on the island, but still relatively simple in construction. That was their destination.

Marcus was breathing heavily by the end of the climb, bringing his bound arms up to wipe sweat from his face and earning a slap along his left ear by one of his guards, sending him stumbling and falling to his knees in the courtyard of Ezmeralda's home. Blearily, he shook his head, glancing around as he rose and noticed a strange grated well a few feet away. He couldn't regain his feet fast enough. He heard a low growl and then cried out sharply in pain as a booted foot slammed into his raw and exposed back. It sent him sprawling onto his face in the sand.

"I'm going to give you one opportunity to choose your confinement. It's going to be a few weeks before your party can make it back to the capital, let alone secure the ransom, so I'd think this through carefully," he heard Ezmeralda hiss from his place on the ground. "You can either choose to answer my questions and stay in my home as my prisoner, or you can rot away in the pit we built below the sands right here," Ezmeralda offered, jumping on the latched door to drive her point home. "Make your choice and make it fast," she commanded, her eyes boring down into his.

"My choice would depend on your questions," Marcus said slowly, working his tongue around his mouth to produce as much moisture as he could. They hadn't given him water in quite a while, deliberately, he presumed. After all, it's what he would do. Had done. "If you'd like my opinion on which labor camp I will send you to, I can give you some great recommendations."

"No need. Those who don't know how to look for us'll never find us, you see. As you know, information is more valuable than any commodity we might lift from passing ships. Recently, Yukonian captains have been seeking information at the ports we frequent about the war effort. Who would know better than His Imperial Highness?" she asked snidely, making no secret of the questions her inquisition would include. "Which one are you, anyway?"

"Does it matter?"

"I suppose not. You're a pampered prince. Nothing more."

"You know, I haven't seen the bottom of a pit since my brother tried to bury me in one as a child. I think I'd prefer the shade to all this talk," Marcus rasped with a taunting smile.

"The shade? My prince, the day has only just begun. That pit is where you will sleep. That pole," she said, pointing to a thick, sturdy stake jutting out of the sand, "is where you will stand until that handsome face of yours is festering with oozing blisters. Then we'll talk about the shade." Ezmeralda smiled and waved to her men with one finger to do as she bid.

Two of her guards slammed his back into the scratchy stake to knock the wind out of him, hoisted him off the ground. It worked. He gagged before they spun him around and tied his hands around the pole, chest first. He caught on to their intentions quickly. The idea was a simple one: his back was already in pain, but the agony of a sunburn on top of those deep cuts would surely encourage his lips to move. They also secured his feet and head. He had to admit that after a few trial pulls at his bonds; it was unlikely he could wriggle his way free. It turned out that the tales told were true–no one could tie knots tighter than the Pirates of Dauhn.

"Well, don't we look comfortable?" Ezmeralda mused with an appreciative sigh as she slapped his back as though he were a comrade. He flinched from the blow, but the bindings left him nowhere to go. "Enjoy the salty air. I'll be back later to see if you've changed your mind."

"Oh please, don't trouble yourself. I'll just stand here and enjoy the lovely view," he rasped sarcastically as she walked out of his vision.

He listened to the sound of her footsteps walking away, along with those of her men. He thought he heard feet and boots on wooden planks and the door closing, so he assumed they had all gone into the house. It was maddening; with the way his head was bound, all he could see was a blank expanse of horizon, sky, and water.

It wasn't long before the sun got to him. He shifted his shoulders, trying to move or unbind himself, but it was a fruitless effort. The sun rose higher and higher above the horizon, and his back was facing directly toward it. After just an hour of his sweat seeping into his wounds, his eyes lost focus. The steady loss of blood from the wounds on his back combined with dehydration and the heat was conspiring to weaken him. He could barely keep his weight on his feet. He knew his knees would give out before too much longer, and then he'd be hanging by his wrists.

It took a little over an hour and a half before she returned to untie his head and press a cup of water to her lips. She let most of the contents slip down her neck in a steady stream for him to watch. "So, still feeling brave?" she purred. She poured the remaining water down his back, grinning as the sudden cold caused him to buck and squirm. "You can have what's left in this cup if you answer one question. I'll make it simple, so pay attention. Who was the girl I released?" she asked, her eyes boring into his as though she was seeking to root out his secrets by sheer will alone.

Marcus knew she was not alone, for he had heard the other footsteps in the sand. He wondered what would happen if he revealed that she could have had two royal hostages instead of one, but he wasn't willing to expose Alex. He could endure if he had to. Eventually, she would have to let him inside. After all, a dead prisoner would not do her much good. He just had to outlast her.

"She was just a girl. A maid. She cleaned things. She had a firm backside, which I liked." Marcus pushed through his cracked lips, his eyes fluttering shut. He pressed his forehead against the beam and forced himself to focus. He had to be careful not to let anything slip in his attempts to anger this bitch. "I think I'm ready for my drink now."

"Open your smart mouth when you're not invited to do so again, and it will be salt water I used to wash this off," she warned seconds before he felt an eruption of pain course through his wounds as she rubbed a thick, oily ointment into his back.

"There. You heard it from his own mouth. The bitch was nothing more than a maid, likely indentured to his family," Ezmeralda sighed with what sounded like relief. Is that what had they been talking about all this time? Were they thinking of trying to find Alex? Before his head could spin any more, she pulled it back so he could accept the cool water she poured past his cracked lips. She was true to her word.

"Yeah, but Cap'n, we've all heard the rumors at a port from those Yukonians that what they're really after that Artorian princess he supposedly ran away with!"

"Yes, but we've also heard the reports that they sent her head back to her own palace in a leather sack. That journey would take weeks, so there is no way her head has made it back there to be disproved. What probable reason could this man have to lie about her? It's not like I could send the lot of you to find her in those forsaken swamps anyway!" Ezmeralda snapped, clearly flustered by the thought that was breeding among the crew that she had made a mistake.

"Yeah Cap'n, what reason could a prisoner have to lie to you?" the man fired back with a snort.

The tension in the air was thick with accusatory thoughts that would not go away until they pried the whole truth from their prisoner's lips. If they needed to, they could track her down, but Ezmeralda didn't appear ready to budge. Without warning, Marcus felt the violent slam of her boot on his back, which snatched his breath away so fast it made his lungs hurt. They walked away then, all of them, and he didn't think they would give him another chance to speak for quite a while.

Marcus reflected how surprising how long three hours can feel while his bare back was cooking in the sun. Marcus was dripping with sweat, and he knew he was on the verge of heatstroke. His ill treatment was stacking up and taking a toll on his body. He was slipping. He had felt his knees give way twice, and he'd only barely been able to straighten them again to hold himself up. Marcus was in poor shape, and it was showing.

"My prince, you don't look so good," he heard Ezmeralda chime into his ear, as though feigning concern. Then he heard her muffled command as she turned her head, "Bring him in for treatment." They unbound him and dragged across the courtyard. His feet hung beneath him, useless. His boots dug troughs in the sand until they dragged him up the stairs. The moment they entered the shade of her home, he felt relief at being out of the sun. He was too weak to struggle, but they threw him onto a small bed and shackled him, anyway.

Once they restrained him face down on the bed, she sat beside him and poured another glass of water over the back of his head. Then she snatched his ear, refusing to let him slip further. "What was a maid doing in your service so far from the front line?" she snarled. He heard the rest of her men step back to watch their captain work.

"My... laundry," he croaked. He closed his eyes as he felt the room spin. He was shivering, but he wasn't cold.

"Oh, no! Can't do that. Only compliant prisoners get to sleep." Ezmeralda grabbed another cup of water and pushed it to his lips. "Drink, or I'll shove a funnel down your throat."

Marcus quickly gave up on any thoughts of making himself ill on purpose. He needed water, so he would take it and just hope she had added nothing to it. He was in no position to fight. So, tied face down on a bed, he didn't struggle as she tugged his head back far enough to pour the water between his lips. His tongue was awkward and ended up pushing half of the first few mouthfuls out to dribble down his chin and chest, but he accepted all the water she gave him in as slow of sips as he could manage.

Once he had downed at least a full glass, she stopped pushing water into his mouth and let him go. "Laundry, you say? Earlier, you said she was a princess. Why would a princess do laundry?" For a second, he almost answered honestly, before his tired mind caught up to what was going on.

"Never said that. Laundry is all she does. Lots of socks and pants. Great at getting blood out," he mumbled into the dirty, straw-stuffed pillow his face was laying against. He closed his eyes, willing himself to be alert, trying to kick and prod his sluggish mind to keep up. "Sometimes she makes my dinner, but she's a wretched cook."

"There. It's settled. I've whipped, roasted, and tortured the bastard and his answer has not changed. I'm done wasting my time with your concerns," he heard Ezmeralda bark at her, men. "Now, get out and get ready to unload the ship. It should arrive in the next couple of hours."

Once the men left, she pulled up a chair to sit beside him, her eyes still fixed on his gaze. "I don't like how you look, as if you have something to hide. It makes my skin itch, so why don't you come out with it and spare yourself a little pain?"

Marcus raised his eyes to meet hers, blinking the grit clear of them as he focused on the hardened icy stare that had reduced soldiers and foes to quivering jelly throughout his career. The blistering skin on his ears and the haggard appearance of his face marred its effect, but the rage and determination that drove him still burned bright.

"Why don't you go fuck yourself with a splintered broom?"

Silence fell between them, and Ezmeralda pulled out a needle that complemented her sadistic grin. "You couldn't possibly know this, but your back is basically one giant blister. Allow me to lance them while you think about your answer." Not waiting for his reply, she began popping boils all along his shoulders, driving the tip of the needle into his skin every few seconds.

"What you also most definitely don't know is that I laced the water you guzzled with a fair amount of juice from a poisonous root called babu. It's not lethal, but you will tell me everything I want to know, like it or not." She dug the needle almost half an inch down into his skin this time.

"Fuck you!" Marcus growled and strained against his bonds. He extended his fingers and struggled to bring them to his mouth. He was desperate to make himself vomit, endeavoring to purge himself with the poison that could put his wife in danger. The spinning of the room took on a more ominous tone now. The fuzziness that was filling his head was not just heat stroke, but a drug notoriously used for interrogating stubborn prisoners. It was dangerous to use; too much and you risk sending the subject into a coma, but if you got the dosage correct, their mind became loose and pliable, open to suggestion. He got one finger into his mouth and tried to drive it back into his throat, thrusting his tongue out to provoke his gag reflex.

"Now, now, I won't allow you to ruin these sheets," Ezmeralda purred, her voice growing soft as the drugs took hold of him. She pulled his head up and his fingers away, refusing to allow him to expel the toxins.

"Let's start with something simple. What was the name of the girl traveling with you?" Her voice floated on the breeze, soft and almost caring. He closed his eyes tight, trying to shake his head, only to discover someone was holding his hair. That was nice of them. Now he wouldn't fall from this cloud he was lying on. She was asking a question; he wasn't supposed to give her the name, he knew that. He had to remember.

"Marjandra," he mumbled, his eyes blinking rapidly until he squeezed them shut, straining to overcome the disorienting wave that was washing over him.

"That's strange. I heard her say Marjorie and Margaret, and now you're telling me another name still. I can't help but feel you aren't being very honest with me. How did you two meet?" she pressed, her voice still soft and as gentle as a feather.

"A dead horse introduced us. I mean, she was cleaning and there was a horse," he muttered, his lips flying open with a small giggle as he sank further and further into the daze that was swallowing him up.

"A dead horse, huh? That's strange. Why was it dead?" she pressed, ignoring his sloppy attempt to cover up what he'd let slip.

"Someone killed it with a spear. How else would a horse die and fall on someone?"

"The horse fell on your maid? That can't be true. I think you're still lying to me," she said in a light, accusatory tone. "A horse would have crushed her."

"She's not a maid," he giggled at her mistake. "She was wearing armor!" A nagging voice in the back of his mind was making a loud, persistent drone as it strained to break him free of the daze that had him firmly in its warm embrace.

"Oh, I must have misheard you earlier. Who was that woman traveling with you again? What was her name?" the pretty voice whispered to him once more.

"Hmmm. She's my wife, of course. Alexandra, Princess Alexandra. My wife. Did I say that?" he rambled, his eyes losing focus as he tried to figure out what that annoying noise was in the back of his mind.

"Of course you did. I was just forgetful. Remind me again, whose head was it you supposedly sent back to her kingdom? Obviously, it wasn't hers," the voice softly sang, soothing away the pain in his back. He almost felt like he could walk now!

"Supposedly it was hers, but I couldn't kill my wife. That wouldn't be right. Killed her rapist instead; fat bastard deserved it." He frowned, the clouds splintering a little as pain ravaged his form. Something lifted him from the cloud he was resting on.

"That's very good. I'm glad you could be so honest with me," the voice commended him as he sat up on the bed, his hands bound in front of him now so she could lead him around for a brisk walk that made him cringe as he came crashing back down to earth. What he knew of the root was that it was potent, fast-acting, but also fleeting. His chest felt like it was sinking as she walked him through the courtyard to the pit he'd chosen hours ago.

"You'll stay down here and swallow nothing they try to give you. You'll speak of this to no one. Know that if you fail, I will have my men rip into that princess until the Yukonians come to claim her for the bounty she is worth. The condition they find her in will make no difference," Ezmeralda warned, as she kicked open the latch.

The toxins still dazed Marcus, but even through that fog of euphoria, he felt the pain of being dumped into the pit. He tumbled and spun in the air in that strange moment of freefall before slamming down onto his wounded back, drawing forth a loud, echoing cry of pain. His muscles seized up, and he saw nothing but little red pinpricks of light for a few long moments.

When his senses finally returned to him, he was unsure of how much time had passed, but Ezmeralda was gone, and she locked the pit behind her once more. He realized he didn't even have room to stretch out, so he forced himself to sit curled up or with his legs half extended. He staggered to his feet. Trying to climb out of this hole would be pointless–he'd need another man his size whose shoulders he could stand on to even get close. He collapsed back onto the floor and allowed tears to slip freely from his eyes.

"I'm sorry, Alex," he whispered to the air as he closed his eyes to hide the world as his tears made tracks through the sand that dusted his face.

CHAPTER 20

Alex had always thought riding on a ship would be a pleasant experience. She was wrong. She and Kaden were both suffering with quiet groans as the ship dipped and rose above the waves in an unending rhythm that left them both with bile in the backs of their throats.

"This is awful. This is just... ugh... Victus? How do I make it stop?" Alex pleaded from her hiding spot, desperate not to purge her small breakfast. She needed what strength she could muster for what was ahead.

"Here, biscuits help sometimes. They'll absorb some of what's sloshing around in there. Eventually, you get your sea legs, Your Highness, at least most do." The hold was empty except for them, everyone else having gone above deck a short time ago. Victus peered out into the empty hold with a contemplative look on his face. Finally, he turned to look at Kaden and Alex.

"I'll be right back. We might be near the shore. I'll find out," he said softly and slipped off his boots and padded out into the hold, tiptoeing to the stairs that led above deck. She watched him crouch at the base of the stairs for a few long moments, his head cocked to the side, before he spun and leapt silently up the stairs. He darted back down after a few long seconds and silently returned to their hiding place, where Alex was sucking on the biscuit he'd given her.

"Good news, Alex. We don't have to count on you gaining your sea legs. We are being towed to the dock right now," he whispered with a smile.

"Really?" she groaned and pulled herself up, her stomach still churning as her center continued to experience the rise and fall of waves that were no longer here. "Kaden, get up," she muttered, tossing him the biscuit after she bit off half.

He slowly rose to his feet, bracing himself against the side of the ship. They were a sorry lot, and they were going to have to fight an entire pirate crew in a matter of minutes. She was afraid. She didn't think they were ready. "Victus, we're going to need your help until the nausea wears off. You'll need to cut their legs out from under them, but let me deliver the final blow. We'll need as many bodies as we can throw at them, and right now, we only have ours."

"I didn't figure Kaden could do much while we were under here. His fighting style requires more space to roar and swing like a bear," Victus murmured with a smirk at his Artorian counterpart. "Unless you want hamstrung corpses, perhaps I should focus on leading their parries high, giving you easy openings to dart in and claim the kill?"

"You're right. We need them to run unhindered. Give me a clean shot, if you can, but don't let yourself get hit for the sake of this task. We have the advantage. The hall they have to come down is narrow, meaning they'll only be able to file in here one at a time. This will work until we have enough of them to seize the deck."

"I've yet to find anyone outside the capital, aside from Prince Marcus, who can match me in a duel. I doubt these pirates will best me," Victus retorted with a small smile as he stood out in the open as bait while Kaden worked his way toward the side of the door where he could easily ambush if things got crowded.

The sound of footsteps coming down the stairs made Alex's spine stiffen. Moving quickly to the side of the door, she kept her eyes on Victus, waiting for him to make the first move.

"She says we gotta unload all this shit and then go back to port? What the fuck for?" one man bellowed, not catching sight of the scrawny warrior.

"Pardon me, gentlemen, I seem to be lost. Can you tell me where the tavern may be?" Victus called out, his face placid though his hand was atop the hilt of his sword.

"The hell? How did you get down here?" a burly, mean son of a bitch demanded to know as he rushed forward to draw his blade and confront the stowaway.

Victus went from calm leisure to deadly action at the drop of a pin, his face remaining as stoic as ever. His rapier snapped out of its sheath, darting out to pierce the wrist of the man trying to draw steel. He drove through the flesh and sank his blade into the wood of the doorframe.

"That wasn't very polite, it was a simple question," Victus remarked, and his eyes flicked to Alex to see if she was going to take the last step.

"Necromorse," she whispered softly, and spun around to slam her blade through his chest. She watched as he spasmed and choked, his eyes rolling to the back of his head when he suddenly went limp. Alex paused, looking dumbfounded and afraid. Why wasn't it working? Had that priestess lied to them?

She heard a chime of steel and looked up to see Victus parrying a blade that they had aimed at her head. Kaden stepped in quickly to wrap the man in a bear hug, disabling his arms, but not before the man opened his lips and scream.

"Attackers below!" the pirate bellowed, before Kaden squeezed the air from his lungs.

Panicking, Alex slit the man's throat before he could say more, like how many of them there were or where they were hiding. Reaching up, she ripped the rapier out of the man's wrist and tossed it to Victus as she uneasily braced herself for the fight ahead. Why the enchanted sword had failed them, she didn't know, but it didn't matter now. Now, she just had to hope they could fight their way through this on their own.

"Well, I always preferred counting on cold steel anyway," Kaden rumbled and retrieved a cutlass from one of the dead men and took up his post.

"If we are counting steel, I believe they have significantly more of it," Victus murmured softly, unruffled by this turn of events.

A swarm of footsteps raced down the stairs to chase down the source of their mate's cries. Two pirates were dead and two men standing with a woman in the hold. They surged forth, but before they could cross the tight threshold of the door, her first victim rose to his feet with a harrowing purple glow in his blank eyes. Alex felt it then: the tug of his soul trying desperately to drag her down as a chorus of whispers filled her ears. Out of the corners of her eyes, shapes appeared, the shapes of men cut down by this blade, taking their celestial stand with the wielder.

"Kill them," she commanded, watching with a satisfied grin as her new puppet carried out her command.

The dead pirates turned and rushed in a stumbling, ungainly manner toward their former comrades, who shouted in fright at the vision of dead men rushing after them. She met the first dead pirate with a cutlass buried in his chest by his old friend, but it didn't stop him from clamping his teeth around the man's throat and tearing it out with a hungry moan. The death and gore that filled the hold soon spread onto the deck, and the rising dead continued to carry out their grisly mission.

She smiled a wide grin of joy and turned to look at Kaden and Victus, only to see concern in her old mentor's eyes and a reflection of that concern in the eyes of her new protector. Victus reached down and picked up a cutlass, turning the flat of the blade to show her the eerie smile that was stretching her lips without her knowledge.

"We need the blade to save your husband, but none of it will be worth it if we lose you."

Alex was out of breath, though she'd done nothing at all to exert herself. It was all mental, though, to look at her. One couldn't be sure. She stared hard at her own reflection, swallowing the unnatural smile as she watched the purple ring around her pupil grow just a little brighter.

"You're right. I'm sorry. Let's get above deck. Let's find Marcus," she said, biting her lower lip to stop from smiling. Alex couldn't deny that she felt twinges of excitement every time she heard the strangled cries of another victim. She couldn't forget what her goal in this was. She couldn't allow herself to fail. Wherever he was on this island, Marcus was counting on her, and she would not let him suffer the consequences if she lost herself to such a blade.

Victus led them up out of the hold, with Kaden taking up the rear guard behind her. She saw Victus pause and glance back over his shoulder, shock and disgust upon his face, before he smoothed his features and stepped out of her path.

Dead pirates were spilling out onto the dock, stopping to rip the guts from the animals they had brought aboard the ship to feed the island. The deck of the ship was awash in gore, with severed fingers, bits of intestine, and other signs of violent deaths, making the deck slick with blood. An alarm bell rang on the island, fires lighting in a few watch towers as the pirates rallied to defend against this strange attack.

Alex was giggling with glee at the small rivers of blood she chased to the front of the ship. They were just little ants to be used for a greater purpose. She would build this army to reclaim her throne and...

"Alex!" Kaden shouted. One undead pirate was staggering his way toward him. Despite a clearly shattered ankle, the ghoul still had a firm grip on his sword and appeared to be ready to use it on Kaden.

"Stop!" Alex cried, regaining her focus and the attention of her undying slave. "Go with the others. Find your captain and bring her to me!" she roared, her voice taking a tone no one, not even Kaden, had ever heard. She was quickly becoming a woman possessed.

"Kaden," Victus called out, motioning the large man over to him. Alex saw them looking at her, but she was finding it hard to remember why they were concerned. "Keep watch over her. I am going to find Prince Marcus. I don't trust these puppets to leave him unharmed, and I am much stealthier than you. Try to remind her of the dangers of that blade. She is in a battle of will, and I think she's losing." His voice was concerned, and his brow buckled. Then, he spun and rolled over the side of the ship, landing noiselessly on the dock and darting off into the chaos.

"Kaden, what's happening to me?" Alex whispered. She shakily collapsed to her knees, stabbing the cursed blade into the blood-soaked planks of the deck. Everything seemed so blurry, and it was becoming difficult to hear her own voice over the chastising whispers in her head that were telling her she needed the sword to reclaim her kingdom. No mention of Marcus, only the throne she had lost.

"Nothing. We just gotta remember why we're here, right?" Kaden placed a comforting paw on her shoulder, lending her his grounded strength.

"Yes. We're here to save Marcus, aren't we?" she asked, her bewildered purple eyes stretching up to meet his.

"That's right. Don't give in. Don't forget. You are not a slave to this blade," he gently rumbled, hesitating to be harsh on her now with such a weapon in her white-knuckled grip.

"No, you're right. I'm not its slave. We're partners." She giggled softly as she nuzzled her cheek against the pommel of her new ally.

* * *

Marcus reflected that solitude could be one of the cruelest forms of punishment for a captive, if done correctly. They could have just sat him in a small room in clean clothes with a bed or chair. Solitude would have eventually broken him down. His mind would crack as he would become starved for contact with another human.

Instead, they threw him down a small hole in the ground after ripping his back open with that whip. Sunburnt boils further lanced and opened his flesh. The poison still muddled his mind, and the solitude was taking on a whole new depth. The only way he knew time had passed is when the hole finally returned to shadow, and eventually, the cool darkness of night set in.

There was nothing for him to do but sit and dwell on his pain. He couldn't shift or move to be more comfortable. All he could do was sit there and suffer, thinking about all the things he did that led to this moment, blaming himself.

Confusion turned to anger. Even hate.

So, when he heard the crunch of her boots on the sands above, he kept his head ducked down, not wanting to give her the satisfaction of seeing how haggard he was after just one day of this torture. He wanted her to think of him as a defeated, weak monarch. He wanted her to drag him out of this hole so he could try for just one swing at this bitch. One chance to crush her throat. That would be enough. It had to be.

"I just wanted to thank you again for your honesty this afternoon. I'll have your wife bound, gagged, and in that hole with you in two days. Just you wait. She can't have gone very far in those swamps. Why, it wouldn't surprise me if she's already spending some lap time with some of my men back at port who just couldn't bear to see her leave." Ezmeralda's voice was light and taunting. She was digging at him, prodding the bear in its cage.

She obviously yearned for a reaction. Her words were crude. The sly twisting of the knife about the information he shared was the most adept bit of mental war she waged upon him. Marcus refused to look up. He wouldn't give her the pleasure of seeing him respond. He just kneeled there, curled up in a puddle of his own waste and soiled clothing as he waited for her to shove another stick through the bars of his cage.

Then, a burst of red light from the setting sun flooded in as Ezmeralda threw open the hatch above him. What was happening? Had the toxins of the babu root taken him? Was he lying here comatose from exposure?

"Say something or I'll have you ripped out of there and flogged until you're begging to talk!"

Even though her command had come out as a snarl through the grit of her teeth, Marcus didn't move a muscle. If she thought he was unconscious or dead, she'd pull him from the hole and he might have a chance. A chance for what? He didn't know, but anything was better than this. Maybe if she had told none of her men yet what he'd revealed, he could still save Alex. Maybe there was still time! Preserving his own life somehow meant very little if he couldn't save hers. It was almost instinctual. He had to make this right.

So, when he heard Ezmeralda sigh in exasperation and say, "Time to go fishing. Find me a line, and you, prepare to go down there." he didn't move. He only smiled ever so slightly at the thought of getting out of this damn hole.

Sand cascaded over the edge of the pit onto the back of his head as someone above positioned themselves on the very lip, as though preparing to jump. Marcus braced himself for the manhandling to come, but then it never happened. Alarm bells from town echoed all the way to his tiny prison, making those above him pause.

"What the hell is going on down there? You two, let's go! We'll come back for him later," and just like that, she left him alone again in his maddeningly small prison with a lifeline left dangling just out of his reach. He sat there for several long minutes, unwilling to look up or move, afraid that this was another way of testing to see if he was truly awake. Once he was confident that they were gone, he tried to get his feet under him, but after hours stuck in this same cramped position, his muscles rebelled.

Gritting his teeth against the searing pain, he pushed out with his legs and pressed his tortured back against the side of the pit. Bearing down, he grunted in pain so tremendous that it brought tears to his eyes. He kept trying to extend his legs and brought his hands down to push and pull himself upwards. He scoured his back raw and ripped flesh from it as he slowly dragged himself back to his feet.

By the time he was standing upright once more, he was clinging to the wall of the pit, panting for air as he turned his face upward to catch the last glimmers of dusk. His face set in grim determination, he dug his fingers into the earth of the pit and tried to drag himself up and out. The gods rewarded him with a cascade of loose soil in his face, and losing his balance sent him crashing back against the wall once more. The fall knocked the breath out of him, and pain radiated from his back.

Gritting his teeth, he reached up again and strained to find a hand or foothold that would support his weight. Again and again, he pulled down fists of loose sand, coating his face and chest in a thick layer of it. He leaned against the side, surrender washing over him as a sob of frustration escaped his lips. His hands curled into fists and he hammered them against the walls of the pit with what strength he had left. It wasn't fair!

Then, a hallucination. It had to be. He could hear Victus calling out to him in a whispered voice from above the pit, but Victus was far away by now. It made no sense! He was back on the mainland protecting Alex. Tilting his head up as a shadow blocked the last of the sun's dying rays, his eyes widened as a range of emotions came crashing down on him—relief, anger, confusion. Those were just three, but they were the strongest.

"Your Highness! We need to get you out of here, now! Can you grab a hold of this?" Victus called as he tossed down the rope Marcus had been hopelessly grasping at for the last few minutes. Marcus grabbed the rope and quickly focused on one thing at a time; he could be angry with Victus for leaving Alex back at the swamp, or he could get out of the damned pit. But before Victus could be of any help, he suddenly spun around to catch a sword neither of them saw coming until it was almost too late. The song of their blades crashing together rang all the way down into Marcus' bones, giving him chills, but they were nothing compared to the surge of rage he felt when he heard her voice again.

"Did you really think I would leave my prize prisoner alone just because you goosed the town? I may just be a simple pirate, but I'm not so easily fooled. Whatever you've done down there, it won't be enough. All you really did was volunteer yourself as my new whipping boy." He groped his way up the pit as quietly as he could, inch after agonizing inch.

"Oh? Do your men have much experience dealing with cursed blades and the undead? Because I must admit, it's a first for me," Victus quipped, the smile audible in his voice. Marcus was confused. No one had a cursed blade, except Ezmeralda and that dagger. And undead? What was going on?

"What are you going on about? It seems you have forgotten that I am the one in possession of the cursed weapon, but it is not a sword. It's a dagger." He could practically hear her lips curling as the soft sound of that dagger being pulled from its sheath filled the air. "I think I should use it now. It might not damn you, but I hope you won't miss your companion. Betrayer." She hissed that word almost as though she were speaking another language.

"No!" Marcus cried out and pulled himself over the lip of the pit, desperate to grab at her feet to stop her, if he still could. Yet, despite hearing his cry, Ezmeralda stayed perfectly still. A silence fell over the beach as an eerie wind blew in from the mainland. There was a long-standing quiet that chilled Marcus to the bone. Then, a gasp of pain broke the silence, and she collapsed to the sand, gripping her chest. Beneath her hand was a growing patch of blood that should have bloomed on Kaden's chest.

"The curse. That witch. She threw it back at me..." Ezmeralda gasped with her final breath, a look of comprehension and horror stretching across her face.

"How?" Marcus breathed in disbelief. He stared down at her dim eyes in fascination and horror.

"We have to hurry, Your Highness. The highlights are that we met a witch in the swamp after arriving back in town. She gave Princess Alexandra some gifts, including a talisman for Kaden to wear that caused that curse to backfire. Now, come on." Victus grunted as he leaned down to help Marcus sway to his feet.

"A witch?! What?" Marcus stumbled, barely able to keep his feet moving. His entire body screamed out in protest.

"Your Highness, if I stand here long enough to explain, we'll get caught. We have a long journey home; I will go into more detail later. Now, if you'd be so kind as to walk a little faster, we might get out of here before the other gift from that witch drives your wife insane." Victus turned them down a side alley and through a backyard, aiming for a rather steep hill. "This is going to hurt, Your Highness, but the main road is a little bloody." He gripped Marcus around the waist and rolled them over the side of the embankment. Marcus didn't even have time to cry out before a flash of red made the world go black.

• • •

Marcus... Marcus is dead beneath the sands where these rats left him to rot. The men charged with protecting your life have failed and now there is nothing for you to hold on to. Just relax and allow me to make them suffer. It's for you, all for you.

The voice took root in the back of Alex's mind that would not let her believe for even a moment that there was any hope of finding Marcus alive. Too much time had passed. He was gone. How long had it been, anyway? Hours? Days? Weeks? She knelt there on the deck of that ship with her forehead mashed against the hilt of her blade as great, soul-shattering sobs shot out of her lungs. Everything hurt, but a sliver of her soul remained, even in the darkness. Her mission was to find him, not to punish. She could not lose sight of that.

The sun had set several minutes prior before she finally found the strength to pull herself to her feet. With her shaken mind set on finding Marcus herself, she stumbled down the gangplank and slowly made her way to the dock. She would see for herself where they were keeping Marcus. She would find him, and she would bring him to rest in her arms once more.

She floated through the gutted town like an ethereal specter of death. Those who she didn't slay were hiding in their little holes to wait out the unearthly attack. One such person must have seen the glow of her blade and realized she was the key to this madness. Kaden flanked her to the right, but this attacker came from the left.

She could see through the eyes of many now, but that cost her dearly with her own peripheral vision. The attacker waited for her to pass before lunging out of his hiding spot like a viper. He plunged a dagger into her back, a scant inch from her heart. Alex let out an inhuman screech that carried throughout the island. Her knees buckled, but not before she swung around to cut down the boy of eleven who'd attacked her.

She crumbled to the ground, crying in pain as the blade delivered toxins throughout her body, making her instantly feel feverish and weak. "Alexandra?!" she heard Kaden cry out. He kneeled beside her and placed his hand on the hilt of the blade in her back. "Alexandra, I'm sorry to have to do this. Hold still!" Kaden ripped the blade out and pressed her down to the ground to stop the bleeding.

As she lay there in shock, she whispered in a voice belonging not to her, "Every life is now mine. I will avenge my husband's death by painting this island red with the blood of every man, woman, and child upon it. Kill them, kill them all..."

"Alex, no! Stop it! We have to find Marcus, remember? He's the reason we're here!" Kaden snapped at her as he pressed down harder, desperate to keep her from bleeding out. But it wasn't her blood that she was concerned with.

"He's hurting me. Shower me with the traitor's blood." She hissed the command as three ghouls appeared from the front and four others came from the back. They were being surrounded. Her call summoned every undead pirate at her command to the center of the town, where they were all determined to carry out their appointed task.

"Alex, snap out of it! Please!" Kaden begged. The undead were nearly upon him. With a cry of frustration, he wielded the short cutlass he had bought on the ship to sever the wrist of the first undead who approached him, and then he took possession of its broadsword. His blade tore audibly through the air with every powerful swing, but the blows he delivered only kept his multiplying opponents down for a few moments before they staggered back up. He could only cut so many in half, but even then, they grabbed at his feet to hold him still.

'Kaden. He is the man responsible for all of this. He failed to save you when you needed him most. Do you not recall this sound?' The voice asked her. The painful sound of the twinkling music box crept through her head like a deafening horn that unburdened her from the sounds of Kaden fighting for his life.

'No! Stop it! Stop it, please! I can't...' Alex thought, powerless to even move her own lips.

Oh, but you can and you will. I have waited centuries for an opportunity like this, and while you may not realize it yet, you have already lost.

• • •

"Just a little further. That's right, lift your feet. You can do it, Your Highness." Marcus could hear a voice calling to him. His body was moving, but the pirates had practically crippled him with pain. His eyes slowly fluttered open as awareness gradually returned to him. He burned with agony, but nothing seemed to be broken.

"Victus?" Marcus said.

"Yes, Your Highness?"

"Never do that again," Marcus rasped and lifted his head to look around the strangely deserted pirate town. They were moving down a side alley, but there were no signs of life. "Where?"

"Dead, most likely. Or undead." Before Marcus could ask for clarification, they heard the sounds of battle up ahead. Above it all, a familiar voice cried out.

"Damn it, girl! Wake up! You're stronger than a damned piece of steel!" A fleshy sound of impact and a chorus of groans followed his voice. Marcus did not know what was happening; it was all like some unreal fever dream. Victus looked ashen as he peered around the corner, cursing before he picked up Marcus once more.

"Your Highness, Marcus, your wife is losing her fight against a cursed blade. Her blade summoned these undead, but she's losing control. She's trying to kill Kaden. We can go around and reach a boat, but it will mean the two of them will surely die," Victus explained slowly, watching the anger simmering in his master's eyes. "Or you can try to break through to her while I try to hold off the undead? We will probably all die, Your Highness."

"Take me to my wife." Marcus' determination gave strength to his limbs as he and Victus moved out into the open.

The sight before him was terrifying and strange. The bodies of recently killed pirates were up and walking around with great gaping wounds in their necks and bellies oozing and gushing blood, yet they walked on as though nothing was wrong. He watched as one dragged himself up towards Kaden's blade that was buried in its guts. Kaden had to use the blade in his other fist, smashing the pommel into the creature's face three times before it fell back.

Victus dragged Marcus as quickly as he could, dropping him next to Alex before drawing his rapier and dashing off into the battle. He pinned a creature through the ear just before it could bite Kaden's neck—this was unlike any battle Victus had ever fought.

Alex was lying on the ground, her eyes wide and unmoving as they took in the scene she had set in motion. Tears flowed freely into the sand, though it didn't seem that she was even aware of them. Marcus collapsed atop her, his own face becoming wet with tears as he gripped her face with his hands.

"Alex! Let it go! I'm here now, you did it! I'm safe. Please, come back to me!" he begged. He stroked and smoothed her hair, shutting out the battle behind him.

"Ever since I lost Meridian, I thought I knew I had to be cursed. You changed that. We should hate one another, but I don't hate you. I would trade places with you, if I could. Don't leave me now. I can't lose you. Please Alex, come back to me!"

"Foolish boy. You think your bride is still here? I have already claimed control." Alex's lips were moving, but the voices that passed through them were the harrowing voices of many. Just then, a stillness rushed through the beach. The undead stopped moving and lowered their blades, allowing themselves to be attacked by Victus and Kaden until the undead fell in on them and held them fast. Their great numbers and strength made overcoming the two warriors a simple matter.

"See?" the voices asked as she pushed Marcus off her with an otherworldly strength not proportionate to her small body. Pulling herself to her feet, she held the blade in a death grip and stared down at a broken and bloodied Marcus with a sickening grin.

"I will shatter what remains of this tattered bond once and for all by claiming your life with the edge of this blade." She raised her blade high into the air, the surrounding undead mimicking her action. This was it. He was going to die. He couldn't save her. Resignation shuddered through his body because he knew he couldn't hurt her, not if there was even a piece of her left in there. He just couldn't.

"Stop it! No!" Alex's own voice cried out. Despite her desperate cries, she lifted her blade in unison with the undead all around her, until suddenly, she wasn't. Something happened. The blade erupted in a brilliant red flame and shattered into glowing grains of golden sand. All the corpses under the blade's control collapsed to the ground and the blade's destruction released their souls in that very instant. A calm only death could summon raced across the island, leaving only four lives behind.

Alex swayed on the edge of consciousness. Piles of gore and blood lined the beach, seeping beneath her boots. She crumpled with a sigh that brought both the promise of life and everlasting death to the world around her. Alex twitched but didn't utter a word. She dangled in the shadow of death.

None of what he had just witnessed made any sense. He didn't know what saved them and he couldn't ask. For now, his bride lay unconscious on the beach, bleeding out into the sand beneath a blood-red moon.

Marcus summoned what little strength he had left to crawl to her and collect her in his arms. He reached out with one trembling hand to put pressure against the wound on her back until his own injuries overcame him and his vision faded. The last thing he saw was Alex's face, which was still strained, as though she were amid a violent debate. Agony was writ across her face.

CHAPTER 21

"Well, she seems to have recovered from the toxins, but it might take a while for her to regain consciousness. I can give her some yarrow for the fever. Fortunately, the poison on that blade wasn't fatal. It was a numbing toxin meant to immobilize her, but you say that she kept fighting?" the witch asked Marcus, who strained to push himself up from his cot.

Alex lay nearby, but her soul wasn't with them. He could tell. The old woman had laid her on a small bed, knowing she would benefit more than he from a cushioned back. His face was rugged and his eyes were bloodshot. He couldn't get the sound of the voices that had passed through her lips out of his mind. Kaden and Victus were right beside her as well, but none of them knew what to do.

"Yes. That cursed blade had claimed her as its thrall, but in the end, the blade burst into flames and shattered," Marcus explained.

"I saw it as well. One moment, she held the blade over her head, ready to strike, and then it was suddenly aflame. When she collapsed, I found this," Victus interjected as he gently lifted her right ring finger. The ring the witch had given her for good luck now had a glistening amber stone in the bear's open maw.

"When I tried to take it off of her, it burned my fingers," Kaden whined, rubbing his enormous thumb and forefinger together.

"Then you probably shouldn't touch it," the witch curtly replied. "But that should be impossible!" She stared at Alex's hand, flipping it this way and that in search of something that she couldn't seem to find.

"What do you mean by that? What are you looking for?" Marcus asked.

"Burns. Activating that ring should have covered her in fresh burns, but it would seem it spared her," the witch explained. With a grunt and without another word, she picked up a jar of green, gooey swamp mud and applied it liberally to Marcus' sun-ravaged back.

"Ack! What are you doing?" Marcus snapped, tensing up because he expected to be confronted with a rush of pain. Instead, it was quite a cooling, soothing sensation that had his back tingling and itching within seconds.

"It's swamp mud that I enchanted with the legs of three frogs, a toadstool, the tails of two fish, and the wings of a flightless bird. You should be mobile again in no time." It would be awhile yet before he could move around without pain, but he hoped he would be off her table in short order. Already his dizziness was fading.

"They're only new battle scars. Don't worry about me. Tend to my wife! Cast out whatever cursed spirits are inside her and that ring! What did you do to her with that sword?" Marcus asked angrily, glaring at her with eyes hard as polished shards of ice.

"What has happened to your wife is not my fault. It destroyed the sword, just like I knew it would, and banished the twisted the spirit inhabiting it, just as I knew they would be. As for your wife, she's just tired. Exhausted, really. Why should any of this surprise you?"

"Because magic is nearly gone from this world and the few artifacts that remain don't possess this sort of power!" he exclaimed. He needed to calm down, so he pinched the bridge of his nose and took several long breaths. Finally, he looked up at this strange witch, who had both helped and harmed the woman he cared for.

"So young, and already so blind. Magic is not gone from the world. It is hiding from those who might seek to abuse it. You should know–your family required every capable priest and priestess to enlist, regardless of their age or their strength. Why should they make their presence known to you?" the witch shot back with a pointed finger, accusation thick in her voice.

"As you yourself said, what happened wasn't possible. It should have burned her, right? Now my wife suddenly manifests the ability to cast fire the day after she meets you? I am to believe you didn't do something to her with that cursed sword from the age of the wizard kings?"

"I'm flattered you think I possess such a talent, boy, but if I did, your wife isn't someone I would waste it on." The witch slammed her pot on the table so hard a crack raced up its side. "I may have lost a child in this war, but I've since learned it was not all your family's fault. A man supposedly named Nicholas, who threw an infant princess's body into a hearth, started it. She awoke in her own kingdom knowing the names, faces, and histories of nobles who had died over a hundred years ago, in a court that didn't know her from a rat on the street. Your giant confirmed all of this while you were sunbathing."

"But does that really mean that she is the one? The princess that..." Victus shut his mouth when he noticed Marcus glaring at him. He groaned and sank his head into his hands, shaking it in confusion.

"This is all so strange. Can she really be from the past?" Marcus asked in an exhausted voice.

"Yes, I believe she is the princess who disappeared from the Luxorian palace over a hundred years ago. The lost child who sparked this entire war. The Raybrandt family was visiting Luxor to arrange a marriage between the child and the Luxorian prince, but..." she reminisced about an old legend they all knew well. In recent years, it had fallen out of popular knowledge in Artoria, but most in Luxor still knew it because they had held the fabric of their culture together better than Artoria had.

"I always found that legend suspect. Why would the Queen of Artoria stay if she knew they would kill her for the death of the prince? It was foolish," Victus said. He kept his voice down in case Alex woke up and heard him speak ill of her dead mother.

"Because she was a mother before she was a queen," the witch answered solemnly. The room fell silent as the memory of a tortured ghost filled their hearts and minds. They went that night without song, dance, or tales of bravery, only much-needed sleep aided by a witch's brew.

The witch tended their wounds and fed them well for the next several days. Marcus grudgingly conceded that he was in no shape to tend to himself in his present condition. He slept leaning against the bed of hay on which Alex still slumbered. Six days quickly passed, and while the brief respite had been enough to allow the witch's medicines to heal him to where he could travel once more, his wife still slept.

"What is wrong with her? Why hasn't she woken?" Marcus asked, fear tainting the strength of his voice.

"I can't say. My gift is seeing into souls, not healing them. I don't know of any Empaths left in this region. They were among the first to go."

"I know one. I'll carry her to the palace if I have to. Are you certain that an Empath can awaken her?" Marcus asked. He looked at the witch with renewed hope and determination.

"No, I cannot say for certain. However, an Empath has the best chance of reaching her now. I met one when I once suffered a fever that lasted for five days. I still dream about her face and the light that radiated from her as she guided me back from the brink of death. How typical of the palace to horde one of the few remaining Empaths for itself."

"She's a noblewoman, and she has hidden her ability from as many as she can. She's my friend and one of the few people I trust. I will thank you not to lump me in with the crimes of my family. I've never relished my rights as a prince, but I've done all I could to attend to my responsibilities."

"Very well. If this Empath will exhaust herself to rouse your bride, you have perhaps earned her trust. You may also have mine. I'm sorry I was quick to judge you."

"No, I'm the one who's sorry. My family has certainly committed enough atrocities in the name of power to merit a poor opinion among those they've held beneath the heel of their boot for so long," Marcus sighed. He turned to look back at the witch, a small smile on his face. "I should thank you, and I do, profusely, for what you have done to care for my wife and to save me. I don't even know your name."

After a long pause, she uttered, "My name is an old one. You needn't know it. I would offer you a token or artifact of power to take with you to ease your travel, but the artifacts I have left are all distorted. As it is, I'm afraid it will only be a matter of time before the object on your wife's finger will draw the attention of those you'll wish to avoid. Anything more will just shine the light brighter and she's not ready for that."

"Can't you take it off of her, then?" Marcus asked.

"No one who values their own skin and bones should touch that ring. Don't worry, it will keep her safe. However, your visit has convinced me of something. All these objects I have tasked myself with keeping secure are too dangerous to remain in this world. I have no successor, and I cannot allow them to stay here for anyone to claim once I pass into the next world. I hope it will help her sleep easy to know that I will see to the dissolution of these artifacts before I die. As a priestess, not a witch, it is my duty." She smiled at Marcus for the first time, almost reassuringly so.

"Very well. We are in your debt. Thank you." Marcus bowed stiffly to the priestess, who had saved them, wishing he could offer more. "And I'm sorry for calling you a witch..."

"Forgiven." She said with a wave. "And if you are truly in my debt, then I will ask for repayment right now. That music box you carry–leave it here," the priestess said as Kaden and Victus walked outside. Marcus froze in the doorway, his hand hovering over his bag. They had found it in Ezmeralda's house after the slaughter, before any of the pirates had figured out what to do with it.

"How do you know about that?" he quietly asked.

"I could hear its tune the moment they brought you into my home. Why you didn't just leave it on that island is beyond me. Tell me, why would you want to protect such a dark artifact?"

"Because one of my men used it against Alex, and I think that maybe if she could destroy it, it might help her recover," Marcus confessed. He clutched the devilish box tight, the wood creaking beneath his grip.

"Prince Marcus, I am a priestess of revelation. While you have slept in my home, the spirit I pray to has gifted me insight into the path before you and hints of what is coming. I can tell you that many trials will await your bride at the Luxorian court. Your bride is strong, Prince Marcus, but perhaps now is not the time for her to worry about destroying this box."

Marcus stared into her eyes for a long time, measuring her intent, and his hand tightened even more around the music box. "Maybe you're right. I can't say I enjoyed keeping this thing so close. If you only knew how much harm this box has caused." Marcus blinked away tears. Images of Meridian and Alex flashed through his mind. To rid himself of their haunting screams, he thrust his hand out to surrender the box.

She took it from his hand gently and carefully turned it from side to side with half-closed eyes. She ran her fingers along the edges of the box before letting out a small, sad sigh. "I think I shall send you a friend. Keep an eye out for her. She is young in appearance, but is clever and powerful. She will help Alex prepare for the many battles she has yet to face."

"Don't trouble yourself. I don't know that my father will welcome her to court. I am more than capable of protecting my wife with my own two hands," Marcus warned. He scooped Alex into his arms, desperate to be on his way.

"Very well. One last thing. Please give your large friend my gratitude for returning my dagger. It'll save me a great deal of trouble having to track it down."

"Will you be safe here all on your own?"

"Not to worry. It will not be so easy for bandits to find my home now that I have the Pearl of Illusion back. You must be sure to thank your blond friend for that. Now, step outside and see what I mean."

He could see Kaden and Victus beyond the open door, searching for something. He carried Alex to the door, and as soon as he crossed the threshold, a strange tingle ran through him, disorienting him and leaving him wondering which direction he was facing. Shaking his head, he looked up to see legitimate fear in the pair's eyes.

"Marcus, there you are! We were afraid we'd somehow gotten lost. Where did her house go?" Victus asked, clearly exasperated and stressed at the thought of having lost his charge once again.

"What are you talking about?" Marcus asked. He turned around, expecting to see the hut right behind him. Instead, he was only looking at the trunk of what appeared to be nothing more than a moss-covered, three-hundred-year-old oak tree in the middle of the swamp. Her message had been clear: get Alex out of here and find her a home within the walls of the palace.

"I think her house is exactly where it needs to be," Marcus said. "Come, we have a long road ahead of us."

The journey took almost a week, and although they could jostle her awake for bites of food or sips of water, she never stayed conscious long enough to work out where she was. Often, her brief moments of lucidity were spent calling for her mother, a woman long dead. Marcus was her greatest comfort in those moments. He would hold her, kiss her softly, and agree to promises she wouldn't remember asking for just to keep her calm. Only when she was calm again would she slip back into a dreamless sleep. It was as though she was making up for all the rest she had lost since that horrible day in Tripsburgh.

When they had nearly reached Valencius, the group set camp to work out a plan of attack. Sunset was a few hours away, so they had time to think before they acted. Their mission to sneak Alex into the walls of the palace was difficult because she still hadn't woken from her slumber. Kaden was taking his turn, holding her by the fire, trying his best to coax her to open her mouth enough to accept a strip of rabbit or a sip of water.

"Come on, sweet girl. Open your mouth. It's rabbit meat! You like rabbit." He tried to inform her as he waved a chunk of meat under her nose.

"Kaden, before we get to the palace, we should probably talk about the way you are with Alex." Victus spoke to him as he would to any protective father who was holding his injured daughter.

"What about the way I am with her? Does your master have a problem with it?" he shot back, looking directly at Marcus with fire in his eyes.

"No, Kaden, I think it's wonderful that she has someone who cares for her as you do," Marcus reassured him. "The problem is our destination. The palace is a place of intrigue, double-speech and backstabbing; no one addresses problems head-on. They consider themselves to be above such squabble. Their blood is too pure and divine to be spilled. Instead, they look for targets close to those they wish to harm who lack noble breeding. If you act like a doting father and she smiles and laughs at your jests as though she is an adoring daughter, it will mark you as a target. The moment someone wishes to harm Alex, they will maim, cripple, or kill you, all for the sake of sending a message to the one who loves you most."

"What about your little lap dog? I've never seen a man follow another man with such adoring eyes!" Kaden snarled defensively.

With a face devoid of emotion, Victus explained, "I am a commoner who Marcus trained to wield a sword. I defend him with my life, and I am a devoted bodyguard who will gladly die in my prince's stead. However, Prince Marcus does not take me drinking. He does not join me at the dinner table for gossip or casual conversation. He commands and I obey. No one would ever think that Prince Marcus feels as strongly for me as Alex does for you."

"And just how do you expect Alex to feel about this? She's never had to taper her feelings. We have not taught her to fear an attack that is so veiled, so indirect. Alex is not ready for this and she might never be!" Kaden snapped, clearly annoyed.

"She will probably hate it more than you do, Kaden. I expect her to kick, scream, and rant about it at length," Marcus lamented. "Some ladies of the court who are friends of mine can help her learn to adapt to the conditions there. I hope she comes to love it."

"Ha! You expect her to open up to a bunch of noblewomen? You really don't know her very well."

"She is going to have to learn to behave like a princess. Who better to learn from?"

Victus stepped in. "As for you, it's crucial you accept the way things are before we step into the palace. You can't coddle her. You are her guardian and a representative of Artoria, nothing more. It would be best if we could get you a position in the Palace Guard. It was a duty you once performed well, and you would always be nearby if she needed you."

"Accept this? I am her guard, not the warden of some fucking palace in the middle of Luxor! No one knows her better than me!" Kaden roared.

"Exactly! No one knows her better. Do you think anyone knows Prince Marcus as I do? The difference is that I have trained for most of my life to serve in this environment," Victus explained, anger sparking in his eyes. "Tell me, would you be able to stand at Princess Alexandra's shoulder and just watch as a man pressed himself close and leered down at her while making remarks that implied ill of her? Could you watch while another besmirched her honor, insulted her, or came close to threatening her? Could you stand ready to act, yet not show it, when a man you know wishes to kill her steps within arm's reach so that they can speak about matters of court? That is what life in the palace will be."

"Do you know how many times I have had to stand stone-faced while a man I know wishes to kill Prince Marcus calls a private meeting with him? Men, I know, have slipped poison into his food, yet I just stood and smiled as they shook his hand? That is the life we are about to step into. You are a great warrior and you possess an indomitable heart, Kaden, but you lack restraint. I can hold myself at bay, ready to act, but not imposing. You would loom over her like a great bear and snarl and glare at each foe who approached her, thinking you were protecting her when all you were actually doing was hurting her. This is not Artoria, and it is not the battlefield. The rules are different here." Victus tossed the knife which had held his bit of rabbit down into the earth next to the fire.

"She's going to pull a weapon on her first day. You realize that, right? You realize everything you described is just as intolerable for her, don't you?" Kaden said, his voice softer now.

With a tired sigh, Marcus said, "She will have to learn. I am hoping I can keep her from wearing a blade to avoid just that. Don't be too angry with Victus, Kaden. He's stood watchful guard over me for many years and has seen too many attempts on my life, including all the attempts made by my brother. He's just trying to spare you the pain of bringing harm to Alex because of not knowing how to act in our world."

"Very well. Who do you propose will stand guard over her, if not me?" Kaden asked with crossed arms and a raised brow.

"I will," Victus said confidently. "Prince Marcus will have his personal praetorians by his side again when the army arrives. Until then, I will try to keep them together so I can protect them both."

"Now that my brother is dead, I am the sole heir to the throne. Attempts on my life should be less frequent and the nobles will be more amenable to me," Marcus said with a rueful laugh. "No one is truly safe from palace intrigue, but Alex will face a tremendous challenge on her very right to the protections afforded to her by her noble birth and marriage to me. We have to protect her however we can."

"And what if she hates me for leaving her with you? She doesn't know you like she knows me." Kaden's defenses were crumbling as they assaulted the situation with logic and forethought that he couldn't deny.

Victus said, "I will tell her it was my idea, and that I convinced you of it. If she hates me, all the better; that way she won't be showing weakness by doting on me with affection. Many courtly ladies despise the guardians their husbands or fathers have given them. It's practically tradition."

"I doubt it will even come to that. She is impulsive and willful, but she is no fool, Kaden," Marcus interjected. "She may be angry for a while, but once she calms down and assesses the situation with a clear head, she will realize that we have made the smartest choice we could make. Enlisting in the Palace Guard means you are still on hand to defend her if things go wrong. I will see that you receive a good placement on the guard. You will probably have to endure some ire from your fellow guards initially, but we have other outlanders in service."

"Very well. I'll agree to be removed from her side when she wakes. It won't do her any good to wake up without me there, especially after she passed out on the beach with her undead attacking me."

"Of course, Kaden. It will take a few days to get you into the Palace Guard, anyway. I am hoping my friend Althea can bring her out of this daze by then. The sun has nearly set. We should start for the city soon."

"Your Highness, if we all go in together, the odds of the princess reaching the palace alive and unmolested are slim. Let me go on ahead and arrange a way for us to slip in undetected," Victus suggested.

Marcus looked at his old friend for a long moment and then nodded in agreement. "Be careful. Senator Estradian should be able to help. Trust no one else."

"Of course, Your Highness. I will be back as soon as I can." With no further words, he slid into the forest as quiet as the shadows he hid within.

Hours later, Victus made good on his word and returned with a plain brown carriage that a local merchant might ride in, but certainly not someone of noble birth. Kaden lifted Alex into the back with Marcus, with the curtains drawn and her head resting upon her husband's chest. Kaden hung off the back of the carriage as a footman, and Victus sat in the driver's seat, the cowl of his cloak pulled low over his face. The team cautiously crawled toward Valencius.

When Marcus eased back the curtains to watch the approaching city, a warmth grew in his heart as he saw the outer walls of the city came into view. The blocky, solid construction was not fancy or intricate. It was no-nonsense, solid workmanship intended to defend the commoners who lived behind those walls. He had always thought of himself as being like those walls–the youngest son of the royal line, the one who stood for the people even though he received no credit or admiration. They passed beneath them with no issue, into the city proper.

The main highway through the city led straight to the palace, a broad thoroughfare lined with beech trees and willows, flowers in small square gardens beautifying the merchant district. Their ancestors had paved the road in white stone that positively gleamed in the light of the rising moon. The last shops were closing up for the day; a few last-minute transactions were good-naturedly haggled as the city slowly wound down after a day of bustling activity. Marcus smiled as he watched the city flow past him. Monuments of past victories blurred together with taverns, businesses, homes, and inns. It was a city full of life and noise. It was his home.

Ahead of them rose the palace, an immense stone structure that spread out in the city's center. Fluted columns, great archways, and towering spires adorned it. Servants filled the interior with small gardens and open walkways, a visible sign of the progress and wealth of the empire. It had been a long time since he'd walked those halls, and he had to admit that he missed them. Victus took them around to a small garden on the side of the palace, where a short walkway led to a side door.

It was a servant's entrance. A place where they might get caught, but not by those who would notice their arrival or have the time to care. The only man standing there to welcome them wore a dull, scratchy, brown cloak with a luxurious emerald cloak peeking out from underneath. He waited for Marcus to emerge before easing his shoulders a bit.

"Prince Marcus. Welcome back," he said, his eyes lingering on the unresponsive princess's soft face before meeting Marcus' eyes with an unreadable look.

Marcus held out his hand with a smile. "Senator Estradian, thank you for your help. But why are you here?"

"The walls are alive with whispers and eyes tonight, my prince. We must speak quickly before they realize where we are," the shadowy senator explained as he gestured for Marcus to follow him off the trail a few steps. "Your bride is in grave danger, Marcus. Rumors have already spread that her death was false. The other families on the council are already making noise about it. I don't know where the other four families will fall, but you know I will stand by your side. Of course, the Rustionage house will never support sparing her life."

"She's been in danger for our entire journey to Valencius. Hell, Quintus, she's been in danger since before she became my prisoner!" Marcus barked with a small, tired groan. "We have to get her to the royal apartments where I can protect her until she wakes. I need Althea. Can you call on her for me?"

"Of course. Now, we should go. Already the whispers are spreading of this meeting. Let's get you safely inside." He hurried them along and stood aside to allow the prince and his party entry to the palace. He didn't allow them to linger in any one spot for more than a couple of seconds as they hurried through the halls with their heads down. At long last, they reached the safety of the royal apartments. The halls outside this room were buzzing with talk, but in here, she was safe.

• • •

On the third day since their arrival in the capital, Alex finally awoke to find Marcus holding her hand with his head resting on the mattress. At the door slouched Kaden and Victus, who'd been on guard nonstop as rumor had spread about a princess everyone believed to be dead. Even now, her guardians' eyes were open but barely comprehending their surroundings. They were barricading her in this plush room of blue and silver, but she didn't know why.

Alex couldn't know that the five families beyond that door desperately wanted to see her dead or bent over in submission. All she knew was that there, in that room that was bathed in light, she, her friends, and her husband were all still alive. In the confines of the Luxorian palace, Alex dared to hope that she had finally found a home. But resting on her chest was a letter sealed with the Raybrandt family crest, and it changed everything.

ABOUT THE AUTHOR

When E.K. is not obsessing over the *Transcending Fire* universe, she's likely playing with her baby, replicating the latest cooking craze she saw on YouTube, reading the latest Kindle releases, or planting more tropical plants in her garden somewhere in Northeast Florida. She dreams of traveling the world with her husband and son, and maybe, if she's lucky, she'll finally get to build a snowman.

NOTE FROM THE AUTHOR

Word-of-mouth is crucial for any author to succeed. If you enjoyed *Transcending Fire*, please leave a review online—anywhere you are able. Even if it's just a sentence or two. It would make all the difference and would be very much appreciated.

Thanks!
E. K. Blalock